PLAIN JANE

"WICKEDLY MACABRE AND BLISTERINGLY PACED, *PLAIN JANE* MARKS THE DEBUT OF A THRILLER FOR THE NEW MILLENNIUM.

BRASH, FUNNY, TERRIFYING, AND SHOCKING, HERE IS A STORY BEST ENJOYED WITH ALL THE LIGHTS ON.

DON'T SAY I DIDN'T WARN YOU!"

NYT TOP TEN BEST SELLER
JAMES ROLLINS

PLAIN JANE

CRISTYN WEST

PLAIN JANE

An Off Our Meds Project/published by arrangement with the author

FIRST EDITION
Copyright © 2010 by Carolyn McCray
All rights reserved.

Printed in the United States of America.

ISBN: 1452854343
EAN-13: 9781452854342
LCCN: 2010907246

Any inquiries can be made to:
1387 Hanover Lane
Ventura, CA 93001
Or...

Visit our website at:
www.plainjanethenovel.com

10 9 8 7 6 5 4 3 2 1

ACKNOWLEGMENTS

My very first acknowledgment must go to Gary. Somehow through everything, he raised me right.

Then, of course, must come Jim. My best friend for over two decades. Mentor, hero and fellow video game junky.

And Dee Dee, always loud and proud. Who has somehow convinced me to #ack go out and meet new people #weird

Last but not least, Ben, my business partner and moral compass. He's always there, even when it's way awkward.

Prologue

The man forced himself deeper into the darkened storefront. He could not chance the brunette spotting him as she approached.

Joann was late. The man knew her schedule because he had watched her office from the roof of an adjacent building. Watched that boss of hers give the brunette a new account right before seven. The lazy bastard knew that Joann would stay hours to input the client's information then run a full set of actuaries before she left. Not because the brunette had to, but because Joann would never leave a task unfinished.

That sense of responsibility was only one of the many, many traits which attracted the man to her. You only had to glance at the brunette to know that she was worthy. Worthy of his time. Worthy of his attention.

As Joann drew closer and closer to his position, any sense of frustration over the long, cold wait melted. The sight of her dark brown eyes, slightly drooped from long hours in front of the computer, was why he risked positioning himself so close to her route home.

He needed to be near her. Near enough to smell her Obsession perfume. The fragrance he had sent her. Of course Joann did not know it was from him. The brunette thought she had won it from the Avon Woman's Week Website contest. But he knew. Knew a piece of him caressed her skin. Lingered at her throat.

Slowly, ever so slowly, the man closed the chasm.

Close enough that he noticed the night chill force one of her delicate hands into her coat pocket while the other clasped her jacket tight around her neck. Joann had been rushed this morning due to a call and had forgotten her scarf. The long purple one. Her favorite.

The man noticed such things. Knew such things because, unlike every other male in her life, the man took the time to discover such things.

Breath caught in his throat as she neared. The man could not let his excitement reveal his presence. His fists tightened as the urge to reach out and caress her skin felt near to overwhelming him.

To many Joann might have seemed average, perhaps even plain, but the man did not care what others thought. He knew her to be perfect. Had the brunette used a bit of rogue, or was the flush to her cheeks brought on by the crisp night air?

As she hurried along, a small plume of fog punctuated the brunette's every breath. Even this act of breathing was perfect, just as she was.

So petite and delicate.

Joann could not be taller than five foot three. Short enough that if the brunette ever kissed him she would need to stand on the tips of her toes. Slender enough that he could encircle her waist and pull her against him with a single arm.

The man felt a slight buzz as his body urged him to take a breath, but he could not. Not while she passed. Passed so closely that if the man wished, he could have reached out and stroked her shoulder-length hair.

He could have touched the tender flesh beneath her ear then trailed down the curve of her shoulder. But that would not do. He could not let Joann know he watched her, followed her. He could not let her know that he even existed, not until he was ready. Not until she was exactly where he wanted her.

The click of her low heels carried the brunette down the street, but the man did not follow.

He knew exactly where she headed.

Just like last night and the night before, he would wait until Joann crossed the street at the light and disappeared around the corner to her apartment building before he caught up. The man could not take the chance she would spot him on the empty street. Not before he found the perfect moment to introduce himself. Not a single moment before then.

Letting out his long-held breath, his vision became obscured by the cloud of fog. As it cleared he found Joann looking back over her shoulder. Panic gripped him. Had she seen him? Felt his warmth from the shadows? The brunette's lips turned down, eyes scanning the street behind her, but they were not yet fixed on his position.

Holding his breath, the man watched as Joann abandoned her survey of the street behind her. Clearly, though, the brunette had become alarmed.

You could see it in her shoulders, in her rushed step, in the way she clutched her purse to her body.

The man hissed out an exhale. Slowly enough to keep the steam from betraying him. His eyes glued to the back of the brunette's head.

Keep walking, just keep walking.

Movement across the street diverted his attention. Lively chatter filled the otherwise deserted avenue. He had forgotten it was Thursday. Midnight Movie night at the Crestview theater.

The opposite sidewalk filled with Tim Curry wannabes and enough black leather and red velvet to choke a transvestite.

The man's eyes flickered to Joann. She moved at a near run. But still he hung back. Safely tucked away from prying eyes.

Their relationship needed to stay secret, at least for a little while longer.

Abruptly Joann crossed the street and melted into the growing throng. His stomach twisted. Why had the brunette done that? Was she going into the theater to make a call? The man knew Joann did not have her cell-phone because she had forgotten to charge it the night before and had been forced to leave the phone at home.

Risking exposure, the man stepped out from the deep shadows. He had to take this calculated gamble if he wished to keep her within sight.

Even so exposed, the man could barely make out Joann's beige coat amongst the sea of Rocky Horror red and black. To cross the street could raise suspicion. Not crossing might mean losing her forever.

Shrugging his collar up as if to protect him against the gaining wind, the man trotted across the street, trying to act as if he was meeting someone casually after the film. Perhaps to apologize for being late. At least that was the impression he wanted to project as Joann made her way through the thick, rambunctious crowd.

Abandoning his usual disdain for others, the man dove into the mass of laughing, giggling revelers. He could not lose her. Lose Joann.

Yet for every step he made forward, the brunette seemed to make two. How he wished Joann had remembered her bright lavender scarf now. In the second it took to right himself as he tripped over a drunk in heels, the man lost sight of Joann.

Not bothering to contain his urgency, he brusquely pushed aside the moviegoers, making for the far side of the crowd. Finally the throng parted, and he stumbled onto the empty pavement.

Desperate, he searched the street. No Joann. He swung left, then right, then back towards the crowd. But not a single clue as to where she had disappeared.

Joann was gone.

CHAPTER 1

Officer Mickey Macaine's elbows settled against his duty belt as he shifted his weight onto the heel of his boots. This was going to be a long ass night, most of it standing on Crestview Ave. It was only two-thirty in the morning and they already had three noise complaints from the neighbors about women and *men* dressed in fishnet stockings, arms linked, singing some piss-poor tune from the damned homo movie.

"Keep it down," Macaine intoned for the fifteenth time, certain that it would take another fifteen before this rowdy crowd dispersed.

His attention became piqued, though, when a mascara-smeared woman staggered toward him. These moviegoer get-ups made the working girls down the block look like cloistered nuns. Therefore, Mickey let the chick bump into him before he spoke. "I'm sorry, ma'am. You need to exit off Fremont."

The blonde's words slurred as she leaned heavily against his puffed out chest. "But my car's down there…somewhere."

"I'm sorry, but that's a residential --"

"Sarah! The car's down here!" A man yelled.

The cop was slightly disappointed as the woman pulled away. Mickey could have squeezed in another few minutes of contact with her before sending her along.

"Oops. My bad," the girl slurred, then flashed a smile that totally made up for any inconvenience.

Maybe he might come to one of these midnight movies himself. Attention focused on the chick's skirt so short that you could see the rounded crescents of her ass, Macaine ignored a sound from behind.

Who cared when you had a view like this? But a louder clang made Mickey crane an ear.

Did one of these yahoos get past him?

His lieutenant would have his head if the neighborhood watch lodged another loitering complaint. But had he really heard a sound? Or was it just the rush of blood coming back from his crotch after his close encounter with the blonde?

Halfway to the intersection, Macaine heard it again. This time he was certain. Certain that the sound was metal against pavement.

The cop clicked on his flashlight. The sounds were definitely coming from the alley. *Way* down the alley. And was that a gasp? Panting?

Maybe he would get lucky enough to catch a couple banging away. Besides the thrill factor, it would make a great story for the bullpen.

Still, Mickey unhooked his nightstick.

Not because he thought he was going to need it, but because it always looked cool. "Police. Show yourself."

More heavy breathing. Maybe he should call for back up? But his hand did not reach for his handset. Not while there was still a chance these noises were some S&M couple going at it like dogs in heat.

"Police," Mickey growled. "Last chance to keep this out of the public record."

Another sound. That did not sound like sex. That sounded pained. Angry. This time Macaine unhooked his gun.

Not because it looked cool, but because he might actually need to use it.

There it was again. Definite sounds of a struggle.

Instinctually the cop changed his stance.

Gun out, arm forward.

"Police. Step out, *now*." Macaine stressed that last word. He needed them to know he was serious. Besides the for-shit lighting, a dumpster blocked his view. Carefully Mickey picked his way around it.

Sure enough, it was a couple. Girl on the ground, guy on top. Relief swept over him, until the cop realized that the glistening pool on the ground was not rainwater, it was blood.

"Step away!" Macaine grabbed his handset. "I need backup in the alley behind Crestview and Van Wheller."

The man not only ignored him but continued beating on the brunette. And the more Mickey's eyes adjusted to the dark, the more blood he saw. So much. *Too* much.

"Step back, or I will be forced to shoot." And Macaine meant it.

But not only did the man stay on the ground, he leaned over the woman's face. Was he kissing her bloody lips?

Sick bastard.

Mickey popped the safety off. This guy only got one more warning. "Last chance." Macaine cocked his gun. Was this really going to be his first shooting? Was it really going to be tonight? The man went back to beating on the woman.

Yep, he guessed it really was.

The cop's finger tightened on the trigger.

"No!" A woman's voice shouted from behind.

Mickey's eyes darted over his shoulder. A brunette ran full tilt toward him. Even before he saw the gun in her hands, held out to her side in perfect academy position, Macaine knew that she was a cop. She ran like a cop. Sounded like a cop.

"Don't shoot!" The gold badge clipped to the petite woman's belt sparkled as she put a hand on Macaine's outstretched gun arm and urged it down as the fucked-up guy still beat on the woman.

"He's F.B.I."

CHAPTER 2

Detective Nicole Usher forcibly pushed the uniform's arm down. She could not let him shoot Kent. At least not before she got the chance.

"He's one of us," Nicole reassured the cop, although he did not look close to believing her. She did not have time to convince him. Not with a woman down and the profiler performing CPR in a urine soaked alley.

"I wouldn't go that far," a new voice came from behind. "But don't shoot."

By the baritone timber and obvious distain, Nicole knew the newest arrival was Ruben Torres, her partner, and least favorite fan of Kent Harbinger.

The beat cop's arm wavered, but Ruben's wide frame convinced him to finally lower the gun.

Despite her hope that Joann was still alive, the closer Nicole came to the grisly scene, the more obvious it became that the brunette was well past saving. Blood pooled around the woman's head and ran down her side. The slick lake did not end until it washed up against the brick wall. Deep red saturated Joann's clothes. Kent's shirt was smeared with it.

The most telling sign that Joann was beyond any of their help was her blank, glazed stare. Unblinking. Pupils fixed and dilated. Nicole had seen it too many times before.

Seventeen times in the last two years. Five times in the last four months. Now twice in three weeks. The killer was accelerating his behavior, becoming reckless and all the more dangerous for it.

"She's gone, Kent."

Sirens wailed in the distance, like nails on a chalkboard. It was the sound of their defeat yet again.

For a moment Kent stopped his compressions, then leaned over and continued giving Joann mouth-to-mouth. Could not he see he was too late? Could not he see that no amount of CPR would bring Joann back?

To anyone else Nicole might have offered a compassionate word, a reassuring pat on the arm, but Harbinger was not just anyone. He was an F.B.I. profiler known for his ability to immerse himself so completely into the perversion of a serial killer's mind that he could select and stalk a victim before the madman could.

Yet a price had to be paid for such a talent. Each time the profiler went this deep into a case, he lost a part of himself. How could he remember the concept of love when his job demanded that he pick a woman and hunt her down like prey?

This focused on a task and so detached from reality, Nicole couldn't trust that Kent knew friend from foe right now.

She firmed her tone. "It's over."

Harbinger rose up from the brunette's mouth and put his hands back on Joann's sternum as his own breaths came in great heaves. Nicole feared he would start compressions again. Finally his head tilted forward in defeat. His eyes squeezed shut. His pain palpable.

"She's gone."

Nicole chanced a tentative hand on his shoulder.

Two years ago the gesture might have meant more. Now she just needed to get Kent away before he contaminated the crime scene any further. This was the freshest kill to date. If they were going to gain any new insight, they needed to vacate *now* and turn the body over to forensics.

They owed it to Joann.

Ignoring her, Harbinger pulled the brunette's blouse up. "Kent!"

The profiler appeared far beyond listening to anyone, let alone her, as he ripped the buttons from Joann's shirt. The wailing sirens merged as if singing a lament. Crying out to stop the sacrilege that was about to occur.

He jerked open the stained silk to reveal a huge gash deep into Joann's pale abdomen. Blue and red lights flashed as the patrol cars descended on their position, casting bright splashes of color on the otherwise dreary alley.

It felt all too surreal.

The unnatural position of Joann's legs. The huge, bloody gash across her belly, the look of obsessed determination in the profiler's eyes. Nicole dug her fingers into Harbinger's arm.

"Damn it!" Nicole tried to pull the profiler from the brunette before he not only contaminated the autopsy but desecrated the body as well. Had Harbinger lost all sense of himself? Of basic human decency?

"The M.E. will tell us if he took his trophy!"

Seeming oblivious to the fact that she had his arm, Kent prepared to force his bare hand into Joann's bloody wound. Short of shooting the profiler, Nicole was helpless to stop him.

Her partner, however, had no trouble grabbing Kent by the collar, and hauling the profiler to his feet.

"Oh no you don't, you sick fuck," Ruben growled.

CHAPTER 3

Ruben's hands shook with rage as he slammed Kent against the rough brick wall. Enough was enough.

He might only have an Associate's degree from a community college versus Kent's Cum Laude graduation from Yale, but that did not mean the profiler was always right.

Or even sane.

"I've put up with your 'I'm so brilliant that no one can even *try* to understand me' crap."

He searched the profiler's face for some reaction, but found only boredom. Kent acted as if he did not have the academy's champion boxer at his throat. Shit, he acted as if he did not have *anyone's* hands at his throat.

Fine. If Ruben could not physically intimidate the prick, he was not beneath pushing some hot buttons.

"And your "let's pretend coming back doesn't hurt Nicole" routine is getting stale..."

Ruben stopped short. His voice had cracked at her name, and he was not about to let Kent have the satisfaction of seeing him out of control.

It had been four long years since Ruben was forced into the background as Harbinger swept into town, high-jacking his first major case. Adding insult to injury, and seemingly without effort, Kent lured Nicole away as well. First a promising career then a promising relationship had been sabotaged by the profiler.

That was the past, Ruben reminded himself. Harbinger had been out of commission, out of their lives, for so long. In two years he thought that he'd grown enough as a detective and as Nicole's lover to not be rattled by the profiler.

Obviously he had been sadly mistaken. Kent, however, didn't need to hear any of that betrayed in Ruben's voice. Voice measured and even, he continued, "I won't allow you to violate that woman again."

"If you hadn't noticed, she's not a woman anymore," the profiler stated flatly. "She's a corpse."

Without thinking of the consequences, Ruben bounced the back of Kent's skull off the wall. "Because of *you!*"

How could this creep have been recruited out of *high school* by the F.B.I.? Reminding himself that the only upper hand he had over Harbinger was some form of emotional control, Ruben kept his anger in check.

Instead of physically lashing out, he indicated to the dozen or so cops who descended upon the scene. "We had twenty cops on alert. An alert that you insisted upon. But you could not bother to call in because --"

"Because as good of a profiler as Kent is..." Nicole elbowed her way between them. "He's no psychic."

Kent shrugged as if Nicole had stated the profiler did not play the piano very well. Seemingly uncaring that just a few feet away the E.M.T.s pronounced Joann dead. A woman that Kent failed to protect.

"Damn it!" Ruben shoved the profiler hard against the wall, but Nicole put a hand over his closed knuckles.

CHAPTER 4

"Ruben, come on," Nicole coaxed. "We've got a canvas to roll out and --"

"This asshole does it for the rush," her partner growled.

"And that outburst was helpful, exactly how?"

Nicole knew her tone was harsh, but here was not the place to be having a testosterone-fueled standoff.

Dozens of cops, E.M.T.s, C.S.I.s, and firemen crowded the alley. All trying to pretend this little altercation wasn't happening. Their showdown needed to end *now* or it was going to be on the nightly news.

She squeezed her partner's hand, but Ruben refused to break his stare. The profiler had really gotten to him this time.

"Rube, please," Nicole said, her tone more consolatory.

Her partner's eyes met hers. She understood his frustration. Kent could get under your skin like bamboo shoots. However, they needed to hash out Harbinger's difficult personality traits another time.

"This isn't helping."

Ruben shoved Kent against the wall in the same motion that released the profiler. Even so, her partner did not back away, not even a step. The two men were no longer in contact, but locked in combat nonetheless.

Her partner stood several inches taller than Kent and had seventy pounds on the leaner profiler. Ruben was the type of guy who not only had a gym membership but actually used it. Whereas Kent relied upon his genetic heritage to keep fit.

Despite her partner's clear physical advantage, Kent seemed completely ignorant of Ruben's towering presence. And there was nothing that annoyed her partner more than being discounted. Nicole made sure to position herself between them as Kent leaned his head back against the wall. As if the profiler might take a nap.

Nicole hesitated as the air stilled. Activity buzzed all around, yet an eerie calm blanketed the area. The C.S.I.'s camera flashes added strobe. Faster and faster. They too must have sensed the change in the air. A storm approached. A storm that would wash away vital evidence.

Reminded of the real issue, Nicole set her jaw. The boys were just going to have to suck it up.

"Now if you two are done --"

Then Kent did the unthinkable. He yawned.

Nicole wedged herself deeper between them before Ruben's shock transformed into anger. While she was trying to think of something, anything, to defuse Ruben's increasingly short temper, her cell-phone rang.

Nicole flipped open the phone. "Usher."

"Status?" Her boss asked.

"I'm sorry, *Captain*." Nicole stressed the last word to keep Ruben in check. "Joann Forme, the woman Kent had under surveillance, is dead."

Nicole heard a loud sigh on the other end. Followed by a long pause. Her Captain believed in counting to ten before responding to bad news.

"Are you going to explain that despite a trained F.B.I. officer providing round-the-clock surveillance and twenty officers on-call within a mile of this woman, somehow the killer was still able to get to her?"

"I promise you, sir. We *will* explain tonight's events."

"Within the hour."

"Yes, sir."

She snapped the phone closed, harder than she needed, "We're due back by two so let's direct our hostilities toward the killer, all right?"

Ruben glanced at Kent, who still stared up at the brooding clouds. Finally her partner gave a stiff nod and strode over to the beat cop who discovered the grisly scene.

Nicole waited long enough to make sure that the cop held Ruben's attention before she turned back to Kent, but the profiler had vanished.

Immediately she looked to Joann. Luckily he had not gone back to the body. She searched the growing crowd of blue uniforms, but no sign of him.

Besides being the special agent who had apprehended the highest number of serial killers in the last decade, Harbinger's other specialty was disappearing when things did not go his way.

Desperate, Nicole looked down the alley in the opposite direction and found Kent's retreating form.

Nicole trotted to catch up. "Where in the hell do you think you're going?"

Kent ignored her. She grabbed his arm. Why did he always make her run after him? Why did he always make her feel like a little girl trying to get an absent daddy's attention?

"Damn it, you are not going to leave me to answer to Glick alone." Kent tried to walk off. This time Nicole jerked him so hard that he had to face her. She was done chasing.

"Not *again*."

CHAPTER 5

Kent stared blankly at Nicole even though he knew exactly the shared past she meant. Not only did he know the reference but took her accusation like a kick to the 'nads.

Anger flared. At the killer, at himself, even at Nicole for dragging him back into a case like this.

Joann's sticky blood dripped from his hands. The metallic taste lingered on his lips. A woman he had grown to know more intimately than most husbands know their wives had been killed on his watch. How could Nicole expect him to stand here and have a normal conversation? If he opened his emotions even a crack, the dam would break. He would break.

A profiler was not allowed that luxury. As long as the Plain Jane killer was still on the loose, Kent had to contain his anger, his pain. He had to bottle it and use it as fuel to drive him deeper into the killer's mind.

Closer to the killer's truth.

Standing here attending to Nicole's feeling of abandonment was not going to help him catch Plain Jane.

Nicole must have sensed the emotional wall he had erected. Her words were meant to be stern, however, her tone already sounded defeated. "You've got to come back to the station with me."

Kent looked down at his clothes. His pants were soaked through with dirty rainwater, grease, blood, and who knew what else from his failed attempt at resuscitation. His shirt and coat were streaked crimson with Joann's arterial blood. Even if he did not need to get the hell away from here, he could never show up at the station looking this much the worse for wear.

He looked up into the eyes of the woman whom he had once hoped would be the mother of his children. That was years ago, though. Now this woman just sighed, silently agreeing that he was not fit to present to her Captain.

"Fine. I'll explain to Glick, *again,* that you had no way of knowing for certain if Joann was Plain Jane's next victim."

Nicole paused, waiting for confirmation. Kent gave a non-committal shrug even though her statement was patently false. He had *known* Joann was the killer's next prize. Known it in his gut every time she tucked her hair behind her ears. Known it in his groin each time she flashed that lop-sided smile. Kent had known Plain Jane could not resist Joann's perfect blend of humility and inner beauty.

"Even if Joann *was* the target, you had no way to know if the killer was going to strike *tonight.*"

Again Nicole waited for confirmation.

Kent thought the clarification was more for herself than for Glick. She wanted reassurance that there was nothing they could have done to save Joann.

Again he shrugged.

Again he lied to Nicole. For Kent had known tonight was the night. He knew Plain Jane could not resist Joann any longer. The urge to kill. The urge to slash her throat and get up to his elbows in her belly was near to overwhelming.

Kent had known because his hands had wished to reach out to her. He had almost betrayed his presence on the street. The need to know her had grown that strong. His and Plain Jane's desire merged into one. Yet Kent still could not keep Joann from that long, sharp knife.

"Anything else?" She asked, searching his face. Kent forced his muscles to go slack.

Nicole did not need to know his sense of distress. If she did, the detective might balk at his next course of action.

As the silence lingered, the air closed in around them. The barometer fell as rapidly as the temperature. It was only a matter of minutes before a deluge. Nicole inhaled as if to speak, then sadly shook her head, dropping the hold on his arm.

Free, Kent continued walking down the alley.

Away from the body. Away from his failure.

Nicole was not done with him yet. "Still..." Her voice lingered on the air as thunder rumbled overhead. "When you lost her, you should have called for back-up."

As a heavy rain began to fall, Kent turned to Nicole, the scent of Joann's perfume fresh in his nostrils.

For the first time tonight, he did not lie to the woman he once loved. "I know."

CHAPTER 6

The killer charged down the stairs, two at a time.

Panting more from excitement than from exertion. The five-block sprint was not as much of a rush as coming that close to being caught.

Hurrying over to the sink, the killer snapped off bloody gloves, rinsed them over and over again under hot water, then balled them together and set off down another set of stairs to the furnace.

Opening the door, the killer threw the gloves into the blasting heat, then pulled off a long, blood-smeared overcoat and tossed it in as well. The fire flared brighter, burning hotter for a brief second. Just as Joann's eyes had done before being extinguished forever.

CHAPTER 7

Kent crouched in the bushes outside the morgue's loading dock. The building seemed squat and quite unattractive even for government work. All dull steel and rough concrete. Artistically as dead as the denizens inside. Meat packing plants had more character than this place.

At some point, someone must have realized that this building was a place where friends and family came to claim the bodies of their loved ones.

That "someone" had planted enough foliage to create an arboretum, not realizing that greenery alone could not shake the building's sense of despair. No matter the flowering shrubs, no happiness could come of this place.

But Kent was not here to criticize.

He was here to claim his own dead.

Perhaps everyone else could wait until Dr. McGregor rolled his ass out of bed at seven, but the profiler could not wait those four hours. He needed to know now.

Unlike metropolitan centers like L.A. or New York with their round-the-clock medical examiners with nearly instantaneous answers, the remainder of the country still had to make do with good-ole-boy docs.

Doctors who turned off their pagers at midnight. If you planned on dying after the witching hour, you didn't count on an autopsy until after McGregor had his breakfast.

Clearly the good doctor did not understand that the killer's timetable depended on his success or defeat this night. If Plain Jane had his trophy, Kent and the police might have another four or five days, maybe a week, to stop the lunatic before he struck again. If the killer left the crime scene empty-handed, Plain Jane would be out again, maybe even tonight.

If that were the case, Kent needed to know. He needed to be on the prowl again. Trolling the city for short, quiet unassuming brunettes.

No one else, not even Nicole, seemed ready to act upon his urgency. Glick had made it perfectly clear when Kent came on the case that his role was solely as that of an advisor. He had a better chance of bossing the janitors around than he did of ordering anyone in the department to do his bidding.

Glick had tied his hands. If he hadn't, Kent would have wakened the medical examiner himself. This idiotic following of bureaucratic protocol could get another woman killed.

A growing fury reduced the his vision to a pinpoint.

They were to blame. Glick, Torres, Nicole.

Well...

Kent gulped, remembering his own tragic decision. Nicole had been right. When he lost track of Joann in the Rocky Horror crowd, he should have called for back up. However, Kent knew if all those cops descended on Joann to protect her, the killer would have evaporated.

Worse, had Kent shown his hand that boldly, Plain Jane might have been able to make him. How safe would the women of this city have been if the killer knew the face of the man who hunted him?

And they were running out of time. If Kent was correct in his calculations, Plain Jane would only make one more kill in this city before pulling up roots, replanting months from now, miles from here.

Plain Jane had already changed M.O.s three times in three different cities. He was getting bolder, no longer hiding his true aim. The killings would never lessen, only grow.

Sighing, Kent knew those were all the logical reasons he had not called for back up. However, crouched behind a bush in the pouring rain, Kent could admit the real reason he had not called for help. The sole reason, which he could never share with anyone, not even Nicole, was his delusional belief that he, and only he, could keep Joann safe. He had slipped so deeply into the killer's mindset that his reality had warped. Tunnel vision could not even describe it.

There was him and Joann. No other. The rest of the world was but a blur, meaning nothing and contributing nothing. Joann was his and his alone. The back-up police force felt so insignificant as to not even register on Kent's radar. Joann was his only concern.

And now he sat here in the mud, waiting for her body. Maybe breathing in her Obsession one last time might give him a sense of peace.

Refocusing, Kent stared at the morgue. It was the one and only building he needed to get into tonight, yet it was the single building he could not enter.

A two year-old restraining order barred him from entering the morgue or even approaching within one hundred feet. Even if that were somehow lifted, the D.A. would never officially sanction what Kent needed to do for fear of contaminating the chain of evidence. That, and the minor fact that Kent had no medical training.

For the span of a breath, anger welled again at Nicole. If only she had not stopped him at the crime scene. Just a few more moments in that retched alley, and he would have known if Plain Jane had claimed his trophy.

As quickly as the anger rose, the hot burn faded. Not that Nicole was not to blame, but Kent could not dwell again on the detective. He needed laser-sharp focus if he had any hope of catching the killer.

Kent could still feel the firm grip of her fingers on his arm. Damn, she had been pissed. He might even have a few bruises. But the touch that lingered most was the gentle laying of her hand upon his shoulder. Why the hell had she done that? Why had she reached out to him like she used to? He'd been perfectly content glowering at her and her partner-boy-toy. Perfectly happy to secretly pine for her unattainable affection.

For months they had worked at arm's length. Alternating between apathy and begrudging acceptance. Their relationship was right where he liked it.

Now she had to go and cover for him again. Just like the old days. Just like the old nights when he would hold her until she fell asleep, then watch her breathe in and out. He would lay motionless beside her, gaining a sense of quiet and peace, before he left their bed to go stalk another killer.

Damn, but she'd felt good in his arms. The smell of her hair. The taste of the sweat on her skin after she had worked out. His body remembered the sensation even better than his mind. And this was not the echo of some pervert's lust when he stalked victims. This was his own desire. His own need. And that is what made it so painful. Nearly unbearable.

Kent shook his head, trying to clear Nicole from his thoughts, but simply ended up scattering rainwater from his hair. That's why he could not allow his mind to touch upon the detective. It always led him down a path he couldn't follow.

Gritting his teeth, Kent forced himself to stare at the morgue's loading dock. The body should have been here by now. Did Nicole suspect his plan and have the corpse shipped to the F.B.I.'s body shop in Kansas City instead?

His concern had been premature, as the medical examiner's van hydroplaned into the parking lot. A spray of dirty water washed over him as the transport skidded to a stop. Kent did not even bother to wipe the grunge off. His renewed pin-point focus would not let him. Nothing else mattered.

Joann, or what was left of Joann, had arrived.

A young morgue attendant, one that Kent did not recognize from two years ago, rushed out the thick double doors. Protecting a 'Slipknot' leather choker, the slim attendant pulled his white coat over his head.

The storm's fury had withered to a sprinkle as the driver, wearing a beat up and stained yet officially licensed N.A.S.C.A.R. jacket, got out of the van and opened the door.

"Got another one for you."

"Man, would people stop dying or what? It's going to be a week before we process all these stiffs."

The driver seemed unimpressed by the younger man's bluster. "They want a preliminary report this morning."

"Yeah, right."

"By 9A.M."

The wiry attendant did a double-take before he answered, "Are they huffing formaldehyde?" When the driver did not respond, he continued, "I've got three homicides for McGregor to cut before this one."

"They want to know if she got sliced by Plain Jane."

"Oh man, you're kidding!"

"Nope," the driver said flatly. "They need to know first thing if he took his usual trophy or not."

Kent recognized the look on the attendant's face. His expression held a respect that almost bordered on fascination. He had felt it earlier this evening, huddled in that storefront, waiting for Joann to pass.

"Wow, this is my most favorite corpse to date." He opened the bag and passed his finger along her slit throat.

As perverse as it sounded, Kent felt a dagger of jealousy. No one should touch Joann like that. No one.

"Don't worry, babe. You are first on the hit parade."

"You are one sick bastard." With that, the driver got back into the van, leaving the attendant to wheel the body back towards the morgue.

Kent's muscles tensed.

The long wait forgotten.

Soon he would be with Joann.

CHAPTER 8

With the wagon gone and the kid heading inside, Kent made his move. Keeping between the stucco wall of the morgue and the thick foliage, he made sure the security cameras could only register his shoulder.

Then Kent's luck changed for the good. The heavy-metal loving attendant pushed two Shure noise-canceling earbuds into his ears. Kent knew because he owned three pair of the same brand. They were the only thing that kept his neighbor's late night amorous adventures to a reasonable level. Now Kent just needed to keep out of view of the cameras.

As the attendant keyed in the door's code he began air-guitaring. With this guy's A.D.D., breaking into the morgue was like stealing candy from a premie. Timing it perfectly, Kent crept in alongside the gurney as the attendant half-pulled the body behind him and half-stomped to some unheard beat.

As the rich air of the rainstorm met the acrid odor of death, Kent's nostrils clamped down. The stench of formaldehyde vied for supremacy over bitter antiseptics.

His masterful break-in almost complete, Harbinger felt his trench coat catch in the closing doors. He jerked the garment, but it was stuck. If he delayed any longer even the head-banger was going to notice his very unauthorized presence. Trusting the kid's iPod to mask the sound, Kent ripped the edge of his coat off.

Kent slunk forward. He had to keep the gurney between him and the camera positioned above the intake desk. Another few feet and he could take the first sharp right and be free of the attendant.

"Boy, what are you dragging in here?"

Freezing, the profiler knew that voice. O'Fallon. The world's oldest security guard. Kent and the gaunt gentleman had tangled horns before.

O'Fallon jerked the plugs from the kid's ears. Kent had to scramble to stay out of the old man's line of sight, which brought him dangerously close to the camera's view.

The kid nearly shouted his answer. "Just rolling in another satisfied customer, O'Fallon."

Kent kept low under the gurney. O'Fallon might have been hard of hearing but for an octogenarian, he had surprisingly good eyesight.

"Then what's that in the door, *boy?*"

"Just some crap kicked up by the storm, *old man.*"

Tensing as the security guard's heavy footsteps approached, Kent glanced around for an escape route. A hiding place. A nook. A cranny. Anything. He did not need much wiggle room.

Kent had won plenty of bets back at Quantico by disappearing into nearly thin air.

Unfortunately, this morgue's tile floors and stainless steel-lined walls were all sharp angles and open space. Even the nearest air vent was a good ten feet away.

"I'll have no cursing, boy," O'Fallon warned as he made his way around the gurney.

Kent cursed as he shoved the gurney into the attendant, forcing the kid to stumble into the aged guard. Head down and tilted away from the camera, the profiler sprinted the length of the hallway as the two untangled themselves.

"Harbinger!" The guard shouted. "You just violated your T.R.O.!"

It appeared the old man's memory was as sharp as his eyesight. Fortunately, Kent had an even better sense of recall. Without hesitation, the profiler took a left, then a fast right for eight paces, then another quick left to a door that led to the back parking lot. A photographic memory came in handy, given his frequent run-ins with local law enforcement.

Even though a sign over the emergency exit warned an alarm would sound, the profiler hit it at a full run. No bells. No buzzer. Harbinger was glad to see they took security of the building as seriously as they had two years ago.

Kent burst into the renewed storm and made for the tree line. He could hear muffled shouts, yet he did not worry. The video surveillance would show his break-in. But enough evidence to pin it on him?

Never.

There was not any proof he had ever been inside the morgue. No proof except the small, torn corner of his overcoat. Proof that he violated a restraining order.

Given his abject failure to protect Joann, Kent could not give the D.A. any other excuse to pull him from the case.

Despite the nearly hail-like rain, he shrugged off his torn coat. He did not bother to bury the evidence. The weather would wash away any DNA. Sometimes, granted rarely, but sometimes it came in extremely handy to think like a criminal.

Making his way into the wooded park, Kent glanced back at the morgue. Despite his initial failure, this night was not over. He still needed time alone with Joann's body. As much as he hated to admit it, he would need help.

Her help.

CHAPTER 9

Across from Glick, Nicole sat as if she were a statue upon the chair. Her waist at a perfect right angle. Her knees bent at another ninety-degree angle. Her left ankle crossed over the right. Both hands lay in her lap, atop a F.B.I. textbook Harbinger had written on the apprehension of serial killers.

After the cold alley, Glick's office practically steamed. Too humid. Too claustrophobic. Crowding the small room were the Captain's pseudo-wood desk, five dented file cabinets, and an old fashioned radiator. For a City Counsel that insisted it was tough on crime, they certainly did not fund the fight very well.

The detective wished she could take off her jacket, but with Ruben sitting right next to her, she did not want to draw attention to herself. His anger, frustration, and distrust of Harbinger already carried over in waves.

Nicole gripped Kent's book tighter. She wanted plenty of ammunition to counteract any accusations Ruben might hurl. Without Kent at her side, his book was the next best thing.

Even though Nicole knew the statistics from the text by heart, it still hurt to lose Joann. Knowing that it could take officials months or even years to realize that they had a serial killer on their hands did not make Nicole feel any better.

Nor did the fact that once you identified a serialist, you were destined to lose another five, maybe six more victims before even coming close to capturing a proficient killer. Sometimes the number doubled. Sometimes decades elapsed. Sometimes the bastards eluded capture completely.

But not with Harbinger. The most victims this profiler had ever lost before on a case numbered three. Joann shattered that record to bring the total to four. Though you would never know it to look at him, Nicole knew Kent felt regret. Guilt. Even shame. She could see it in his eyes; Joann's death had shaken him.

It turned out his arrogance was a double-edged sword. It carried Kent to victory after victory, but in defeat it drove him to obsession. The investigation became oh-so-personal. He was no longer a cop after a suspect. It was now Kent against the Killer.

Worse, when Harbinger felt guilt he became reckless. Defying authority, more than usual. Breaking laws, even more than usual. Keeping her at an emotional arm's length, way more than usual.

Nicole dragged her thoughts out of the past. They had enough problems now that she did not need to dredge their history for more. Her gaze flickered up to make sure Glick had not finished with the report. His salt and pepper hair seemed to have gained more salt over the past few months to the point his bushy mustache was nearly white. His heavily lidded eyes scanned the document, giving it his customary diligence.

Well, his newfound diligence.

It was not two years ago that the Captain would have railed at them like any worthwhile superior officer. But after three heart attacks, two following altercations with Kent, Glick must have realized the bluster just was not worth it.

With his dark blue tie loosened and the top button of his shirt open, you could see the tip of his scar. A quadruple, triple bypass. Heart surgery did not get much more serious than that.

Which was why it pained Nicole to have failed her captain. You could see by the way his jaw worked that Glick's frustration doubled her own. While she only had the victim's family to answer to, he had an entire city.

Worse, an entire City Counsel that had been none too subtle about their displeasure. Being splashed across the news that their fair city was the serial killer capital of the world was not doing the tourist trade any good.

Ironically it had been this heightened level of political pressure that had allowed Nicole to convince Glick they needed Kent on the case. She had thought she was doing her Captain a favor by bringing in the lauded profiler, but by the vein throbbing on his forehead, Nicole was not so sure.

On numerous occasions, usually right after she said she had a headache and did not want to spend the night at his place, Ruben accused her of pulling Harbinger out of retirement for her own personal reasons.

Had she?

A few months ago she might have vehemently disagreed, but now? Now, all she could think about was Kent. Think of where he might be, right this minute. Think of what trouble he could be stirring up. Think of how she should be out there with him hunting a predator rather than in here performing damage control.

Nicole knew the rumors that circulated the bullpen. Her colleagues thought Kent to be some sort of Svengali. Using his nearly mythical intellect and stubbled good looks, Kent had mesmerized her so deeply that she could look past all his flaws.

What no one seemed to understand was that it was exactly those flaws that called to her. She had gone to an Ivy League college. She had been around enough brainiacs to not be so easily impressed by sheer intellect alone. Plus, if you put

Kent and the other men she had dated over the years in a line-up, the profiler's looks did not even crack the top five.

No, only Nicole knew the real basis of her fascination. She was not exactly proud of it, so she did not broadcast it to the world. It was almost safer to let other people think she could be so easily seduced by success.

For it was not what Kent gave that attracted Nicole, but what he withheld. The profiler would give her mere glimpses of his genius, but hold back that most vital detail. He kept her coming back for more. Professionally and emotionally.

She knew the impulse was dysfunctional, but a single back-handed compliment from Kent meant more to her than all of Ruben's declarations of devotion.

CHAPTER 10

Ruben tried to keep his eyes forward, watching Glick read their very preliminary report filled with even more preliminary conclusions, but no matter how much he willed his stare ahead, his eyes flickered to Nicole.

Even though his partner dressed in a stern pantsuit, there was no mistaking Usher for anything but a woman. Her open blazer allowed a bit of cleavage to show. And it was truly a miracle that she could run in those three-inch heels. But just try to take them away from her. Nicole was sensitive about her height. She did not want to look small. Frail.

How anyone could look into those green eyes and think her weak, Ruben would never know. He waited for her to glance over, but Nicole was far more successful keeping her gaze across the desk at their Captain.

A mumble from outside the office drew Ruben's attention. At least half-a-dozen uniforms still hung around the bullpen, mostly officers fresh from being released from their T.O. These young bucks certainly weren't waiting for Ruben, Nicole, or even Glick. The word must have gotten out that

Harbinger had been summoned to the Captain's office. The naive officers hoped for a sighting of the infamous profiler.

<u>Infamous, my ass</u>. Ruben wanted to retort, but that would pretty much prove him as unstable as Kent.

A grunt from the Captain brought Ruben's attention back to the room. Glick must have gotten to the part where Nicole tried to justify why Harbinger hadn't called for back up.

Again Ruben's eyes strayed to his partner. Her eyes were cast down, fixated on the hands crossed in her lap, where a finger toyed with a single string from her bookmark. Over and over again she entwined the thread around her fingertip, then released it. A nervous habit. One that she only displayed when Harbinger invaded her life.

How he hated seeing her like this. Her heel tapped ever so quietly, like a schoolgirl nervous about being called to the principal's office.

By the set of her lips, Ruben knew how alone she felt. Once again, Kent had fucked up and, once again, left Nicole to clean up the mess. After her difficult childhood, raising her younger sister, and then working her way through college, she deserved far better than this. Far better than a profiler who abandoned her at every turn.

Tonight though, she proved that, yet again, she could not abandon Harbinger. While Ruben took the statement from Officer Macaine, he had watched Kent and Nicole's argument. Ruben knew the depth of her fury at Harbinger, yet within a few words, he witnessed the profiler turn Nicole from a self-assured, professional, experienced detective into an uncertain, defensive, and worst of all, *submissive* woman.

Although Ruben had to admit Harbinger had that affect on just about anybody the profiler decided to go up against.

Kent was an ass, but an ass with a resume to rival Holmes. Even the F.B.I. had been too small a pond for the profiler. With half a dozen high-profile arrests under his belt by the age of twenty-five, the boy-wonder had been recruited into a classified think tank.

Damn it, why could not the bastard have just stayed tucked away with those other eggheads? But no, someone had to go and randomly poison the nation's beef supply, forcing the president to personally ask Kent to come out of retirement to solve the apparently unsolvable crime.

A laugh rose from the bullpen behind him, then just as quickly the titter died. Despite Kent's abject failure to save another victim, the station was still abuzz at the very idea Harbinger would deign to make an appearance. However, even the most junior officer knew that tonight was not for levity.

It galled Ruben that whatever social skills Kent lacked, he made up for in reputation. How the profiler had cracked the beef poisoning case was the stuff law enforcement legends were made of.

After the president's desperate call, Harbinger had boarded a plane in Chicago completely ignorant of the facts, yet by the time he landed in D.C., Kent had solved the crime.

Yep, the prick had cracked a masterful scheme that had brought the stock market tumbling a thousand points and dropped the meat industry to its knees while he sipped champagne in first class.

Without any fanfare, Kent had come off the tarmac and handed the agents, who were waiting to whisk him off to Quantico, a list of leads scribbled on a napkin.

Despite the president's orders, the profiler refused to go back to headquarters with them. Instead, as only Harbinger could, Kent went into an airport restaurant and ordered a steak.

Rare.

The bastard had been that damn sure he knew the pattern of the poisonings, he ordered a fucking Porterhouse. Before Kent had finished his meal, a group of domestic terrorists, who had evaded seven separate task-forces for over eleven months and traveled all over the country undetected, had been arrested.

But the story did not end there. When Harbinger received the congratulatory call from the director of the F.B.I. himself, Kent told his old boss that he was billing the agency for a full day's wage and taking the afternoon off so that he could go comic book shopping.

Ruben sighed. It was probably that last part that had sealed Harbinger's reputation with the young officers.

It truly was a great story. Who else but the profiler could have realized that the terrorists had spiked poison into the anti-bacterial fluid that meat handlers used to sanitize their hands? And not every bag, but every third one delivered.

He might have had a begrudging respect for the profiler, had he not met the man behind the legend.

Having to actually to work with that level of genius made you just want punch the guy rather than worship him.

How could you put your theory forward or think to disagree with a man whose advice had been sought by presidents and kings alike?

It was a little hard to imagine that you might have something meaningful to contribute when Kent had the Secretary of State on speed dial.

Ending Ruben's revelry, their Captain closed the file. "I'm not even going to bother to ask where Harbinger is."

Ruben snuck a peek over to Nicole whose eyes were up from her hands, but averted from their Captain's gaze. She had no good answer to that question, and they all knew it. Ruben noticed her finger wound the string into a tight coil.

Glick continued, "As you know, I try to be the kinder, gentler Captain, but I need an answer as to how we let this woman die, or I *will* start yelling."

Surprisingly, Nicole glanced over at Ruben. While just a little flattered, he could not help her this time. Not with Kent.

Not with another death under the profiler's belt. "You don't want me going first."

To her credit, Nicole re-grouped, straightening her back, abandoning the string. "Sir, the very fact that Kent was within moments of the killer shows his methods are working."

"This is the fourth victim on Kent's watch."

"We all knew there were going to be losses." Nicole hurried on, "His technique is to hunt the victim --"

Ruben could not help himself. "So far, so good."

"Thanks for proving my point," Nicole snapped.

"I wasn't."

Flushed, Nicole turned to face him. "Can you do that? Can you watch a sea of women and pick the one, the *same* one as the killer? Because if you can, I'd like to see it."

Ruben's ears burned as his jaw clenched. What had gotten into her? Where did she get off talking to him like that? Throwing his inadequacies back into his face?

"I don't think that was --" Glick tried to interrupt, but Nicole turned on him as well.

"Kent has the unique ability to find the victim first, then back-track to the killer."

"I know the jacket liner, Usher. What we --"

Nicole jumped over their Captain's words again. "He cuts off the killer at the proverbial pass."

"Or not," Ruben interjected.

Glick cut off Nicole's retort. "It's not his profiling skills that are the issue. We've got to face the possibility that he's becoming more of a liability than an asset."

"What?"

Ruben tensed as the Captain glanced in his direction. With the slightest nod, he agreed that Glick should continue. Bracing himself, Ruben knew that Nicole would be angered, maybe even irate, with the both of them. But their intervention was not just for the scared brunettes in the city, it was for

Nicole as well. Someone had to break the sick influence Kent had over her.

Glick pulled out a large stack of files and flipped through them. "Twelve peeping tom reports. Five stalking complaints." He overrode Nicki, "And a shop-lifting incident."

Ruben tried to suppress his anger and project a more sympathetic tone, "He's out of control."

"If the press or the public ever found out that we not only allowed but, worse, *encouraged* this kind of behavior --"

"We've already had four other F.B.I. profilers before Kent." Nicole didn't bother to hide her exasperation.

Both men shifted uncomfortably. If Nicole was upset at this part? Well, this talk was not going to unfold well at all.

Glick measured his words out slowly and carefully. "Ruben has done some solid police-work and perhaps might be better suited to run the case."

CHAPTER 11

Nicole sat shocked, horrified, and more than a little confused. The words coming out of her Captain's mouth could not be the ones she thought she heard.

"Excuse me?"

"Torres has some angles on the case that I think Kent might have overlooked."

Fury and betrayal overrode all else as she turned on her supposed partner. "And you were going to tell me this, when?"

Ruben shrugged. "You don't like anything that contradicts your stubbled Sherlock."

Nicole tried to speak, but the Captain's volume rose higher than she had heard for two years. Since Kent had left. "We'll hear from Ruben *and* Kent. We'll look at their profiles side-by-side and decide in which direction to take the case."

"That's not --"

"We'll hear them *both* out, Usher." Glick's tone could not be argued.

Choking back a hundred retorts could only Nicole nod.

As graciously as she could, Nicole rose and exited Glick's office, making sure to shut the door behind her. Tears of frustration sprang to her eyes, but she held them back as she passed the six or seven young cops that lingered in the bullpen. It was bad enough to have been humiliated back there; she did not need to repeat the experience in front of this eager crowd.

Once past the gaggle of onlookers, Nicole dug through her purse. Where in the hell were her keys? She wanted out of here. Now. Before Ruben came chasing after her, trying to placate her with how he had gone behind her back for her own good. She did not know how much more male manipulation she could stand right now.

Crossing to her desk, Nicole tossed the drawers. She found a stapler she thought that she had lost. Her favorite pen reclaimed, but no keys. She was so intent on her task that she did not hear her partner's approach.

"Nicki," Ruben's tone sounded almost as bruised as her feelings.

"Don't."

The good old logical, thoughtful Ruben tried to make a reappearance. "If I thought he was even slightly sane I would back off, but Nicki..." She could not see it, but she heard a deep sigh from her partner as Ruben continued, "You saw him tonight. Saw what he was like."

Emotions constricted her throat as she checked the middle drawer again, but the words came out easily since she had defended Harbinger with them a hundred times before. "You know as well as I do that Kent has to strip his psyche down so far that he --"

"*You*...don't." His tone cut. "Save the misunderstood genius spiel for Glick."

Nicole paused in her frantic search when she realized her hands were shaking. Was it fury at a partner whom had betrayer her? Or the fact that he might be right about Kent?

Ruben stepped closer so that he could place his hand on her shoulder. "We all gave him another chance. It was Harbinger that blew it, not us."

Tears stung again as she noticed a glint from the corner of her drawer.

Grabbing her keys, "I'm out of here."

Ruben wasn't going to be denied. "Where to?"

"Home."

"What happened to Thursday nights at my place?"

Nicole could not believe that Ruben would choose this night, this moment, to bring up their stagnant relationship. For weeks, no for months, neither of them had brought up the fact that they had not had sex in forever, or the fact that their 'dates' had devolved to the point where the only time they went out was to get the occasional beer with the rest of the squad.

She wan't about to change that dynamic. "I'm going home. *Alone*."

"You so sure about that?" Nicole did not rise to the bait, but Ruben continued as he walked along side her toward the exit. "Maybe Kent is hiding down in the shadows of the garage for a secret rendezvous?" She ignored him, but her partner refused to relent. "Let me guess. You two are off to some dark, mysterious locale?"

"I am not amused," she tried to warn him off.

"A funeral parlor? Morgue? Oh wait, perhaps a picnic at a cemetery?"

That was it. Nicole turned on her heel. "You don't know jack about him and obviously not much more about me."

Instead of seeming angered, Ruben just looked sad. "He's not the same man he was, Nicki."

Why were all the men in her life spending so much time trying to protect her that they forgot she could protect herself?

"Did it ever occur to you that I'm not the same woman?" Nicole was done. Done wrangling. Done arguing. Done getting her feelings hurt. "You know what? No matter his flaws, Kent never would have stooped to playing politics behind your back."

Not waiting for her partner's retort, Nicole stormed toward the door.

Ruben's words were just loud enough for her to catch, but quiet enough that Nicole could pretend she didn't hear them. "No, because that would require him to actually *care* about someone."

CHAPTER 12

Kent heard Nicole coming down the garage stairs before he saw her. She was hurrying. Rushing her steps. Traveling far too fast for her mood. Far too fast for those clunky high heels.

Oh, Nicole might be a great athlete, but graceful when pissed off she was not. Almost on cue a loud clang resounded from the staircase. That would be her foot slipping off the end of a step, then her banging her elbow before catching herself with a last ditch grab from her now numb wrist.

Sure enough, a pause in her footsteps and some muffled cursing. Kent knew her too well.

He knew once out of the stairwell exactly how many steps it would take her to get to her car. He knew she'd started using a new shampoo, because even though she took the time and energy to shop at a beauty supply house rather than picking up her hair care products at the grocery store, Nicole could not resist a bargain. He also knew that she carried a Nine West purse. Once she discovered this brand had penholders sewn right into the inner pocket, she'd never buy another brand.

Kent knew that and so much more. How Nicole could go days without applying make-up but would not be caught dead without her nails polished. Religiously, she bought the same color as the salon and had a bottle in her purse, her car, and at home. That way if Nicole barely even chipped a nail, she could repair it in heartbeat. How many times before bed, and over his protests, had she pulled one of those bottles from her nightstand for a touch up?

The thought brought a grin to his troubled lips. He knew her habits. Knew her moods. Knew her body better than she did. That's how he knew she was only a few days away from her period. She would be at her most emotional, but also at the height of her sexual appetite.

A few years ago that combination would have guaranteed they take not one, but two or three rounds in her goose-downed bed. He knew all this as well as he knew his own name, but there was one thing he did not know.

How he could convince Nicole to help him.

Especially with what he had in mind.

CHAPTER 13

Nicole winced as she pushed the Mustang's key into the lock. That blow to her elbow was going to bug her for a few days. Just another reminder of the disaster this night was chalking up to be. She could not wait until she crashed into bed. Maybe by daylight she could get some sense of perspective on Joann's death and Kent's abandonment.

She went to turn the key, then paused. She did not so much hear a breath or see a shoe tip, as much as Nicole just knew Kent stood behind her. The night just would not end.

"If you came all the way down here, you could have at least taken some of the heat during the meeting."

"You should be more careful."

Kent's voice had never sounded so sexy. He could infuse words with honey and musk. Sweet and sultry. It took the sting out of almost everything that had happened tonight.

"I could have taken you six ways to Sunday," she said.

"Really?" Was that amusement on his lips?

Then she found out why. Kent held out a gun, butt first towards her. Why would he do that? Her hand flew to her holster. Her gun was missing.

No, not missing. It was being handed back to her.

Embarrassed, Nicole snatched the gun from him. "You better show up to the briefing tomorrow."

Kent not only ignored her words, but he used the distraction as she re-holstered her gun to grab her keys. Before she could stop him, Kent had opened the driver's side door and hopped in as if it were his own. Just like he used to.

"Whoa. Where are we going?" Nicole asked as she made her way around to the passenger side. The profiler could give the most perfect, dead-on, teenage 'duh' expression when he wanted to, but she was not as intuitive as he was, so Nicole had to ask. "Where?"

"Where else?" Kent rolled his eyes. "The morgue."

Nicole's hand dropped from the handle. "Of course."

"You getting in or not?"

The argument with Ruben came back in a rush. How her partner had foreseen the profiler waiting for her in the garage. Her own words declaring she wasn't the same woman she had been two years ago. Now was the time to prove it.

The 32-year-old Nicole would have jumped in the car and gladly gone on the wild Kent-ride, but the 34-year-old detective took a step back from the car.

"Go be morbid on your own time."

"I already did."

From the look on his face, Nicole knew Kent was not lying. But the situation still did not make any sense.

"Then why drag me there?"

Obviously Harbinger wasn't used to her saying 'no.' And didn't sound very happy with it. "Get in or not."

Kent getting bossy actually steeled Nicole's resolve. She took another step back to make her intent clear. "Let me know how it goes."

CHAPTER 14

Kent felt incredulous, which was odd, because he'd never experienced that particular emotion before.

Whatever you called it, it felt damn weird. A mixture of surprise, bewilderment, and just a hint of pride that Nicole had actually stood up for herself.

Tonight, however, was not the time to hear her roar.

He needed her.

Perhaps if he just told her that. Told her how much he needed her. And not just for breaking into morgues, but other, less gruesome things. Maybe if he just told her that, she might help. But that would break his cardinal rule.

Never, ever, even under threat of torture, be emotionally honest. If someone actually knew how you felt, they would have a hold over you. Like the hold he had over the psychos that he hunted. Once Kent knew a basic truth about them, he had them by the short hairs. He would never allow another person to have that kind of control over him.

Not even Nicole.

Kent looked one last time in the rear view mirror to find Nicole had not budged. She wanted to play chicken? He could play chicken. Kent turned on the engine. Put the car into gear. Revved the gas, but still the detective did not move.

Exactly how ballsy had Nicole gotten?

He inched the car forward and checked the mirror again. Still no movement. Damn her. Hitting the gas, he squealed out of the garage.

He did not need anyone that badly.

CHAPTER 15

Nicole was surprised to find her feet still planted solidly on the ground as Kent drove off. The detective let out a breath that she did not even realize she was holding. She had done it. She had stood her ground.

A small smile spread across her lips until Nicole realized she had no way to get home to celebrate this historic moment. She was not about to go upstairs and beg a ride off Ruben. She could check, but Nicole knew she did not have cash for a cab. It was a hell of a walk home, especially with her ankle still sore from the near fall in the stairwell.

With no palatable options, Nicole just stood there. Tired and a little shaky. If this was what victory felt like, it was not exactly motivating her to go for another win.

Was that the sound of a car? Engine sounds echoed off the garage's low ceilings. Nicole's mood brightened. Maybe a squad car was coming in for the night. With luck, she could get a lift home from a uniform.

But the arrival turned out to be far more complicated. It was Kent, backing her car down the ramp. Nicole stayed in place not so much due to stubbornness as to shock. Kent had never come back.

Never.

Kent stopped the car right beside her. "O'Fallon recognized me." His gaze met hers. "And, well, I was not exactly welcomed."

If she were in a better mood, there was probably a story in there that would be quite amusing. When she did not respond, Kent continued, "The brain incident of 2003? I trust you remember?"

Oh, Nicole remembered it all right. Not an era that she wanted to revisit. "And you want my help, for?"

"A distraction." He shrugged. "I need some quality time with the body."

"Imagine my surprise they didn't let you in."

All the humor left his face. "The trophy..." The words caught in his throat, and the profiler had to restart. "I have to know if he has his prize."

There it was. Kent's siren call. Everyone else, including her, was willing to wait until the morning for the report. What did Kent understand about the killer that none of the rest of them did? Normally that intrigue would have been enough to lure her into the car, but now, tonight?

She was just tired and sore.

The more Kent massaged his ego, the more hitching a ride with Ruben sounded appealing.

Nicole headed towards the stairs. "Read it in the report like everyone else." The profiler's eyes narrowed. Kent had that lean and hungry look. Nicole wasn't impressed this time. "Waiting four hours for the autopsy isn't going to kill you."

CHAPTER 16

No, but it might get another brunette killed.

Kent watched Nicole walk across the garage to the stairs. What was she thinking? The nation's most prolific serial killer had been interrupted.

How could he gauge the killer's reaction if he didn't know his level of frustration? Was he happy, coveting his latest trophy or back on the prowl? Didn't Nicole understand?

Obviously the detective didn't since she kept walking. He was losing her. Kent had only one card left.

"I'll come tomorrow," he called out.

Nicole stopped but did not turn around. What more did she want from him? What more did he have?

"To the morning briefing." She still refused to turn around. "That's what you wanted, isn't it?"

Nicole turned the upper half of her body, but kept her toes pointed toward the stairwell. Toward Ruben. "On time?"

He couldn't help but smirk. "Don't push it."

CHAPTER 17

Ruben watched Nicole drive away with Kent.

Why was he not surprised?

He hadn't meant to eavesdrop. He had come down to apologize. But then, imagine that, he found Kent standing right next to her. Just as he had predicted. Ruben had thought he was just being sarcastic during the fight with Nicole, but obviously a part of him feared that she quickened to the profiler's ultra-dangerous aura.

Worse, Kent was not just a bad boy. The profiler was a downright awful boy. Harbinger did not just ride motorcycles, he would hot-wire one to bring on a date.

How could anyone sane, compete?

When Kent had driven off, leaving Nicole standing there all alone, Ruben's heart skipped a beat. For once, the profiler was showing his true colors. The deep selfish streak that for some reason seemed beyond anyone else's comprehension to see was coming shining through.

Ruben knew he could never be Nicole's knight in shining armor; however, tonight he had the chance to at least be a guy with a silver Lexus who could make sure she got home safe and sound.

Those hopes were dashed in their infancy when Kent backed all the way from the street to Nicole's parking spot. An action which spelled the end to Ruben's rescue fantasy.

He'd seen it in his partner's eyes. Instead of being pissed that Kent had not only stolen her car but left her with no ride home, Nicole had somehow seemed content. Maybe even a little gratified. Maybe a lot.

After everything Harbinger had put her through, Nicole seemed ready, even eager, to get back on the profiler's emotional merry-go-round.

Ruben knew a lot of men would just give up on her. Back off. But he was not most men. It was not arrogance or some masochistic urge that kept him in the game. No, it was the fact that despite Kent's allure, ultimately, whether Nicole wanted to admit it or not, the profiler would hurt her. Not just hurt her, but jeopardize her career again. Ruin her life again.

And when that day came, Ruben would be sure to be there to catch her. <u>Again</u>.

CHAPTER 18

Nicole knew assisting Harbinger was a bad idea. A *really* bad idea. Helping Kent break into the morgue was possibly the worst idea since...

Well, since the brain incident of 2003. But the truth was she never felt more alive than she did right now, knowing that Kent was somewhere in the shadows behind her.

Following her.

Unlike the profiler, she knew the door code and let them in into the morgue without incident. They made their way to the intake desk, keeping to the back halls. Nicole in the lead. Kent trailing in the darkness.

Even she needed to avoid old man O'Fallon. He might be well past retirement age, but the security guard would know if she showed up at the morgue in the middle of the night, Kent could not be far behind.

Instead they targeted the new attendant. It didn't hurt that the kid had a crush on her. While Nicole tried to avoid the morgue after the ugly incident several years ago, her job brought her here frequently. Between the memories and the rank odor, Nicole always had to go home and take a hot shower afterward. She had no idea how anyone could work here full-time. You would have to be a morbid son-of-a-bitch with a poor sense of smell.

Yet here she was approaching the desk, making certain that O'Fallon was not nearby before she showed herself. Luckily the elderly guard seemed to be off on one of his many 'cat-naps' he took during the long night shift.

Nicole came out of hiding. "Hey, Joshua."

The younger man continued to stare straight ahead at the bank of security monitors. Well, they couldn't have him doing that if Kent was going to break into the crypt. Nicole tapped the young man on the shoulder.

"Joshua."

The attendant practically fell out of his seat. The kid jerked the buds out of his ears and the tinny sounds of death metal floated on the air.

"Detective Usher! I didn't hear you buzz me."

"Nah. I know the codes."

Joshua fumbled with his iPod, trying desperately to turn it off as he spoke, "Yeah, duh. Of course you do." Finally the music stopped. "Do you have a new body? Because I'm all about new bodies. I mean I'm --"

"I need to review the paperwork on Plain Jane."

The attendant's chest puffed up. "No worries."

"Torres and I got our wires crossed, and we didn't double-check it."

"I'm telling you, everything is five-by-five."

"This is the city's most prolific serial killer, Josh. The documentation needs to be more like ten-by-ten."

Nicole forced a flirty smile.

CHAPTER 19

Kent watched as Nicole leaned forward on that last 'ten'. She had pushed some cleavage together.

The attendant's eyes dilated and his cheeks blushed. Nicole didn't have a lot going on in the chest department, but what she had, she knew how to use.

After several seconds completely slack-jawed, the attendant snapped back to attention. "Of course, let me get it."

As Joshua turned away, Kent snuck down the hall, past the desk and into the corridor to the right. Silent, up on the balls of his feet, he easily alluded the kid. Even in the pitch black, Kent made his way to the crypt without a single misstep.

Not hesitating, Harbinger pushed open the door and strode across the crypt to the rows of coolers. Rapidly, he read the names on the doors. The attendant had not been exaggerating; they had nearly a full house. Kent did not linger on any one name. These others did not concern him. The only one that mattered to him was Joann Forme.

The woman he had stalked for over a week. Nicole was not the only female whose bathroom he snooped around. He even knew that Joann was only two days from bleeding. That was how he knew the killer was going to strike tonight. Besides the trophy, Kent was beginning to form a theory that the Plain Jane wanted his women at their sexual peak.

As much as Kent loved to cultivate the perception that his insight was near psychic in origin, it actually arose from long, boring hours of observation. Sometimes so many hours that other lives were lost in the interim.

You could not rush genius.

Kent had come so close to saving Joann because of the hundreds of hours he had logged on the last three victims. Claudia Simons, Julie Gamos, and Maria Villa. From them he had learned that it was not just their petite form that drew the killer, but their pert breasts, high on the rib-cage. The killer also required a fairly narrow waist sloping into full hips. A nice ass did not hurt either.

All of those characteristics plus one other that still eluded Kent drew both the profiler and killer to Joann. It was then that the profiler realized he had been standing in front of the brunette's crypt, a hand on the lever.

Kent did not have the luxury to brood. Nicole's cleavage was not going to keep the young attendant fascinated forever. She just did not have that much to go around.

He jerked open the door and rolled Joann's body out of its temporary tomb. The sound echoed in the small room, filling it, making it seem even smaller. Cool air rushing out from the interior gave rise to goose bumps along his arm. Or was it the sight of the woman's pale face that stood out against the bright red slash across her neck?

The press might have dubbed these victims as Plain Janes, but to Kent each held their own beauty. Joann's small button nose. Her baby smooth skin, now marred by bloody hair matted against her cheek.

Despite his sense of urgency, Kent gently pulled back the unruly strands. Joann would have been horrified to have her hair in such a mess. Unlike Nicole, this woman only used one brand of shampoo and conditioner. A boutique brand, priced at over a hundred dollars a bottle, just like the celebrities used. A price she should not have been able to afford on a bookkeeper's salary.

As if hiding some state secret, late at night, Joann would go on-line and buy the expensive products on eBay. Hell, just last night she had gotten free shipping thrown in. Kent could not help but grin. Joann had looked so proud. A small victory in a small life.

Pulling her purple scarf from his pocket, he draped it over her slashed neck. A small tribute to their bond.

Quickly the smile fell. This was not a wake. He had work. Snapping on a pair of latex gloves, Kent silently apologized to the brunette for what he was about to do.

CHAPTER 20

Nicole read the intake form again. For the fifth time. Where in the hell was Kent? A piece of paper tossed into the hallway was supposed to be the signal that she could wrap up this charade. Each time she glanced to the hall, still no paper.

She was not sure how much longer she could keep Josh distracted. For what seemed like forever, while she had been checking out the paperwork, she had made sure the attendant was checking *her* out.

However, there was only so much shifting and strutting in an under-wire bra you could do before it began cutting off circulation. She needed a new strategy.

Then movement on the security screen caught Josh's eye. Over his shoulder, Nicole could see the image of Kent moving around in the crypt.

The attendant pointed. "Oh man, that freak again!"

Before she could stop him, Joshua flew down the hallway. Nicole had no other option but to rush after him. She caught up right at the door to the cooler, praying they burst into an empty room, but they found Kent elbow deep in the brunette's belly.

The most shocking site, however, was the sheer joy on the profiler's face as he pulled pink tissue to the surface.

"It's still here." He urged the mottled tissue toward her. "He didn't get it."

Several moments passed before the surprise wore off and Nicole realized what Kent was showing her.

Joann's uterus.

CHAPTER 21

Kent tugged at the ovarian ligament, trying to expose the womb better. Didn't Nicole realize what this meant? The killer had been thwarted. Denied his prize. His trophy. Kent's mind reeled with the implications.

"Dude, get another hobby!"

The attendant's outburst brought Kent back to the present circumstance. "It's still here."

Joshua pointed. "Um, that's against the law, right?"

"Uh, oh yeah." This seemed to break the detective out of her shock. She drew her gun. "Step away from the body."

Kent did not like taking orders, even if they were fake ones. "What? At least I put on gloves this time."

Nicole tilted her head to the side.

"Um, you know how to use the gun, right?" Josh asked.

Oh, she knew how to use it all right, Kent thought as Nicole leveled her aim at his head. "Step away. Now!"

Not so much to obey her as that his job was done, Kent let the uterus slip from his hands, snapped his gloves off, and tossed them into the red-lined medical waste receptacle for three points, but strangely no one cheered.

"Hands behind your back."

Playing along, Harbinger turned and was mildly surprised when he felt Nicole's knee in his back, pressing him up against the gurney. She was getting into this role-playing gig a little too enthusiastically.

"Do you think... Do you think he's Plain Jane?" the attendant asked.

Efficiently, Nicole slapped the cuffs on his wrist, tightening them more than Kent would've liked. "No. The creep only gets up close and personal after they're dead."

"Oh, so he's a necro..." The attendant stared at him with a new sense of revulsion and wonder. "Cool. I never met one face to face before."

Nicole urged Kent towards the door. "Let's go. You have the right to remain silent --"

Joshua looked to the bloody mess.

"This is the best job ever."

CHAPTER 22

Once they were out in the parking lot, Kent tried to pull free of her grip. "You can take the cuffs off now."

"I could…" Nicole shoved him toward her car. He was going to know who was in charge, at least for now.

"You have to," Kent demanded.

Even though she tried to keep him facing forward, the profiler slipped from her grasp and turned around. For a guy who had never lifted a dumbbell, Kent was deceptively strong.

His entire posture changed, and even though he leaned against the car with his hands cuffed behind him, you would never know he was the one restrained. Who needed to actually be in control, when you could just act like you were?

"I interrupted him. He'll be out again." Kent implored. "Soon. Maybe even tonight. Maybe *now*."

Nicole did her best to keep up. "He's never struck so close. He's gone at least a week between kills." But she only ended up playing his foil.

"He's never been denied his prize before. He *needs* it."

"As much as you needed to stick your damned hands in Joann's belly?"

"*More*," Kent emphasized.

That damned hungry tone. A palpable need that radiated from the profiler like an irresistible pheromone. Even though she intellectually knew that the hunger was not for her, there was no telling her body that. Kent was never as charismatic as when he was honing in on a killer.

But she had walked this path before with him. One that lead to pain, self-destruction, and abandonment. If not for his sake, then for her own Nicole needed to find a way to work this case differently. She wouldn't repeat the mistakes of the past.

"If I un-cuff you, you're going to ditch me aren't you? Not even bother coming to tomorrow's briefing, are you?"

CHAPTER 23

It was Kent's turn to study Nicole. He had cranked up his rogue, lone wolf vibe to high, and still she resisted him.

There had to be a reason.

"What's so important about this briefing?"

Nicole met his stare full on. "Every once in a while, you do need to *participate* with the department. With your colleagues. With me."

"You're not very good at lying, you know?" Her valiant effort to fool him amused Kent.

"Whatever," she said as she pulled out the cuff's keys.

He rebuffed her attempt to turn him around. The one thing he knew how to do for certain was make Nicole squirm.

Her face flushed. "Don't you want to be un-cuffed?"

Kent did not oblige an answer. Instead he locked eyes.

There could be only one winner of this little power struggle, and he certainly was not going out on the prowl for Plain Jane after being a loser.

Finally Nicole shrugged. "Fine. We'll do it your way."

Round one. Kent.

He pressed his advantage as she reached behind him to get to the cuff's lock, forcing her into close proximity.

Round two. Kent

Their body heat mingled as the air around them cooled. The storm did not seem quite over. Kent bent his neck to bring his lips ever so close to her ear. "I repeat. What's so important about tomorrow's meeting?"

His breath upon her neck had the desired effect as she fumbled the keys. The only way she could unlock the cuffs now was to lean into him. Force their bodies together. His lips turned up into a smile as he felt the points of her breasts rub against his chest as she fished for the cuff's lock.

Round three. Kent.

Husky, he moved her hair back from her face with his chin, rubbing stubble across her cheek. "You always were better at putting them on than taking them off, weren't you?"

The top of Nicole's ear turned a bright red as her breath came at a quicker and quicker pace. Obviously she remembered the nights he referred to as well as he.

Leveraging her flustered state, Kent made his move. He grabbed her hands and with a shift of his weight, pulled Nicole around, forcing her back against the car. He stood over her, pressing the entire length of their bodies together.

Round four. Kent.

He could feel the heat of Nicole's body through her thin silk blouse. Unbidden, his loins stirred. *That* was definitely not supposed to happen.

Round five. Nicole.

Worse, she had the presence of mind to continue working on the cuffs. It would not do to have Nicole less rattled than he by their close proximity. He had to keep his mind focused on why he had cornered her in the first place.

"Tomorrow's brainstem-storming session, why is it so important that I attend?"

Nicole could not be deterred, though. She not only ignored his question but finally got the key in the lock. There was an audible click. When she tried to pull her arms from around him, Kent resolved not to be outdone this night.

Flicking the metal from his wrist, he grabbed Nicole's soft hands before she could squirm free. With practice only gotten from a certain amount of illegal activities, Kent closed the cuffs around her wrists.

With a click, Nicole was now his prisoner.

TKO. Kent.

CHAPTER 24

Nicole tugged and tugged. Not only had Kent somehow cuffed her hands, he had locked them to her Mustang's door handle.

"What in the hell do you think you're doing?"

"You don't like?" Kent asked, seduction warm in his voice. "Have you changed that much in two years?"

Desperate to ignore the pulse pounding in her ears, Nicole tried to free herself, but knew it was futile. There was no reason to scratch her chrome door handle.

Kent smiled. "Mellowed out to please Zorro?"

Nicole frowned. Kent had reached all new heights of exasperation. She refused to play this game.

"Why do you want me at the meeting?" he asked.

Setting her jaw, Nicole mimicked Kent's earlier behavior, staring ahead, as if this whole scenario just bored her. However, the strategy backfired as Kent's eyes lit up. She forgot how much he liked a challenge.

"Well, if you won't talk, then…" Kent's finger traced her neck, along the edge of her blouse to the top button. "I'll have to increase the stakes."

Nicole could not keep her chest from heaving. Could not keep goose flesh from rising in response to his touch. She could keep from speaking, though. Kent would be forced to stop before he got too far by morgue security. She was not worried. Was she?

Still, his fingers played with the top button of her blouse. Nicole stared defiantly into his eyes, but Kent did not hesitate to unbutton it. A gasp escaped before she could stifle it. The defiant stare was forgotten as she looked down at what Kent was doing. His fingers ever so tenderly opened the blouse to reveal the curve of cleavage.

"I'll undo them all," the profiler threatened softly.

Still she held strong.

Kent unbuttoned another, revealing the lace edge of her bra. "Let that Conquistador of yours find you like this."

"You wouldn't," her voice trembled despite all effort to steady it.

Obviously he would, as he tugged the third button open.

Nicole's will broke, and the words spilled out over one another. "If you can't prove yourself at the briefing, Glick is pulling you off the case."

Kent's expression was unreadable as his finger traced down the edge of her bra. "See, that was not so hard after all." Despite her acquiescence, he still unbuttoned another, exposing her front-loading bra. "Still trying to protect me, Nic? Just like old times? Hmmm?"

He pressed his thumb against her bra's clasp.

She could scream, but did she really want someone interrupting him?

"Bored with your pedicured boy?" His index finger leveraged against the other side of the clasp. Just a little more pressure and the bra would spring open.

All this one-handed. She couldn't do that, and there was no way Ruben would even attempt it.

He rubbed his rough cheek against hers. "Miss our old times, Nic?" Kent waited for a response, but Nicole no longer possessed language skills. It did not matter that she could not answer him as she did not really know. What were their old times but a blur of passion and pain?

His thumb and fore-finger worked the latch, straining the fabric, pulling it across her nipples, hardening them.

Nicole did not think it possible, but Kent leaned in even closer, bringing his lips next to her ear. Another millimeter and he would be kissing her. Telling her that he loved her, just like he used to. Only heightening the romanticism of the gesture, a light rain began to fall.

Kent's tone was not altogether kind. "Don't ever try to manipulate me, Nic." He pulled back to look her in the eye. "You don't have it in you."

To complete his demonstration of power, Kent twisted the clasp until it almost opened, then let it fall back to her skin, still locked as he backed away. A mixture of relief and disappointment flooded through Nicole as she watched a man she once loved pull away from her.

Kent wasn't just backing up, he was walking away.

Embarrassment replaced arousal. "You can't leave me like this!"

The profiler kept walking as rain drops splashed on her face, making it hard to tell if she was crying or not. "Kent!"

He didn't turn around. "The key's up your sleeve."

CHAPTER 25

Had any morgue attendant ever, ever, ever in the history of morgue attending gotten as lucky as he had tonight? Joshua wondered as he watched Detective Usher squirm to get out of her restraints.

First to have a Plain Jane victim come in on his shift. That put tonight on the map right out of the gate. Then some psycho broke into the morgue?

That was, like, the first time in over two years.

Joshua had thought the coup de grace had been the perv sneaking back into the crypt and getting caught red-handed, literally, in the victim's belly. Little did the attendant know that he would be treated to an off-the-hook peep show to boot!

For the seventeenth time, Joshua made sure the VCR recorded the parking lot camera's feed. For once this antique electronic equipment came in handy. It provided a permanent recording of tonight's parking lot action.

And it was not even over yet. Detective Usher still squirmed to un-lock the cuffs. Her movements were kind of like a slow S&M go-go dance. Joshua could not have imagined a better scene. The unforgiving rain soaked through her shirt. And while he could not see them clearly, those dark nipples of hers stood out in stark contrast to the clinging bra.

How did he get so lucky? But he'd almost jinxed himself. When he first came back from the crypt after he cleaned up the mess, Joshua noticed the perv and Usher having a fight by the car. Being a generally good citizen, Joshua almost called O'Fallon to help her.

Then he realized that not only was the detective *not* putting up much of a fight when the perv made the cuff switch, he was pretty damn sure she was into it.

Hey, maybe that's how cops blew off steam. Who was he to judge Usher's life-style?

And did it get hot or what? Joshua was honestly surprised the rain did not turn to steam when it hit those two. Then the perv, right when it was getting good, walked off. Which simply confirmed the attendant's opinion that the guy was cracked. Who walked away from a body like that?

Wet and hot?

Joshua watched Nicole struggle some more. He could hardly wait to get home and put some music to this show.

"Anything happen?"

The attendant jumped at the security guard's voice. The old man should have been down until at least five.

Flicking off the monitor, Joshua answered, "Nope."

"Thought I heard some clanging around."

"Hearing things…again."

O'Fallon's face clouded. Joshua knew how it goaded the old man to think he might be going senile. Which usually accounted for most of the fun the attendant had on the graveyard shift. But not tonight.

Risking a glance to the VCR, Joshua made sure the red light still glowed brightly. Damn, wouldn't the geezer go back to bed before Usher ended her live show?

O'Fallon yawned. "As long as everything is quiet."

"Oh yeah."

The old man was not ten steps away before Joshua flipped back on the monitor, only to be disappointed that not only had Usher gotten out of the cuffs and re-buttoned her shirt, but she was already back in the car.

He could only hope the tape caught the end of the show.

Hell, who needed pay-per-view porn when you got on-the-job-action like this?

CHAPTER 26

As a wan light shone through the bullpen window, Ruben tried to keep himself busy with his paperwork. After getting no sleep between Joann's death and now, he had downed four extra-tall coffees in a row.

He had a caffeine buzz that urged him to pace in front of the packed house that had gathered for the briefing. Although nine-tenths of them weren't here for his insights. They waited for Kent's grand appearance.

Ruben glanced over at the near-to-bursting crowd. He had never seen so many cops, both uniforms and detectives, crammed into the bullpen.

Focusing on the board, he adjusted Joann's autopsy report. Ruben wanted all the information to be perfectly in order. The backgrounds, original police reports, autopsy reports, and family interviews. Everything. It needed to be assembled in the correct sequence so his talk went smoothly.

No matter Kent's predilection for bizarre, unorthodox behavior, Ruben knew that he still needed to provide a commanding presentation for Glick to take the award-laden profiler off the case. And Ruben did not just want Kent playing second-string. He wanted the lunatic off the case completely. Out of Nicole's life completely.

Out of *their* lives completely.

Ruben peeked to the clock again. 9:12. He looked to his Captain who looked to Nicole. His partner, in turn, looked to the door. No Kent. No hint that Kent was even going to show up. Typical.

Wouldn't that be perfect? The vaunted profiler simply forfeiting his position?

Glick would have to pull Harbinger from the case.

Ruben looked to his Captain. How much longer was Glick going to give Kent? They had a lot of ground to cover.

"He's late," Glick demanded of Nicole.

Of course, she rose to his defense. "I'm sure --"

"He's not coming."

"Not coming?" a hidden voice asked. Ruben recognized the voice but could not believe he had heard it. Kent continued, "I wouldn't dream of missing this."

Ruben sighed. There was no doubt it was Kent, but where in the hell was he? The room was filled to capacity, but no profiler. Then Ruben tilted the profile board to reveal Kent lying on a desk, reading a comic book.

Things definitely *weren't* going Ruben's way anymore.

CHAPTER 27

Kent stayed recumbent, seemingly intent on his comic as he soaked in the room's reaction. Ruben was way too easy to read. If the detective were a cartoon character he would have steam coming out his ears and strange icons bulging in and out of his eyes in a distorted caricature.

Nicole grinned despite herself, and the rest of the room...well the rest of the room was abuzz.

Ah, he had not made an entrance this good since his first day teaching advanced profiling techniques at Quantico. In huge, bold letters, he had scrawled across the blackboard "Powers of Observation," then hid up in the rafters. Students had filed in, clearly a little concerned that their new professor was not at the front of the classroom.

Concerned turned to freaked out when one brave student braved a journey up to the podium and found blood smeared across the syllabus and a trail of red foot-prints leading to the emergency exit.

He didn't even reveal himself when the dean showed up to investigate Kent's mysterious disappearance. The profiler didn't even budge when security was summoned to the scene of the mysterious 'crime.'

Harbinger had just sat up there silently laughing his ass off at the supposed brightest and best scrambling around trying to organize a manhunt. Finally he couldn't contain himself. It had been his own snort of amusement that had given him away.

Yeah, that had been a great entrance. Of course, shortly thereafter he'd been fired. But still. The look on the dean's face alone was worth it. Okay, maybe he should not have lied to the students and told them he had used HIV infected blood as the lure. But come on, the scare those students got would ensure that they never investigated a potential crime scene without gloves ever again. Unfortunately, the bureau did not see it his way and off to the think tank he went.

Out of the corner of his eye, Kent looked over the sea of blue uniforms and typical detective suits. They were all still trying to figure out how he had gotten behind the board and exactly when.

You know, sometimes fieldwork really was rewarding.

Glick recovered first. "Are you going to join us?"

Kent snapped his comic closed, very dramatically, as he swung upright. "And miss Wonderkin's solving of the Sphinx's riddle?" He slapped the desk for emphasis as he rose. "Not on your life."

"Enough of the drama, Harbinger. Get over here."

He complied. Ruben didn't even try to hide his glower. Therefore Kent made sure to sit right next to Nicole. Far closer than polite society usually allowed. Ruben looked like he was going to intervene, then re-grouped and turned to the crowd.

"Let me clarify. I am not going to solve anything --"

"Now that's bold," Harbinger chided. Ah, after the night he had, this was going to be fun.

Ruben tried to move on as if Kent had not just interrupted him. "I'm just here to take a fresh look at all the evidence collected so far..."

Torres glared, as if challenging the profiler to speak up.

Kent was going to enjoy this briefing more than he thought. "Don't keep us in suspense."

Even through the detective's naturally dark cheeks, you could see a flush of red. Before Ruben could retort, Glick stepped in. "Enough."

Oh yeah, the profiler was definitely glad he showed up this morning.

The Captain fixed Kent with a frown, then turned to Torres, "Go on."

He could feel Ruben's gaze, but Kent had already opened his comic book and was not about to give the detective the satisfaction of feeling like he had backed him down.

No one got that satisfaction.

CHAPTER 28

Nicole shifted uncomfortably next to Kent. She should have been pissed at him. He had left her hand-cuffed to her car in the middle of a downpour, for hell's sake. It had been quite the stunt he had pulled, but in retrospect, what had she thought trying to play at Kent's level of gamesmanship?

Last night he had simply reaffirmed himself the master and her the groveling student.

Now she worried for Ruben. Her partner had thrown down a king-sized gauntlet at Kent's feet. Just as she had done. Already, before the briefing even began, Kent had scored the first point. The room craned their necks, not to see Ruben, but to watch the profiler.

Despite her and her partner's fight the night before, Nicole still respected the effort Ruben put into living up to his gold badge. She caught his eye and nodded for him to proceed. Waiting for Kent's acknowledgement was nothing more than a losing proposition.

Ruben started, then stopped, took a deep breath the continued, "We have been seventeen victims so far."

"Wrong," Kent chimed in.

"Seventeen *confirmed* victims," he added.

"Nope. Thirty one and counting."

Rushing in before Ruben could retort, Nicole tried to soften Kent's abrupt disagreement. "Only if you include the missing women who fit the victim profiles from the greater Boston area and Toronto."

"Which I'm not."

"Mistake," The tone wasn't aggressive, just definitive.

Nicole had to give Ruben credit. Instead of playing into Kent's tit-for-tat game, her partner turned to their superior. "Captain?"

The older man frowned, his grey eyebrows nearly touching. "Harbinger, you will have to wait for your turn."

In typical fashion, Kent did not acknowledge the Captain as he read his comic book. The profiler could make compliance appear so very defiant. Nicole gave Ruben an encouraging smile. Kent could not keep up this juvenile behavior forever.

Seemingly poised, Ruben pointed to the long row of photos that showed both happy, smiling pictures of the victims and their gruesome crime scene photos, then lastly their autopsy shots. It was a brutal reminder of what was at stake. They were not here to salvage their reputations but to save another brunette from this violent death.

Ruben's tone sobered. "All the women have been between the ages of 29 and 34. Natural brunettes, but a mixture of races. No children."

Her partner could not help but look over to Kent.

The profiler showed Nicole his comic. "You know the meta-message that the red bow on Minnie Mouse's forehead signifies, don't you?"

Nicole cringed. Ruben needed to stop playing into Kent's hand. The profiler could have shamed Einstein at a physics convention. To his credit, her partner seemed to sense this and decided to move on.

"There have been no direct nor casual links between the victims." Ruben pointed to the long sheets of police reports detailing their families, work history, basically the victims' entire lives. "We have run down their work histories, the places they frequent; grocery stores, restaurants, doctors, gyms, clubs, even fast-food joints. Nothing connects them."

Kent made a loud raspberry sound.

"*Nothing*. No common thread. No common connection. They must have been picked at random."

"Wrong again, but thanks for playing."

CHAPTER 29

There wasn't much Kent ever regretted; however, that off-handed barb at Torres was one of them.

Not because he feared his rival's brilliant repartee, but because it opened up a line of questioning that Kent did not want to go down at the moment.

"Really? And what is their connection?"

Keeping defensiveness from his voice, Kent answered, "I didn't say I knew." Then kicked up his arrogance quotient. "I know, however, that I should still be looking for one."

Thankfully, Glick stepped in before Ruben could retort. "Then let's keep the peanut gallery to a minimum."

Acting his usual bastard self, Kent went back to his comic, this time to hide his frustration. While he might let Nicole think he came to the briefing to please her or that his ego drove him to go toe-to-toe with Torres, the actual reason was a little too raw for his taste.

Last night, after watching from the bushes to make sure that Nicole un-cuffed herself and left safely, Kent had roamed the city alone, on foot. The profiler knew that he needed to pick a new high-probability victim, but he did not have much hope that the outcome would be much better than Joann's. He was missing something. Some vital clue.

The killer's motive eluded him. How could he protect these women if he did not know why the psychopath wanted them? Kent knew the superficial characteristics of the victim type, their height, weight, hair color, but the killer had a core need that the profiler could not identify. A slim piece of information that tied all the women together.

In the dead of night, wandering the city, Kent had come to the harsh reality that he was tapped out. Inspiration was fickle and had fled the jurisdiction. Unfortunately, Kent knew of only one way to jump-start it. He needed to be challenged. He needed to be forced outside his previous conceptions of the case. The profiler needed to push against someone. Someone almost as good as himself.

While he would never admit it, even under the threat of death, Kent knew that person to be Ruben. The guy was uptight, but thorough. If there anyone could jog his intuition into high gear it was going to be the detective.

Ruben continued with his analysis. "Based on the systematic, meticulous pattern to these killings, we can surmise that the killer is Caucasian --"

"Nope."

"Between the age of 22 and 29."

"Not."

Damn it, Torres, you're better than this. Give me something to work with.

"And is highly intelligent and attractive."

"Only because the ugly, stupid ones are easy to catch."

Snickers rose, though Kent took little delight in them. If he didn't figure out that small but essential missing link soon, another woman was going to die. Maybe tomorrow, maybe even tonight. If Ruben didn't help him narrow his search, another woman's blood would be on his hands.

Glick's frown quieted the room to silence. "Torres, please continue."

Ruben pointed to Joann's autopsy report. "The coroner confirmed that the killer did not take his trophy last night."

A collective gasp broke out as the Captain looked straight at Nicole and Kent. "But two of us knew that already, didn't they?" The detective squirmed under Glick's gaze, then jabbed Kent with the pencil. That woman really needed to find another way to express disappointment.

Typical Nicole, after poking him hard enough to leave a mark, she then rose to his defense. "He did not get a chance to take the uterus because Special Agent Harbinger interrupted him. We might not be a step ahead of the killer, but at least we've pulled within a half a step behind. This remaining uterus could be the key to solving the case."

A part of Kent was warmed by Nicole's confidence, but another part really did not want any more pressure.

Ruben paused, making sure his partner was done. He kept it pretty close to his vest, but Kent knew it drove Rubin rabid mad when Nicole stood up for him.

"By his choice of souvenirs, we know that despite the lack of rape, there is a strong sexual component to the crime."

Almost on reflex, Kent disagreed. "No, there's not."

Something Nicole said stuck in his craw. The uterus. It was the one new piece of evidence they had. A piece he had yet to figure into the equation. Squinting, Kent read the coroner's report on Joann's uterus as Ruben droned, "We can assume that he expresses his sexual rage since he is impotent."

"No, he's not," Kent said, but his mind barely registered what Torres had actually said. He squinted harder. Was he reading the report right? Despite it being Ruben's briefing, Kent walked over to the autopsy result.

Joann Forme's uterus showed an abortion.

Kent quickly scanned the other victim's medical history. Another had an abortion. And another. And another.

CHAPTER 30

Nicole watched Kent intently. Ruben kept glancing over his shoulder as the profiler rapidly reorganized his ever-so-carefully arranged files.

"He takes his trophy to show power over the women."

"No, he doesn't," Kent responded, but Nicole knew that the profiler was only dedicating a hundredth of his mind to Ruben. Instead Kent fixated on the newly arranged files. He paced back and forth, mumbling in a way that either indicated schizophrenia or brilliance.

Still, Ruben tried to maintain focus. "Which indicates that he had a strong father, but a weak mother, most likely a victim of domestic violence."

"Noppers."

Flustered, Ruben had to look down at his notes before he could continue. "Um... The killer. The killer will have a medical background --"

"Not even close."

"His career is intellectually based and requires a level of an exacting precision not normally --"

Kent turned, "Where do you get this crap?"

Glick strove for calm. "I must insist that --"

"Here's the pattern." Kent pointed to the rearranged files. "It's been staring us in the face for months."

"Harbinger!" The Captain snapped, then regrouped. "If you can't wait your turn respectfully, I will have to ask you to leave. Now."

Nicole tensed, ready to intercede as Kent stared him down. Glick wasn't going to put up with much more.

Surprisingly, Kent simply shrugged. "Fine."

The room silenced as the profiler turned to leave. Kent did not even look over to her as he passed.

Ruben haltingly continued. "The killer power-reassures when he takes the victim from behind, then power-asserts when he cuts their throat."

Suddenly, Kent grabbed Nicole by the hair to expose her neck. Exactly as the killer must have done. Everyone was on their feet, some even taking a tentative step forward, hands on their holster.

But Nicole's instinct to fight him off was suppressed by Kent's almost soothing voice. Like a father explaining one of life's little mysteries.

"He takes them from behind because he can't look them in the face. In the eye."

"Harbinger, let her go!" Glick demanded.

Kent grabbed a red marker and used it like a knife across her throat. By the shock on everyone's face, Nicole knew it had left a bright red line.

"He slits their throat so they can exsanguinate slowly, though relatively painlessly."

Despite his bizarre behavior, Nicole could see by her colleagues' expressions that they were mesmerized.

"He needs them alive. At least for a few minutes."

Ever so slowly, Kent's hand snaked down her side, just missing the curve of her breast. With the care he would take when making love, he untucked her shirt to reveal bare belly.

"He needs her heart still beating when he cuts into her."

Nicole gasped as Kent slashed the marker across her stomach. The profiler tugged on her skirt, pulling it lower and lower down past her belly-button. Nicole had never been more glad that she had bikini waxed.

"A cut which has gotten smaller and smaller. Cleaner and cleaner. Implying he had no medical experience. Instead he learned on the *job*."

Kent knelt so his face was level with the slash he created. His tone was almost loving. "I understand now," he said as he rubbed her belly. "What he takes isn't a trophy. Not a souvenir to masturbate to later."

With great care, Kent drew the outline of a uterus on her skin, then traced over and over again with his finger. "No. He doesn't want a uterus. He *needs* a womb. He needs blood to still be flowing through the source of all life as he takes it."

Everyone seemed too captivated to move, but Nicole's hand, reached out and rested upon Kent's head. "Why?"

Kent traced the outline one last time, then rose and pointed toward the board. "The coroner found evidence of an abortion within Joann's uterus."

Finally, Ruben found his voice. "So?"

"So?" Kent mocked her partner's tone. "Nine other victims had a history of abortion as well."

"But eight did not."

Kent looked at Ruben. "That we *know* of."

The profiler must have known he had the room's attention and he used it to his advantage. "He took their uteri. He took away any evidence that would have proven that they'd had abortions. We only know about those other nine because their families told us."

Kent turned to her. "We got lucky. Now it's time to get smart." Even though the bullpen was crammed, it felt as if it was only the two of them. "We did not ask the other families if the vics had an abortion, because we did not realize it was the causal link. If we re-interviewed them..."

Nicole fed off of Kent's energy, the thrill of discovery setting her brain afire. "But abortion can be traumatic. The family might not even know if the woman had an abortion, especially if it was a while ago."

"We need to subpoena their complete medical records."

Nicole nodded. "Dig around their financials in case they paid cash at an anonymous clinic?"

Kent brought them nose-to-nose. "Exactly."

No matter that they were surrounded by her colleagues, Nicole could feel the heat of Kent's body. His gaze upon her. She knew the rest of the room squirmed. She knew that Ruben was squirming; she just didn't care. The fire in Kent's eyes held her entranced.

A forced cough from Glick brought the room back to reality. "Then you best get started on the paperwork."

Kent didn't look away from Nicole as he answered. "No can do. Let Rogaine-boy handle it. I'll be out."

"Where?" Ruben answered, his tone as bent out of shape as he most certainly was.

Again, Kent seemed to only have eyes for Nicole. "To find her. His next donor."

"That approach hasn't worked very well so far."

"Before I was looking for a generic victim."

"And now?" Bitterness tainted Ruben's tone.

Kent's hand found Nicole's belly and rubbed it oh-so-slowly. She barely heard his response. "I know exactly who he's looking for."

"Who?" Her question was a rush of air.

The profiler kissed the red uterus. "Mommy."

Breathless, Nicole watched Kent stride off. And it was not just her. The entire room was stunned. No one moved. It took the sound of the door closing for even Glick to rouse.

"Alright, people. Let's track down the families, subpoena the medical records --"

"Captain!" Ruben nearly shouted, then lowered his voice. "I didn't even get a chance to --"

Glick pointed to the rearranged board. "Were you going to present anything more concrete than this lead?" Nicole felt a rush of sympathy for her partner as he shook his head. Seldom did anyone's ego survive unscathed with Kent on the prowl. The Captain raised his voice so the entire room could hear. "Then let's get moving."

The knot of cops scattered as if a strong wind had blown through. The energy of the room shifted. Where before there was despair, there was now hope. Where there was disappointment, there was now determination. While not entirely founded, it felt as if the killer lay just beyond their fingertips. Almost within grasp. Or at least Kent's grasp. And Nicole had to be there when he caught Plain Jane.

"Sir --"

"Go." Glick seemed to know her desire. "Stick with him."

Nicole did not need to be told twice. She snatched her keys and was on her way out.

The Captain called out after her. "Make sure he doesn't break the law and if he does..." Glick caught her gaze. "Make sure you're the one to arrest him...again."

Nicole cringed. He'd just busted her for Kent's little stunt at the morgue last night. But if Glick was not going to make an issue of it then neither was she. "Of course, sir."

CHAPTER 31

Ruben watched Nicole rush towards the door. Rushing after Harbinger. You'd think he'd get used to the view.

Beside him, Glick called out to Nicole again, "Usher." The Captain waited until she turned back to him. "Cover up."

With a questioning glance, Nicole looked down, then realized that her belly was still exposed. Embarrassed, she tucked the blouse back in, disappearing down the stairwell.

Everyone else bustled about, fulfilling the Captain's orders. It seemed Ruben was the only one not energized by Kent's dog-and-pony show.

"Where do you think he went?"

Glick shrugged. "Who knows?"

"Then how is she going to find him?"

The Captain turned his gaze to Ruben. A look of sympathy crossed his face as he spoke. "She'll know."

Ruben wanted to argue, but there was no point. Glick was right. Harbinger could be in the Antarctic, and Nicole would find him. For Ruben, she could not even remember his street number half the time. He looked around at the room full of amped cops. And not just the young ones. Even the more seasoned detectives were intent, refocused, confident.

How many more women had to die before they all realized that Kent was nothing more than a charlatan? A peddler of snake oil? Harbinger would either get himself killed or run off, his tail tucked between his legs. At this moment, with the sting of his public humiliation still fresh, Ruben was not sure which he hoped for more.

CHAPTER 32

The work cubicles at the local DMV office were orderly and felt-lined but cramped. Which made scooting his chair just a fraction of an inch closer to Dolores an easy sell.

The fifty-something DMV worker was more than a little flustered by Kent's presence. Just how he liked his prey. This big-haired lifer at the DMV was putty in his hands. She would get him the information he needed, without a stupid, time-wasting warrant.

"I'm sorry..." Dolores gulped, then wet her lips. Kent had picked exactly the right distance between them. "We're looking only at brunettes, five foot to five foot two, and..."

Kent had to help her. He feared she might just swoon if he made her concentrate any harder. "Ninety-five to one hundred ten pounds..." He nudged her, then winked. "A little too thin for my taste, but whatcha going to do?"

Dolores flushed brighter than her "Moulin Red" rouge and looked away. While he didn't move closer, Kent leaned forward. Just enough to stir the air between them. Just enough to let the pheromones waft from his body to her nostrils.

By the wedding ring on her finger that pinched into her skin, Kent could guess she had been married for over four decades. Probably to a high school sweetheart. A boy who had aged into an overweight drinker. Dolores' own nose was a bit blood-shot, most likely with hypertension, and statistically seldom did women drink alone. Which would mean those two probably had not had sex in months, if not years. In this cramped cubicle, a little pheromone went a long way.

"And the age range was?"

Kent smiled his rouge smile, implying they were doing something a little naughty, making them conspirators. "Let's go for twenty-nine to thirty-five. Make it within the 63105."

"That's a pretty limited search range."

He certainly hoped so.

Even though Dolores' fingers were plump, they flew across the keyboard as she input Kent's request. Almost instantly the first picture was up on the screen. Even though this Mandy Pfizer fit the prerequisite stats, she was far too pretty. Plain Jane did not like his women made-up. "Nope."

The next had too large a nose. The next too busty. The next too flat chested. The next...

"Wait."

This one had the look of the last girl left on the sidelines during the dance. She was shy. Her eyes were downcast in the picture, and she was slightly turned away from the camera as if she could somehow hide from the lens.

"Maybe, just maybe." Kent turned to Dolores. "Cross-reference country records to see if she's had any live births."

The DMV worker's penciled-in eyebrows shot up.

"It's a very detailed study."

Dolores' fingers moved more slowly. "You sure you don't need a warrant for this information?"

Kent had to ante up from roguish to rakish grin. "Would I lie to you?"

Blushing scarlet, she hit the key. The search turned up two live births. Plain Jane took only childless women.

"Never mind. Next."

"Sure you're not using this database search as your own personal match.com?"

For an overweight, square-dancing, DMV-lifer, Dolores was giving him a ride for his money. He had to pull out the GQ smoldering vibe. "Do I look like I need any help from a computer dating service?"

Obviously Dolores did not think so, as she continued with the search. Kent rejected the next ten out of hand. He knew the killer's preferences, and none of those women had them. Soon, poor Dolores was typing as fast as she could, the pictures flying by.

"Wait."

Dolores stopped the search on the pretty brunette. Pretty, but not beautiful. Plain, but not boring. Kent studied the eyes, the nose, the lips.

"She your type?"

Kent was in another world when he answered. "More importantly is she *his* type?"

"*His* type?"

Abrupt, "Print up her stats, then move on."

Dolores sounded surprised. "You want more than one?" Kent realized he'd lost her. He went back to rogue.

"The more the merrier." But this seemed to bother the DMV worker more. "Or at least that's what my *Captain* says."

"Your Captain?" Dolores sounded downright scandalized, but Kent knew her tone hid a piqued interest, so he shrugged, drawing her into their little escapade even further.

He made a point of taking in a deep breath. "And what is that lovely perfume you are wearing, Dolores? White Diamonds?"

The DMV worker was back to blushes and stuttering. She was firmly in his court, but was there ever any doubt?

CHAPTER 33

Nicole parked in front of the Out of This World comic book store. This was the third one she had hit and still no Kent. As she walked into the tiny store, she really did not know why they bothered having more than one in the city. Each comic store looked exactly the same. Old and shabby. Rows and rows of comics. Posters of gaudy super-heroes. Honestly, what did Kent see in these children's toys?

Even the guy behind the counter looked just like the last three. A Shaggy look-alike, who was too busy reading the latest Daredevil to bother greeting her. His hand-written badge declared him to be Sebastian.

"Sebastian, has Kent Harbinger ordered anything through your store?"

The man looked over his Lennon spectacles, "And who's asking?"

"Officer Usher. Now, do you have anything for Harbinger?"

Sebastian dug behind the counter, then came up with a sealed first issue Archie comic. "Just got it in yesterday. A kid traded on-line for --"

"Did you tell Kent you got it in?"

"That's what I get paid the big bucks for."

Nicole breathed a sigh of relief. She had him. Kent would never let a find like this wait for long. "When did he say he was going to be by?"

"He wanted me to stay open late, but hey, I've got plans, you know."

"Don't bother covering for him."

"Please, he boosts more books than he pays for."

Nicole glared. He still had not given her the information she needed.

"He was heading to the DMV. Like he's getting out of there before five. Right." The clerk rolled his eyes.

"Thanks."

Nicole turned to leave, but thought better of it. To have any hope of keeping tabs on Kent, she'd need some leverage. She turned back to Sebastian. "Let me have the book."

"Whoa woman, you may have a badge, but there's a limit."

Pulling back her jacket, Nicole showed off her gun.

"Okay, okay. Don't go all Nazi Maus on me."

"Just hand it over and put it on his account."

More carefully than grocery store clerks handled tomatoes, Sebastian put the acid-free-card boarded, plastic-sealed comic in yet another bag. "Here you go, but don't open the bag, or touch it, or breathe on it, or he'll kill me, okay?"

Nicole smiled. She already had her plan. A little lie to Sebastian would not hurt anything. "Promise."

CHAPTER 34

Kent leaned forward as he watched the pictures speed by, his right knee strategically just barely touching Dolores' stockinged leg. He had to keep her too preoccupied to ask many questions.

Dolores stopped on *Nicole's* photo. "How about her?"

"Nope."

"But she fits all of your... I mean your *Captain's* criteria."

He grinned. "Trust me, she's not a hundred and four pounds."

Used to his idiosyncrasies, Dolores continued, but almost immediately, Kent found another possible victim.

"Her. Check her out."

Dolores complied immediately and began accessing country records as a voice startled them both. "Well, well, you couldn't hide forever."

Kent knew that voice. Nicole.

The DMV worker looked up and recognized the detective from the photo. "Wow, now they're coming to you."

Kent winked. "Told you I didn't need a computer's help."

Nicole wasn't amused. "Can we? Privately?"

Rising, Kent urged Dolores to continue. The detective walked past several cubicles before she found an empty one. Luckily the walls were low enough that Kent could watch Dolores' search while Nicole read him the riot act.

"This isn't legal."

"That's pretty much my calling card."

"Damn it! We don't want to just catch this pervert, we want to convict him as well."

The profiler shrugged. "That's your problem."

Several cubicles away, Dolores stopped on a plain brunette and turned back to look at Kent. He gave a thumbs-up. But the next screen showed that the brunette had four children. Definitely not Plain Jane's type. He needed a womb that had an abortion but no live births. Kent nodded for Dolores to continue. A signal that was not missed by Nicole.

"Just give me an hour, and I'll get you a warrant for --"

"Stop!" he shouted.

CHAPTER 35

Nicole took an unconscious step back. Kent had many affectations, but randomly yelling at her was not one of them. Even though they were in the back of the office, heads still turned at the outburst.

"That one!" Harbinger yelled as he rushed to Dolores.

Relieved that Kent had not completely lost his mind, Nicole followed as he studied the newest brunette's picture as if he was certifying the Mona Lisa for the Louvre. And she could see why. This woman could not be more Plain Jane if she tried. The straight brown hair. The lack of make-up.

The profiler was so engrossed in the woman that he reached out and stroked her screen. "There's my girl."

The DMV worker raised an eyebrow but searched the country records.

"Hold on, let me get a warrant first."

But she had already hit the key. "No live births."

"I could have told you that," Kent said. His voice a mile away.

"Yes, but that search may have --"

In typical fashion, Kent abruptly rose.

"Where you going, darlin'?" the worker asked.

"To find *her*."

The profiler was in target acquisition mode. Nicole had seen it dozens of times before, but the DMV worker hadn't. "Don't you want me to print up her details? Name? Address?"

"No need." Kent tapped his temple. "I've got them archived."

Kent strode off as the woman shook her head. "Damn, but that boy is weird." With a slight leer at his ass. "And hot."

"Fax all the others he picked out to Detective Torres."

"Torres?"

Nicole did not have time for one of Kent's groupies. "Yes. T. O. --"

"Honey, I know how to spell it." The woman still seemed confused. "But he just said he did not need them."

"I don't understand."

"Detective Torres?" The DMV worker looked down the empty corridor. "He just walked out of here, darling."

"That wasn't Ruben."

"Sure it was, sweetie. He showed me his badge and everything."

Kent must have pilfered Ruben's badge. The profiler knew no limits. Nicole handed the woman her business card. "Just fax those other records to that number, okay?"

"You got it, sugar plum." Dolores looked at Nicole. "You better hurry, or he's going to give you the slip again."

CHAPTER 36

Confident he had the information he needed, Kent closed his new cell-phone and was about to make his get-away, in Nicole's car of course, but the detective burst from the exit and rushed alongside the moving car.

"Oh no, you don't."

Kent slowed, but did not stop, forcing Nicole to trot alongside. "I promise to have the car back before its curfew."

"Glick says I'm to stay on you twenty-four, seven."

"As kinky as that sounds..." He sped up the car, but Nicole just would not give up.

"Don't make me stop this car."

Chuckling, Kent shook his head at the silly detective who thought she could bully him into compliance. He stepped on the gas and glanced into the rear-view mirror, mainly to enjoy the look of defeat on Nicole's face, only to find her standing there, looking pretty darn confident. Then with deliberate care, she pulled out a comic book from her briefcase.

It might have been over a hundred feet away, but Kent could spot a number one issue Archie's comic. His foot hovered over the brake. What was she playing at? Then to his horror, Nicole peeled off the seal and began to pull the comic from its protective cover. Did the woman not understand what even the slightest exposure to humidity could do to those fragile pages?

Slamming on the brakes, Kent put the car in reverse, halting, level with Nicole. "You wouldn't."

She was playing. "Watch me."

"I'll just buy another one."

"No, you won't." Nicole smiled a smile that was very reminiscent of his own roguish grin. "Because you can't. You've been looking for over five years. Maybe more."

Damn, but she had him by the balls. That was not just a comic in her hands. It was a national treasure. More for the country than himself, Kent opened up the passenger's door. "Don't say I didn't warn you."

"About?" Nicole asked as she slid into the car.

"Blackmail." Kent started the car. "You've taken your first step down the slippery slope."

"I'll take my chances. Where are we going?"

"You're in the car." Kent eyed his comic to make sure she had properly resealed the package. "Don't expect cooperation too."

CHAPTER 37

Ruben tapped the pages of the report on the edge of his desk to straighten them before he put them away.

"Don't tell me," Glick stated. "Harbinger was right?"

Torres did not even try to hide his sigh. "We're still waiting on the last two vics' history, but yeah, Kent does have as much gray matter as he claims." Ruben hurried on before the Captain could ask the next obvious question. "I've already cross-referenced all the victims' abortion providers, doctors, nurses, janitors, and hell, even their accountants."

"And no one in common?"

"Not a single telephone operator." Again Ruben's anger rose and made his teeth grind. The profiler had stumbled onto a hot lead, but now it was up to Ruben to follow it up.

It pissed him off no end that he had run into dead end after dead end. "And I'm telling you. It's like pulling teeth from some of these families to get confirmation of the victim's abortion. We're tracking down college roommates to confirm the last two."

He handed over the folder, and Glick rapidly flipped through the neatly typed pages as Ruben continued. "Which begs the question, how in the hell did the killer find out that all these women had abortions?"

The Captain shrugged. "Guess that's another one for our resident savant to figure out."

Always, everyone counting on Kent. Even the damn Captain. Ruben turned to walk away, but Glick's voice brought him back.

"You know, just because Harbinger is the Nobel Laureate of whackos doesn't mean that he doesn't still need us." Glick looked over his reading glasses to Ruben. "Doesn't need *you* backing him up."

A tight smile crossed Ruben's lips. "Thanks Captain, but we both know that isn't true."

Even Glick had to nod. "Yeah, I guess we do."

CHAPTER 38

Sitting in the passenger seat, especially in her own car, felt strange to Nicole. How long had it been since she let someone else drive? When Ruben and she went anywhere they either drove separately or she would drive. She didn't like feeling out of control.

Even now Nicole struggled to figure out what the hell Kent was doing as they pulled into the shopping mall's parking lot. She didn't want to ask. She wanted to figure it out on her own, but could not. "So, we're going to do a little shopping before we track her down?"

"Watch and learn."

They pulled to a stop, and Kent removed his safety belt then slouched down into the seat, getting comfortable.

Nicole reviewed the file that Ruben had faxed over based on Kent's lead. "This target, this woman...this *Rebecca* is a meter maid."

"I believe they prefer to be called parking regulation enforcers." Kent glanced at her. "You little sexist."

The profiler's mood had changed from night to day, literally. The night before, Kent had been sullen, angry. Even just a few hours ago he was snide and defensive. Now he was on a high. Harbinger had the scent. He was a hound on a fox, baying for the joy of it.

Nicole scanned the parking lot. "Whichever, there aren't any parking meters for miles."

Kent pulled the lever and brought his seat back to an even more comfortable position, ignoring her completely.

"Why would she be here?" she asked.

"Even 'meter maids' have to eat," Kent said as he settled in and closed his eyes.

The detective looked into the glass-encased food court. Hundreds of people streamed in and out, but no sign of a meter maid. "Kent, there's got to be seven hundred places to eat within her grid. Why would she--"

A meter maid's cart driving past them stopped the detective in her tracks. Nicole hated it when Kent was so right that it made your head throb. "How in the hell did you know?"

"I told you. Watch and learn."

Nicole watched, but Kent just lay there. Eyes shut, his breaths slow and regular. "You're telling me you are just going to lay there?"

Kent put his iPod ear buds in.

The only thing Nicole could do was open the glove-box to whip out a few items she kept handy for a stake-out. Getting out the binoculars, Nicole watched Rebecca head towards the Japanese booth.

Knowing they weren't likely to get a lunch themselves, Nicole took out a couple of juice-in-a-box and a large bag of Cheez-Its. It was not exactly the breakfast of champions, but on a stakeout they would make do.

Opening the bag, she offered Kent some, but his eyes were still closed and his head swayed slightly to the music. She could not help but grin. How many times had she seen him like this? Music was his retreat from boredom. If Kent even thought there was a whiff of tedium in his future, he would pop in the earphones and rock out until the world became more interesting.

The only problem was, the profiler also had a habit of losing the devices. At first it was walkmans, then mp3 players. They had started buying them by the dozen.

Nicole's eyes wandered down the ear bud's wire. It looked like he had upgraded to an iPod. A fairly expensive item to replace every other week. And it looked like Kent had even decorated this one. She tilted her head to read the sticker. "Morgue Attendants Get Stiffs All The Time."

Jerking the buds from his ear, Nicole punched Kent in the shoulder. "That's Joshua's!"

"And even for me, there's some pretty weird shit --"

"I can't believe you stole it!"

"Especially track four. Ritualistic killings and --"

Nicole wrapped the ear buds around the iPod. "It's not Joshua I'm worried about."

Despite her anger, Kent looked at the Cheez-Its in her lap. "So is that how you snagged your goateed gaucho? With pre-packaged snack food?"

"Damn it, Kent."

"Sorry, I'm not as susceptible to your charms, woman."

After years of therapy, Nicole knew that his joking was a defensive mechanism to disassociate him from feelings he did not want to experience, but at the moment she didn't care.

"Kent, this isn't funny. You have a problem."

"Yes I do. Two, in fact. You ripped my ear buds out *and* you are holding my comic book hostage."

Before responding, Nicole tried to reel in her temper. Yelling at him had never been successful. Actually, nothing had been successful with Kent, but she'd try one more time.

"I can't keep lying to Captain, telling him that these missing items --"

"Sure, you can."

Nicole tried to rebuke his statement, but Kent talked right over her.

"Because that's who you are." Harbinger met her eyes. His gaze was not necessarily harsh. "You're an enabler, Nic." The profiler's tone turned playful, and his eyes lit up. "Perhaps you should seek professional help."

Nicole lashed out. "You know, Ruben was wrong about you."

"Of course he was."

Trying to find some way to keep from exploding, Nicole picked up the binoculars. "You really haven't changed at all." She stared out the lens, not daring to meet Kent's gaze. "You're the same selfish bastard you always were."

CHAPTER 39

Kent couldn't argue with that statement even if he wanted to. If anything he had become an even more selfish bastard in the two years they had been apart. What had caring about anyone else's feelings ever gotten him? Stuck in a psyche ward, that's what.

He could blame her for that and so much more, but he never did. There had not been a single second in those padded rooms when he cursed her name. As a matter of fact, the only time he spoke her name was when he cried it out in the middle of a dream.

No, he was not going to think about what once was, nor what could be. Kent was not going to go there. But damn it, how could he not think about her, when she was so close that he could smell her mouthwash?

He watched Nicole watch Rebecca. She was trying so hard to stay mad at him, but he could tell in the corner of her eye, there was the slightest hint of a crinkle. She knew he was watching her. She not only knew it, but she liked it. They might have patched things over if the cell-phone had not rung, to the theme of Bonanza, no less.

Nicole answered it before he could snatch it, obviously knowing that the device was not his.

"Ya. Um, Dolores, it looks like I picked up your phone by mistake."

Ever so carefully, Kent opened his car door while Nicole was distracted. He really didn't need to hang around for this bitching out.

Nicole's voice drifted out of the car as he hurried across the parking lot. "I'll swing by later and drop it off."

He had almost made his escape, but he heard the passenger's door slam shut and the sound of Nicole's heels as she raced to catch up. Kent pushed through the door of the food court, hoping that the crowd would tone down his lashing.

Almost to the Mexican food restaurant, Nicole caught up with him. "What do you think you're doing?"

"Ordering a chimichanga, but the 'wet' burrito, now that sounds interesting."

Nicole growled, "We're supposed to be surveilling."

"Even profilers get hungry." Kent waited until the vein on her temple throbbed. "You're going to draw suspicion if you don't order."

Nicole was livid, but she followed his gaze and noticed several people looking in their direction. "Fine." She turned to the guy behind the counter. "Two steak tacos, an order of guacamole with sour cream on the side."

Kent smiled. "You're never going to get down to a hundred and four pounds that way."

CHAPTER 40

Nicole stared as if he was a stranger. "Excuse me?"

He smirked. "Nothing."

The more Kent ramped up the intelligence scale, the more indecipherable he became. She was about to press him, but their order was ready at the other end of the counter. Nicole grabbed her tray. "Now what?"

Again the smirk. "We eat?"

Not only did the profiler become obtuse when he was on a hyper-intelligent kick, but pretty damned pleased with himself as well. But that was the Kent package. If you wanted his awesome intellect, you better be willing to suffer the inflated attitude that went with it.

By the time Nicole looked up to see where Kent wanted to sit, he was gone. She spun around to find him walking in exactly the opposite direction of Rebecca. For the third time, Nicole had to trot to catch up to the profiler.

"You are heading the wrong way."

"Watch and learn."

Well, Nicole watched as Kent took them nearly all the way on the other side of the food court from Rebecca.

Nicole couldn't hold her tongue. "But our mark is way over there."

Kent not only took them as far away from the woman as possible but intentionally picked a table at an angle facing away from the brunette. He plopped down and began eating, but Nicole stood over him.

Finally he put down his burrito. "What is the average area a person can subconsciously process?" Kent hurried. "And I mean sights, sounds, smells, the whole ball of wax."

The detective shrugged. "Three to five feet."

"No, that's personal space. I'm talking about interpersonal buffer zones."

Nicole sat down, both hating and loving these impromptu lessons. "Ten."

Kent nodded. "For men? Married women in familiar surroundings? Single women in a grouping of three or more? Yeah." The profiler nodded towards Rebecca, who had sat down with her sushi across the food court. "But a single woman, *alone*? She's scanning and processing up to twenty feet of information. With an inverse relationship between how far away the stimuli is and the importance or weight her brain gives to that stimuli."

"That doesn't make sense. Wouldn't you care more about something going on closest to you?"

Kent leaned forward. "Imagine you were sitting here alone. What would creep you out more? A guy walking by like that?"

Nicole looked up. She had barely noticed the bald headed man making his way to a seat only a few feet away.

"Or..."

The detective knew the answer before Kent had a chance to say it. Another man, about fifteen feet behind her, was crossing just out of the periphery of her vision. She had to stop herself from looking over her shoulder just to make sure he was really gone.

"Or the guy you think you saw, but aren't quite sure?"

How Nicole hated it when he was right. Trying to salvage some dignity, she commented, "But we can barely see Rebecca from here."

"That's the idea," Kent said as he leaned back in his chair. The profiler must have sensed her frustration and continued. "To be proficient at this? You have to know how the brain works."

Nicole sighed and rolled her eyes a little. The profiler could be a bit preachy when he wanted to be.

Kent did not miss anything and leaned back. "Okay, miss too-good-to-learn-at-the-feet-of-the-master. What are the priority pathways the brain uses to differentiate friend from foe?" While Nicole blushed, he cocked his head from side to side as if eagerly waiting her explanation. "Well?"

The detective tried to shrug if off. "Fine. Go ahead."

"Excuse me? Go ahead, what?"

Okay, this was why just about everyone else on the planet hated Kent. He couldn't just accept victory, he had to lord it over you. "Please...great master. Impart your wisdom."

With a smirk, Kent began. "The brain identifies three main factors when determining a threat. Distance. Movement. Familiarity. Let's take the tattooed gentleman from earlier. He was at the border of your zone, which should have made him less a threat, but he was moving and you had no familiarity with him, giving him a bullet up the charts. In addition, and this is what kicks you in the ass when you first start stalking chicks, the brain knows you got an incomplete look, which sets off an alarm in your head to fill in the picture."

Nicole nodded. She had taken several surveillance courses and they had explained this phenomenon. But, of course, Kent helped her actually understand it.

She reflected back. "The unconscious part of our brain wants to chalk up everybody as friend or foe. When it can't make that call, it turns our conscious mind to the task."

"Exactly. That primordial portion of our brain is really no more advanced than it was back in Neanderthal land. The more foreign and fast moving a person is, the more dangerous."

Nicole could tell where he was going with this. "So you use that knowledge to your advantage. Stay out on the periphery. Stay put."

"Then ever so slowly move inside the perimeter," Kent leaned in.

Nicole leaned forward as well. "Slowly enough that as you move in, you become more and more familiar."

Leaning so closely that his nose almost touched hers, Kent whispered, "By the time you are right next to them, they don't even notice you."

Oh, Nicole noticed him, but that was not the point.

CHAPTER 41

Kent's pulse was pounding in his ear as her scent filled his nostrils. Perhaps this wasn't the best example to give her, as her pupils dilated and her breath came quicker.

Acting as if he didn't notice the effect they had on one another, "It's called acclimation. If you do it slowly enough, they accept you. No red flags. No weird stalker-vibe."

Nicole cleared her throat. "So how long do you think it's going to take for us to get close to her?"

"About ten seconds."

"What?" Nicole demanded.

Ah, how he loved to fluster her. It was almost as good as sex. Her cheeks flushed and even her lips to darken in color.

"What… What about the slow creeping plan?"

"Oh, we don't have time for that." Kent savored having the detective in the palm of his hand. Savored her hanging on his every word. It was about time for another shock. "You're going to walk over there and ask her if she's had an abortion."

Ah, there it was again. Nicole was so agitated that she couldn't even form words. Yep, pretty much like sex.

"You'll engage in small talk, then steer the conversation to abortion."

Nicole found her voice again. "You expect me just to walk up and somehow segue into abortion?"

"You're a chick. Chicks talk about stuff like that."

"Kent!"

Clearly Nicole was past flustered. Time to reel her back in. Using his best scholarly voice, "Women react completely differently to a feminine presence. Especially if you can find some way to build rapport. Common ground."

"Why are we risking scaring her off? Why not wait for a background check?"

Kent settled back into his chair. This was his wheelhouse. "Because before you're done with that taco, Ruben is going to call to confirm that the other victims have had abortions, but he can't find proof that Rebecca has."

He took a sip of drink then continued, "You two will wring your hands about how you're going to get information from her family and friends without them asking awkward questions that you don't want to answer."

Pretending to be put upon, Kent continued, "At this point I would get up and refill my soda to give you time to realize the path of least resistance is to find a way to extract the information from Rebecca herself without tipping our hand."

Dramatically he put a hand up. "But wait, Ruben would then insist that we warn this poor girl of her possible fate. At which time I get embroiled in the argument that if she knows that she is in danger, her altered behavior could tip the killer off and make him go outside his pattern."

Kent ramped up to real storytelling speed. "After much wrangling, we all agree to find out about the abortion, then promise Ruben that we will tell Rebecca of the danger." His tone dropped to a conspiratorial tone. "But secretly you and I agree to keep the information from her until I can see if I can't pick out the killer first..."

CHAPTER 42

Nicole watched as Kent took an exaggerated breath, like he had just run a marathon. The man could put on a show. But a show was all it was.

"You are good, but not that good," Usher accused.

"Oh, but I am."

She raised an eyebrow.

Kent transformed cocky into an Olympic event. "Remember, I'm the one that knew Rebecca would be here."

How glad Nicole was that the profiler had chosen that fact to prove his point. She pulled out Dolores' phone and flamboyantly hit the 'last dialed' button. Two could play at this showmanship game.

A tiny voice answered on the other end. "Parking Regulations Main Office. How can I assist you?"

Nicole disconnected the call. "So much for your psychic abilities. You just called Rebecca's office and asked where she was eating lunch."

Despite having his legs completely taken out from under him, Kent smiled. "That Jasmine. She was quite helpful. Turns out that Wednesday is Rebecca's sushi day."

Knowing she had the upper hand, Nicole relished the rare victory. "Exactly my point. You can pull this swami crap with everyone else, but I know your limitations and --"

Nicole's cell phone rang. She looked at the caller I.D. Crap.

CHAPTER 43

From the way Nicole's smug grin fell into a deep frown, Kent knew that it was Ruben, yet she let it ring again.

"Sure you shouldn't get that?" he asked.

Nicole's frown spread to the creases of her eyes as she answered the phone. "Yah. Hi, Ruben."

She, but Kent didn't need to eavesdrop, he already knew what Torres was saying. As did Nicole.

"All seventeen victims and at least another ten of the missing women from Montreal and Toronto had abortions?" She tried to look away from Kent, but he their eyes locked. He wasn't about to blink until the conversation ended.

"You can't find any proof of whether or not Rebecca has had an abortion, huh?"

Kent couldn't keep his smirk from spreading and spreading as Nicole listened and shook her head, not believing what she was hearing.

Finally, she cut her partner off. "Ruben, I get it. We'll find out on our end." Kent could hear the hollow sound of Torres trying to argue, but again, Nicole stepped over him.

"Ruben! I'll figure out a way to get the information from Rebecca, quickly and quietly."

Now was the moment of truth. Nicole looked up and held Kent's gaze as she finished the conversation. "Of course I'll tell her the danger she's in if she's had an abortion."

As Nicole ended the call, Kent brought the straw to his lips and sucked until it made that annoying sound that told you that you were empty. "I admit. I was wrong. I didn't even get a chance to get a refill."

"Funny, Svengali."

Kent smiled, but they'd had their fun. Now it was time to get to work. "You better get over there before she finishes her California roll."

Nicole rose. "So what am I going to say to her?"

"Hell if I know."

Even from across the table, he could hear Nicole grind her molars. "Kent, you've proven your mental superiority a thousand times over, so now is not the time to lord over how much better you are than us lowly cops."

"Hey, do you want to hone your deductive powers to the point they seem clairvoyant or not?" Kent asked.

CHAPTER 44

Of course Nicole did want that. She did want very, very, very much to glimpse into the mind of a killer. And worse, Kent knew it, so there was no point in lying.

Nicole simply nodded.

Instead of explaining himself, Harbinger handed her a food tray with chips on it. "You're going to need these."

Nicole stared at the guacamole. What was he thinking?

Kent, however, went back to his lunch. "No pressure, but Plain Jane is more than likely here."

"What?" Nicole's pitch had gone so high, dogs from miles away were probably responding.

He just shrugged. "If I'm right…well because I'm right and Rebecca is his next victim, the killer is here. Watching."

Her pulse raced. Her heart was literally going to explode. Nicole had not thought past finding out if Rebecca had an abortion. Her hand flew to her phone. She needed to call Ruben, but Kent grabbed her wrist.

"We've got to lock the mall down and --"

"No," Kent stated. "We can't tip him off, anyway."

"But --"

"If he's here, he's a hundred yards away. Up in one of those buildings with a telescopic scope."

"How can you be so sure?"

He met her eyes. "Because that's where I'd be."

As he removed his grip, Nicole felt her hands shake, the gravity of her task double-fold. Her coaxing information from Rebecca was no longer a simply a theoretical exercise, but was now a life-saving operation.

"You've got to give me more to work with."

Unfortunately, Kent had gone back to his chimichanga. She wanted to shake him, rattle him from his superior cocoon but knew that she simply didn't have the time. Bracing herself, Nicole gripped the food tray and headed towards Rebecca. The brunette read a book as she deftly maneuvered her chopsticks.

Nicole felt a tightening in her chest. The loud, pervasive chatter of the large cafeteria faded. Trays clattering on tables. Children begging for ice cream. The Hot Dog on a Stick girls churning away. Those and so many more sounds seemed to quiet as the world narrowed down to just her and Rebecca. This average, ordinary brunette could very well be Plain Jane's next victim.

The meter maid looked so peaceful. So content. So oblivious to the danger she was in. Nicole had the sudden urge to not walk, but run to the table shouting for Rebecca to leave the city. To run for her life.

But she held her pace. Because if the meter maid knew of the threat, Rebecca would run. If not run, then hide. If not hide, then look over her shoulder every other step. And they couldn't risk that, because the only thing they had going for them was Kent's intuition. The only hope they had at stopping Plain Jane from taking his eighteenth victim was to follow Rebecca. Dangle her as bait.

Nicole could remember the look in the profiler's eyes when he saw Rebecca's picture. She had seen that look before.

His posture radiated assurance. If Kent said this was the next victim, Nicole believed him, so she would stick to the plan.

With each step though she wondered, how did Kent do this? To have someone's life in his hands, and them not even know he existed? In this moment, Nicole realized just how much better a cop Harbinger really was. No one, not even she, had given the profiler credit for the extremely difficult choices he had to make every day, every victim, every killer.

Cell phone ringing, Nicole snapped out of her musing. She looked at the caller I.D. Dolores Huffenfal. Instead of being pissed that Kent had stolen the DMV worker's phone back from her, Nicole answered.

"Admit you liked being handcuffed out in the open last night, and I'll help you," Harbinger's sultry tone even translated over a tiny cell-phone connection.

She might be desperate, but Nicole wasn't going to give in that easily. "Admit you like using people like puppets, and I'll accept your help."

CHAPTER 45

Kent felt a genuine smile spread across his lips. He could show his appreciation of Nicole's spunk as long as she couldn't see him actually appreciating it.

"Touché," the profiler admitted. "Put in your earpiece and drop the phone in your pocket."

Positioning himself behind a fake acacia bush, Kent had a great angle on the upcoming girl-on-girl action. The marionette strings were clearly coming off Nicole's back. The detective would do as he asked.

"Now what?" she asked.

He took a bite of a steak taco that Nicole had conveniently left. "Come on. Girls share everything. Clothes. Make-up. Gum. Figure it out."

Kent watched the detective weave through the myriad of tables towards Rebecca. Even from this distance he could tell that Nicole's shoulders were tense, worried that she was not up to the task.

To be honest, the profiler was a little worried himself. Strength, virtue, and the American Way were Nicole's strong suits. Lying? Deception? Borderline psychosis? Those were definitely not in her wheelhouse. But at some point the detective had to leave the nest. She needed to figure out if she just wanted to be a gold shield or something so much more.

He watched as Nicole looked over her shoulder. He could see panic spread across her face as she searched for him.

"Kent?"

"I'm here," the profiler answered as a father might to a scared daughter in the dark of a storm.

"Where?"

"Don't worry," Kent intoned, no longer fatherly at all. "I'm watching."

One last time, Nicole's eyes scanned the tables.

"Move on, or people are going to notice a crazy woman talking to herself in the middle of the food court."

A faint smiled crossed her face, then she moved on.

Kent had never been so proud.

CHAPTER 46

Nicole quickly closed the gap between her and Rebecca. She wanted to get this over with. Confirm that the meter maid had an abortion and move on. Move on to something she actually had some experience with.

As her insecurities mounted, it felt as if the volume in the food-court had been dialed up. The laughs were too loud. Voices pressed upon her. The end of lunch was nearing and people milled as they cleared their tables, picking up their trash. Too much activity. Too much noise.

How could she concentrate?

She still had no idea how she was going to break the ice as she neared Rebecca's table. Nicole tried to will the meter maid to look up. To say something, anything, to keep Nicole from having to make the first move. But the brunette kept her nose buried in her book, even when Nicole stopped directly across the table from her.

Gaining some strength from the fact that Kent was close by, watching, listening, suddenly Nicole realized why the profiler had given her the food tray. Without saying anything, Harbinger had given her the 'in' that she needed.

"Is this seat taken?" she asked Rebecca.

The woman looked up, startled, "No, um." But the meter maid seemed equally unwilling to be rude. "I mean, of course not." Rebecca quickly gathered her things together to make room for Nicole. "Please, sit."

Kent's voice mocked her. "Okay, that was *awkward*. Be a chick, not a cop for hell's sake."

Nicole set her tray down and sat on the hard plastic chair. "Sorry…" She was not sure if she was apologizing to Kent or Rebecca. "I just…"

"*Girlie* girl stuff," the profiler prompted.

Lips turned down at the chiding, Nicole continued. "I just hate eating alone." Wow, that sounded lame, even to her ears. "It makes me feel like a loser or something --" Nicole realized how that statement might be taken. She rushed, feeling embarrassed, flustered. "Not to say that you are a --"

"No. No. I get it. It's nice to have company."

Nicole returned the grin Rebecca gave her.

Harbinger's sigh was as loud as if he sat next to her. "Okay, not bad, but next time try not to insult the mark right off the bat." Only Kent could sound that irritated with someone who had just actually succeeded.

Nicole took a bite of her nachos as Rebecca deftly cut a California roll in half with her chopsticks, then with a subtle flick of the wrist tossed it into her mouth. The brunette was dexterous, she had to give her that much. Nicole was having trouble managing guacamole on chips without spilling.

"Hello?" Kent asked. "Is this thing working?"

Ever so slightly, Nicole turned her chin to glare in Kent's general direction. The phone was working fine. It was just her brain that was having technical difficulties.

His tone softened. "Babe, we don't have much time. You've got to build rapport and build it fast."

Nicole could tell that he was trying to be helpful. Except she knew what she needed to do, she just couldn't think of a single thing to say. How could she when she sat across from a possible victim? Especially after seeing Joann cut and bleeding to death in that alley?

"Common ground, Nic. Find similarities," he prodded.

Working from the profiler's suggestion, Nicole looked up and noticed Rebecca's uniform. Finally, she found something they had in common.

"So, are you a policewoman?"

"No, no. I'm a parking regulation --" Rebecca stopped herself and chuckled before she continued, "Sorry, I'm basically a meter maid. And you?"

Kent's patience sounded nearly up. "Not *cop* similar. Those breasts of yours are real, right? You're not taking hormones to grow them? *Chick* similar, Nic. *Chick* similar."

Rebecca's smile turned nervous, the longer that Nicole took to answer the simple question. But she couldn't tell the truth. Holy hell, she was a crappy liar. But that's exactly what she had to do. Still nothing came to her. She squirmed. She felt her hands begin to sweat.

What in the hell would Kent do?

Unfortunately she couldn't ask him. How did he do this? All she could think of was Plain Jane watching them. Of her worry for Rebecca safety.

Then she noticed the book.

"I'm a writer," Nicole blurted.

"Really?" The brunette leaned in, obviously intrigued. "I don't think I've ever met anybody who had published before. Maybe I've read something of yours?"

The meter maid was so sweet, Nicole almost felt bad about continuing the lie. "Oh, I did not say that I was a successful... I guess I should have said *aspiring* author."

"What's your genre?"

"Genre?" Nicole was back to floundering.

Shit, on the trail of serial killer, one did not have the luxury of reading for pleasure. She knew that she had talked herself into a corner. If she picked mysteries, for example, Rebecca was sure to ask questions about other mystery authors. Names and details that Nicole just did not know.

Nicole did not need Kent to prompt her, she knew she had to think of something, quick. "Um, yeah, right." Then she had it. The perfect genre. Only Nicole announced it way too fast. "Non-fiction."

Despite her answer, the meter maid still looked worried as she asked, "Is something wrong?"

CHAPTER 47

Hell yeah, something was wrong.

Nicole had completely lost her mind. Kent held his breath. The meter maid was on to Nicole, and if she did not do something fast, something really incredibly fast, the detective's cover would be blown and so might the chance to catch Plain Jane before he killed again.

"No. Yes..." Even over the brittle connection, the profiler could hear the stress in Nicole's voice. 'I'm sorry. I didn't just stop by your table by chance, Rebecca."

The brunette's faint retort had some sting. "How did you know my name?"

"Ouch." Kent could feel Nicole's pain. "Beginner's mistake, Nic. Too much, too soon. Walk it back."

He rose and made his way towards the table. Nicole might need a rescue if she continued down this road.

"Well?" Rebecca demanded.

"Actually, I was hoping to find you here today."

That's it, Kent thought, as the brunette leaned back from the table, a sure sign she was disengaging from the conversation, putting up her social armor, cutting Nicole off at the proverbial emotional pass.

"Okay, now you're really are creeping me out," Rebecca said to the detective.

Between her body language and her tone, Kent knew that the meter maid's felt vulnerable, exposed. Now a guy, a guy would think Nicole was a stripper sent by a couple of buddies for some afternoon fun.

But a woman? A single woman like Rebecca? She would immediately assume Nicole was there to hurt her. Betray her. Chicks and their damn insecurities.

Nicole was losing any foothold she had made, but he was still a good fifty feet away. Short of a sprint, Kent could not make it over there in time to stop the train wreck.

"I'm sorry." It sounded like the detective could barely squeak the words out. "It's just...well this is really awkward for me as well."

"I'm lost," Rebecca admitted.

So was Kent. What angle was Nicole working?

"I'm doing research for my new book." She sounded stronger, more sure of herself. "And I thought you might be able to help me."

Kent slowed as the brunette's shoulders relaxed. Could she really be buying into Nicole's aspiring author act?

"Okay, so this book is about the exciting and dangerous world of issuing parking citations?"

"No." Nicole sounded back on her game.

"Regret after abortion."

"What?" Both Kent and Rebecca nearly shouted.

No one seemed to notice the meter maid's outburst, but a young mother near Kent grabbed her daughter's hand and scurried out of the food court. Hopefully to go home and have a nice long discussion about how to avoid weird-acting strangers at the mall.

"Darlin', put it in reverse," he growled into the phone, trying not to scare off any other patrons, or, worse, alert security to his presence. He was still on their blacklist over a little lingerie 'misunderstanding' from a few months ago.

But Nicole did not back down. "I'm writing a book about regret after abortion."

"Wow. That was bold, Nic."

"*Abortion?*" The brunette sounded horrified.

"Maybe *too* bold," he added.

A painful silence hung in the air.

"Pull back. Reconnect before you lose her completely."

"I'm sorry." Nicole was back to stammering. "I was just under the impression..."

"Why would you think I could... That I had..."

"I know this information is of a private nature."

"Private? How about taboo?" Rebecca shot back.

"Come on, Nic. Drop the damn intellect and show some compassion," Kent begged.

"Taboo because it is too painful to talk about."

"Go find someone else to help you." Rebecca tried to rise, but Nicole laid a hand over the brunette's wrist.

The detective sounded so kind, so very persuasive. "Please, just talk to me."

"Look, I've never..." Rebecca was up and out of her seat. "I've never had one of those..."

There was no way Kent was going to make it to the table in time. Nicole had to pull this one out of the fire on her own. "Deeper, Nic. Dive in."

Kent was close enough to see that the detective meant business. Her shoulders were down and back. Her spine straight. Her voice full and uncompromising. "Nobody gets that angry unless they *have*, in fact, had one."

Oh, there goes the game, Kent thought as he watched Rebecca's face change three shades of red. He was pretty damn sure his face was undergoing such a transformation as well. Nicole constantly bitched about *his* lack of social tact? She was stumbling head over heel down the manners ladder and had nothing to show for it.

Rebecca was walking away.

Desperate, he appealed to the detective. Challenged her. "You want inside my head, Nicole? You want to understand me? What I do? Why it makes me the way I am?" Kent saw her eyes flicker over to him as he continued. "You need to be raw. As raw as her. You need to become who she needs right now."

The meter maid was almost out of earshot when Nicole spoke up again. "I *know*, because I was that angry when my new GYN asked me."

Rebecca stopped, but didn't turn around. Kent held his breath. Nicole's ploy was dangerous. If you were going to lie that boldly, you had to sell it. "Feed her what she wants to hear, Nic. Keep it up."

Nicole's voice sounded shaky. "It's easy to pretend it never happened, but it still eats at you."

Rebecca turned towards the detective as Kent coached, "You've hooked her, now reel her back in, Nic."

"That's why I'm writing this book. To help..." As the brunette took a step towards her, Nicole's voice cracked. "To help myself."

To his amazement, Rebecca made her way back to table. You could not accuse a guy of having something as minor as jock itch and expect to talk him back to the table. You were more than likely to get punched for the effort. But there was the meter maid making a beeline towards Nicole.

Chicks.

The detective continued, "I did what I did because I didn't have any other choice."

Kent breathed a sigh of relief as Rebecca sat down.

"There's always got to be another choice." The brunette didn't sound so sure of herself, though.

Now Rebecca was acting vulnerable, but felt safe. As others streamed out of the food court, Kent sat down again, confident Nicole had the meter maid back in the game.

And she did not disappoint him. "I was losing my job. The father was gone and --"

"Still. There was adoption."

Even from his limited vantage point, he could see Nicole look up and hold Rebecca's gaze. "The father checked himself into a *psyche* ward."

"Perfect! Cull enough from your personal history to make the story believable," Kent encouraged.

Rebecca sounded shocked. "Checked *himself* in?"

"Yeah, right after he trashed my career, he decided he needed a 'break' from reality."

A frown covered Rebecca's face. "I was a teenager. I didn't even know you could get pregnant your first time."

Relishing yet another victory, Kent leaned back. "Damn, I'm good."

Rebecca continued, "My mom went ballistic when she found out. Almost like I had betrayed *her*."

"That's usually a dad's reaction."

"Guess Mom was pulling double duty. I didn't really know my dad."

Nicole patted the brunette's hand. "I'm so sorry."

"Okay, time to wrap up touchy-feely hour," Kent said.

But the detective ignored his prompting and held Rebecca's hand. "Was she equally upset when you decided to termin --"

Kent didn't even have to tell Nicole she should not use that term. The detective self-corrected. "When you decided to do *it*?"

"Okay, sharing time is really over."

The brunette sounded ready to cry. "Actually she couldn't wait for me to have one." She wiped a stray tear from her cheek and tried to sound brave. "She said she wished she'd had that option when she was younger."

"Ouch. That's something a mother should never say."

"Yeah."

Kent shifted uncomfortably in his seat. There was a reason beyond her ability to form a female connection that he sent Nicole in to get the info from Rebecca. He couldn't handle this much emotional honesty. He'd be breaking out in hives if it were him sitting across from the meter maid.

"Okay, this is about all the soul bearing I can stomach. Let's move onto chapter two of Stalking for Dummies."

Nicole again ignored his prompting. "So, did you tell the father before you had the procedure?"

"He was already onto his next cheerleader. You?"

Kent sighed. Chicks. They just did not understand the concept of hit and run conversations.

Nic shook her head as she answered, "With the meds he was on? I'm not sure if he would have even understood."

Kent chimed in, "Okay, now you're just having fun at my expense."

Luckily Rebecca looked down at her watch. "Oh wow, I've got to get moving. Those meters on Third and Watt are about to roll over."

The two women rose to their feet. Nicole fished around in her pocket; what in the *hell* was she doing?

CHAPTER 48

Nicole found her business card holder and opened it without thinking. She just felt so sorry for Rebecca. To open such a large wound, just to send the poor woman back out to work? She wanted to let the brunette know she was not alone. But when Nicole looked down, she realized the card would blow her cover. With a click, she closed it.

"Sorry. I'm out." Nicole grabbed a napkin and jotted her number down, then handed it to Rebecca. "Call me anytime if you want to talk."

She gave a slight grin. "I will. Nice to meet you."

"It was my pleasure."

Nicole watched Rebecca walk off.

"*Finally,*" Kent huffed in her ear.

But as she watched the brunette retreat, Nicole was suddenly unsure of their plan. How could she let Rebecca go, not knowing that a psychopath was on her trail?

It was one thing to keep the truth from Rebecca when it was just an intellectual exercise. But now that Nicole had spoken with her? Touched her hand and her heart?

Now it was not so easy at all.

She pulled her phone's microphone close to her mouth so her words could only be heard by Kent. "We can't just let her walk off ignorant."

"Oh, yes we can."

Despite his words, Nicole found herself walking after Rebecca. "She needs to know the danger she's in."

"If she does, she'll act differently. Tip him off."

Nicole broke into a trot. "Rebecca!"

Kent either didn't realize or didn't care that his anger came through loud and clear. "Damn it! For her and every other brunette in this city, she can't know, Nic."

"Rebecca!"

The brunette finally turned around. "Yes?"

A little out of breath, Nicole caught up with her. "Rebecca..."

"Don't!" Kent yelled in her ear.

Caught between betraying a new trust and protecting the city's women, Nicole found herself speechless.

"Um, some other slightly disturbing revelation you'd like to make about yourself?" Rebecca asked.

"No. Just..."

The profiler rumbled in her ear. *"Don't you dare."*

As much as she hated to admit it, Kent was right. The only solution was to keep the secret, then watch Rebecca, protect her. Make sure she did not end up like Joann, Claudia, Maria. Tonight they were going to catch a killer. And for that to occur, the brunette needed to remain naïve.

She patted Rebecca's shoulder. "Just be careful out there today, okay?"

"This isn't L.A. Meter maid attacks are down one hundred percent from last year. Making the grand total zero."

"Still..."

"I've taken self-defense classes, and the pepper spray is never far. I'll be fine, promise." Rebecca offered her hand.

Nicole hesitated before taking it. She was gambling on this woman's life. How could she shake her hand? But if the ruse was going to work, she had to play along.

With a forced smile, Nicole shook the woman's hand. Then Rebecca disappeared amongst the sea of patrons returning to their day. Only the brunette had a dagger precariously dangling over her head.

How in hell did Kent do this every day?

CHAPTER 49

Kent stepped next to Nic. "There's hope for you yet."

"Why?"

There was real pain in the detective's eyes, but he couldn't speak to that right now. All he could do was redirect her attention. "Using a fictional event like an abortion to leverage the real pain you felt over our break-up? It was post-graduate stalking behavior."

He headed to the parking lot, but realized that Nicole wasn't following. Obviously she was experiencing post-lying depression. "You did the right thing."

"We are going to watch her like a --"

"No we. I'll be watching her around the clock."

"You really expect me to lie to Ruben and Glick about informing her of the danger, then let you go off on your own...*again?*"

"Yeah, pretty much." Kent knew Nicole was scared, livid, and worried, but he didn't have time to baby-sit her mood. "Sorry, babe. Stalking is a solo sport."

"That sounds a lot like last night. Joann. The Joann now in the morgue."

Kent's jaw tensed. His teeth ground against one another. Nicole shot below the belt. "I *won't* lose her."

Angry, he strode off.

"I've still got your comic book."

Nicole had grown balls in two years, but she didn't have the testosterone to back them up. "It'll be fine."

"I'm not afraid to spill coffee on it."

"But you won't."

"Why not?"

Kent turned to face her.

How he hated emotional truths, but one, maybe just one would come in handy right now. "Because you haven't changed in two years either. You're still the same old selfless Nicole you've always been."

CHAPTER 50

Nicole watched Kent walk off. Just like he always did. And she without a decent retort. Just like always. How could the bastard know her so damn well in certain regards and so completely misread her in others?

Sure, she could catch up for the fourteenth hundred time and argue for fourteen hundred hours, but would that accomplish? She had tried righteous anger, guilt, even extortion and each, in turn, had failed. Nicole had run out of both ammunition and energy.

How did you reason with a man, a profiler who just did *not* give a shit? Didn't care about authority, consequences, or even feelings? Before she could ponder such things, a practical concern rose.

Wait a minute. How was Kent going to stay on Rebecca's tail without any transportation? Once outside, she realized she needn't have worried. There Kent was, with *her* keys, driving off in *her* car.

"Of course," Nicole said to no one in particular. Why did this situation feel so very familiar? Why did she let Kent bend her will every single time? Why did she yield each and every time?

Not up for an internal debate of that magnitude, Nicole turned to the man she always did in these situations. Picking up her phone, she hit speed dial number one. Torres.

Was she imagining things or did she hear his phone's distinct Gypsy Kings' ring? Cautiously, she walked around the corner to find her partner leaning against a railing.

"I figured you might need a ride."

Nicole knew she should feel relieved, but instead she felt irritated. It was bad enough to be abandoned by Kent, but to have Torres witness it and rub it in?

"How much did you hear?"

"Enough."

Her cheeks flushed red. Ruben knew she had agreed to lie for Kent as well. This day could not get much worse. "So you are going to tell Rebecca that she may be a target?"

"No," Torres said as he walked towards his car.

Not certain if she heard him right, "Why not?"

"Because Kent, for all his glory, is wrong this time." Her face must have registered her shock because her partner hurried on. "I know, impossible to imagine, but *true*."

"Because?"

Torres unlocked the passenger's door as he explained, "One of the women from Kent's DMV search, a Nancy Halfer, fits the victim profile, has had an abortion, and complained of a peeping tom last week."

"But that could have been --"

"We checked. Kent was busy getting frisked at the Krispy Kreme at the time she reported the lurker."

As pissed off at Kent as Nicole might be, a part of her still rose to the profiler's defense. Kent might be an asshole, but an asshole that was seldom wrong when it came to the criminal mind.

"That's it? A scared brunette that Kent rejected as a victim is your best lead?"

Her partner picked handed her a folder. "And these."

Ruben urged her into the car as he went around to the driver's side. Nicole sat down but did not shut the door as she flipped through the large stack of security camera photos.

They all showed a young man, mainly from the back or other equally useless angles.

"And who's this?"

Torres shut his door. Suddenly the car seemed too small. She knew she should shut her door but kept it open. Nicole needed to feel that she could leave if she wanted it.

Ruben laid several pictures out on the dash. "I combed through every frame of footage from the store that the previous victims had frequented."

Nicole was in no mood for a presentation. "And this was the best you could come up with?"

"He obviously knew where the cameras were."

"Or it's not the same guy," she asserted.

Her partner's tone sharpened. "True, until I cross checked the photos against the list Kent kicked out of the DMV's computer." Tapping each photo in turn, Ruben continued, "These were taken this week...at the pharmacy, farmer's market, and gym that Nancy attends."

Nicole had to admit the man's presence seemed like more than just a coincidence. Just as she vacillated, Kent drove past them in her car.

A fact that did not escape her partner. "Harbinger has made his decision. You need to make yours."

Nicole watched her tail-lights retreat into the distance. Kent had not even looked back. While Ruben had shown that even when he was pissed, he still had her back. In a moment of decision, Nicole closed the car door.

Torres nodded. He must have sensed the effort it took for her to cut Kent loose like that. He turned the discussion back to business. "Nancy has at least three teams of surveillance, twenty-four-seven."

"You've told her then, the danger she's in?"

Ruben gave her an 'of course' look. "You joining me?"

She nodded, then remembered there were a few problems that Kent had left her. "We just have a few errands to run first..." She opened her purse and pulled out Ruben's badge. "And here."

Ruben looked quizzical, "Where did you find this?"

Nicole could not look him in the eye.

His face went from relief to pissed in one point six seconds flat. "Damn it all to hell! He can't --"

"Ruben, please."

"No, damn it. He has got --"

Nicole couldn't take this right now. She was still too raw from the conversation with Rebecca. Too raw from Kent doing what Kent always did. So Nicole did the only thing she could to stop Ruben from continuing his rant against the profiler. She grabbed his hand. Like she used to. Back before Kent reinserted himself into their lives.

"I'm going with you. Isn't that what you wanted?"

"But --"

There would be no 'buts.' Not today. "Turn him in, and I'll find another ride."

Her partner fumed, but ultimately turned over the ignition. Nicole leaned back in the seat. Relieved that Kent was no longer the topic of conversation.

If the profiler wanted to be on his own, then he was going to get his wish.

CHAPTER 51

Kent laid back in Nicole's bucket seat, looking like he was taking a late afternoon siesta, only with one eye peeled towards the parking regulations office.

Sure enough, Rebecca pulled her meter maid cart into the parking lot within seconds. The brunette was punctual. She gathered her things and went inside the angular building.

Unlike the morgue, someone had tried to get cute with the architecture of this building. What those snobs in the magazines called 'a riddle for the eye.' Kent called it by another name… ugly-ass office complex.

Probably so ugly that actual businesses did not want to pay the rent, so most of the occupants were spill-over government departments. Public works, Assemblyman offices, Oversight committees. You know, crap like that.

The profiler knew all this because he had already done his homework. Rebecca's office was on the second floor, west-side. That's why he had chosen this parking spot.

With winter coming on, everyone's blinds were open to soak in the last bit of sunlight before dusk. He should be able to watch as she synched her palm-pilot with the county's databank, uploading all of her ticket information in a matter of minutes. Kent guessed she would then change in the restroom and head home in street clothes.

He made a mental note that if the surveillance lasted longer than a few days, he would have cameras placed in the changing room. Or more importantly, scan for *other* cameras.

Although he seriously doubted he would have the time. If his own apprehension was any indication, the killer must be about bursting. His need for a womb growing with each second. Her womb. Rebecca's womb.

A snake of doubt slithered in the back of his mind. What if he was wrong? What if she was not Plain Jane's next victim? What if Plain Jane stalked another woman?

Just as quickly the mongoose of arrogance snatched that doubting snake and shook it violently. His job allowed no room for error. No room for doubt. Whatever intangible quality Kent could not quite name but recognized instantly, Rebecca had in spades. Even more than Joann. The killer could not resist this one. Not with his frustrated desire demanding release.

As she entered her office, Kent abandoned his napping ruse and pulled out Nicole's binoculars. He watched Rebecca greet her co-workers. She checked her messages. She logged onto her computer. If Kent was not mistaken she checked her personal e-mail before starting her data transmission.

Interesting. That was the behavior of a woman hoping a man had written. Was she dating? He would have Nicole pull her LUDs, both from her cell and home phones, and put up a tap on her e-mail.

Right on Kent's time-table, Rebecca grabbed a bag from under her desk and headed towards the restroom. So she *was* going to change. Kent had that sense about her. Rebecca would feel self-conscious walking around town in her uniform if she was off duty. She seemed more the wall-flower type.

Exactly the killer's type. Shy. A little socially awkward. That's the only way Nicole's bumbling attempt at undercover work could have been successful.

Unbidden, a grin came to his lips. The detective had done a belly flop her first time out, yet had somehow managed to pull it off. What she lacked in experience she made up for in sheer guts. She'd not been afraid to screw up, and that's what had made her successful.

Nicole had a gift he could never claim. The ability to accept the fact that she might be wrong. That she might make a mistake. She was not afraid of the possibility of failure.

Whereas Kent's stomach torqued on itself at such a thought. He was gambling with Rebecca's life. Exactly one day after he had gambled with Joann's life and lost.

In his world being wrong or failing did not involve embarrassment, it involved death.

An image of Joann's throat slit and blood gushing from her abdomen filled his mind. The taste of her iron on his lips. The smell of death on his clothes. He forced it out. He couldn't let that happen.

He *would not* let that happen to Rebecca.

Precisely on time, the meter maid walked out of the building, sporting loose-fitting jeans and a non-descript knit pull-over. She did not shop at the mall or high-end retail. More likely Marshall's. Maybe Target. Not K-Mart or Wal-Mart, though. She had a little bit more ego invested in her presentation than that.

Kent's brain kicked into over-drive. It was like a T1 trunk line had opened. Information flowed in so quickly that he did not have time to process it. He just let all the sensory input wash over and into him. Every second he spent watching this woman gave him hours of information to sort through. Her stride told him so much. Her Chevy Cavalier told him she lived within her means.

Each moment, each and every movement, reinforced his original gut feeling. She was the one. Even more than he had sensed it about Joann, Kent knew. Deep in his marrow.

Rebecca was the one.

CHAPTER 52

Nicole walked out of the elevator and searched the hallway for apartment number three hundred and two. Ruben had been reluctant, but she had insisted they run a few errands before they joined the protection detail at Nancy's house.

She wanted to be rid of everything Kent. Nicole might be willing to put her career on the line for the *profiler*, but the man himself? Him, she wanted out of her life. And this was her first step towards such an independence. Returning the items Kent 'borrowed' over the last few days would wash her hands of his eccentricities.

In front of the correct apartment, Nicole knocked, but no answer. She knocked again. Still no answer.

Nicole announced, "It's Detective Usher."

The door cracked open, the chain still on. An eye darted, checking the entire hallway from its narrow vantage.

"Um... Joshua?" Nicole asked, not sure if it was the morgue attendant behind the door or not. "Work said you should be home."

The young man's voice squeaked as he spoke. "Yeah." He cleared his throat. "I called in sick, but hey, man, if they're going to send the fuzz to check up on me, I'll go in. No prob."

"No, no," she reassured him. "It's about last night."

"I didn't see anything!" His words came out in a slurred flood. "Or post it on YouTube!"

"What?"

"Nothing, nothing." He opened the door a little wider, but didn't remove the chain. "Sorry. What about last night?"

Reluctantly, Nicole pulled the iPod out of her pocket. She had already returned Dolores's cell phone. This little ritual never got any less embarrassing, though.

"Somehow this got mixed in with my things."

The door slammed in her face.

Did Joshua somehow know the truth? Did he know that Kent lifted the item last night? Just as quickly the door opened and Joshua came out into the hall.

"I was going three shades of Tupac crazy trying to find this thing!" To prove it, he kissed the screen.

Nicole could not help but smile at the young man's unbridled enthusiasm. "No prob."

"Thank you, thank you, thank you!"

CHAPTER 53

Joshua suddenly realized he had left the door ajar behind him. He pulled the door as closed as he could. He had to ditch the detective, like now.

Usher smiled, somewhat sadly. "See you later."

"Yeah, later." Could he sound any more unconvincing? Joshua tried to slow his pulse. Slow his breathing. This chick didn't make detective by affirmative action. She was smart and perceptive.

Luckily Usher turned and walked towards the elevator. He stood out in the hallway, like some kind of dope, but he couldn't risk her catching even a glance inside his apartment.

The detective pushed the button for the elevator then looked quizzical, the question obvious on her face. Why was he still standing there?

But what was he supposed to do? Desperate, he gave a little wave, like he wanted to watch her as long as he could. Which under normal circumstances might have been true, but today, well, he was just desperate.

After possibly the longest wait in recorded history, the elevator finally dinged. With an awkward half-wave, Nicole disappeared into the elevator. Collapsing backwards, Joshua leaned against his door. That was a narrow escape. Too narrow for his bladder.

Checking the hall both ways as if he was getting ready to cross a New York street at rush hour, Joshua opened his door, slid his slim frame inside, then slammed it shut.

Inside his apartment, he clenched his eyes closed, and panted a few more breaths as he listened for any telltale noise that Usher or anyone else was coming down the hallway.

Satisfied that his getaway was complete, Joshua opened his eyes. What he saw, Usher never would have understood. His walls were lined with newspaper articles about Plain Jane. Each one a maze of highlighted text and cutouts.

Well, except for the wall that led to the bedroom. That one had his wall of honor. A Sigourney Weaver poster from Aliens. A Buffy wall scroll. And a pink Power Ranger just to keep things real.

But the thing he might have had to sedate the detective for was sitting on the center shelf above his television. His pride and joy. But in retrospect, maybe he should not have put it in quite such plain sight. Most would not have understood. Not like the way he understood.

Cautiously, Joshua removed the item from the shelf and ever so gently stroked the glass jar. What it contained was beyond precious, beyond beautiful. It was perfection.

A perfect uterus.

CHAPTER 54

Kent had already parked Nicole's car two blocks away from Rebecca's house. The giant exempt "E" on the license plate was sure to raise some eyebrows if he parked too near the meter maid's home.

So he'd parked far enough away, then walked his way in, setting up in the neighbor's Hydrangea bushes. Luckily they were less prickly than the morgue's Azaleas.

From his vantage, he watched Rebecca drive into her driveway, then unload the groceries she had bought at the store all the way across town.

A health food nut.

Kent should have known. It was probably another reason he and the killer were drawn. The meter maid knew how to take care of herself. Arms loaded down with cloth reusable grocery bags, Rebecca climbed the steps to her house.

"Time to get up close and personal," Kent mumbled as he pulled out of the shadows, making his way down the street at a leisurely pace. There was no need to hurry as the meter maid put her key in the lock.

Abruptly though, she stopped and set down her environmentally friendly bags. Without missing a step, Kent continued walking past her house as Rebecca headed towards the backyard.

What in the hell had made her change direction and abandon her task?

There was no way he could double back without arousing suspicion, so he continued to the corner then turned right. As soon as he was sure there were no witnesses, Kent hopped the fence, raced across the yard, and hopped the fence diagonal from Rebecca's house.

He didn't even have to think about his route. Once the meter maid was in line at the grocery store, with enough frozen rice-cream mint sandwiches to feed a battalion of vegetarian tree-huggers, Kent sped over to Rebecca's house and cased the neighborhood. He knew which yards had dogs. Which had children. Which had the nosey older neighbor with his hearing aid and binoculars.

So, without hesitation, Kent followed the hedge line to where the two yards intersected.

Wedged between a shrub and the fence, he found a knothole and peeked through. He couldn't see Rebecca, but Kent heard strange sounds emanating from the alleyway.

Was it a struggle? Was that a strangled cry?

Damn it, he couldn't take the chance. Yesterday he might have, but after Joann's crimson makeover? Not again.

Kent agilely scaled the last fence, landing lightly on the uneven pavement. Another crash, and he took a tentative step down the alley.

If he was late again...

If the killer had already struck...

Bolder, Kent broke into a trot as a strange rumbling came from around the house. Nearly at a run, he skidded to a halt just as Rebecca backed into the alley, dragging a garbage can with a broken wheel down the alley.

Scrambling for cover, Kent landed in some pyrachantha bushes. Luckily, Rebecca was so intent on the unruly trashcan that she didn't seem to notice his presence as she stumbled past his hiding place.

He held his breath as the can nearly tipped over. Finally, Rebecca got the wheels aligned and continued down the sloped alley towards the curb. With his heart somewhere between his chest and his throat, Kent watched her finish with the trash, then head to the front door again.

Kent moved ever so slightly to the left, trying to extract his ass from a thorn, when Rebecca paused at the first step to her porch. Her gaze swept the area, lingering near Kent.

Damn, but the woman didn't have just a twenty-foot radius, but something akin to a thirty-foot zone.

Motionless, he ignored the pain from the scratches as Rebecca's lips turned downward. Then, as if she determined the area threat-free, she bounded up the steps and without hesitation picked up the groceries and headed into her house.

It took another ten seconds before Kent let out a hissing breath. Even then his hands shook. That had been close.

He had let his fear almost blow his cover. By overreacting to a perceived danger to Rebecca, he almost endangered her further. Maybe Nicole wasn't the only one a little too close to the case to be one hundred percent objective.

Before he realized it, his cell-phone was open and Nicole's number was up on the screen. Kent knew he should call and apologize. There was no reason she couldn't be on this stakeout with him. She had earned that place when she extracted the information out of Rebecca.

Still, he closed his phone. Even if Nicole called her, what would he say? I'm sorry?

Not very likely.

Those words did not come easily or very frequently.

CHAPTER 55

Sitting in Ruben's car parked across the street from Nancy's house, Nicole looked down at her cell-phone yet again. And yet again it showed no missed calls. No Kent.

"He's not going to call," Ruben said as he watched Nancy's house through binoculars. "At least not in this lifetime." The second part he mumbled. Loud enough she heard it, but quiet enough they could both pretend she didn't

Trying to keep her mind off Kent, Nicole surveyed the street. The dark van at the corner was theirs. It contained an array of surveillance equipment, including face recognition software. Torres was optimistic, unrealistically in her opinion, that when this mystery man of his showed up they could somehow, through shots of the back of his head, identify him.

Nicole sighed deeply. She didn't even realize she had done it until he turned to her.

"Something wrong?" Ruben asked.

"No. Not at all." She tried to sound convincing but wasn't sure if she had pulled it off. Probably because there was something wrong. Or at least something that felt wrong. Being cooped up in the sedan for hours had become stifling.

To just sit here and wait, and wait, and wait. Kent wasn't doing that. He was out, rooting through Rebecca's garbage or stalking her at the movie theater. Something, anything more exciting than this.

"Hey, are there any chips in the stash?" Ruben asked.

Nicole opened the glove-box to find a stake-out kit nearly identical to hers. Food, plastic utensils, and napkins. She rooted through the items but could not find any chips. "Sorry. We've only got peanuts left."

Ruben took the food. "Kind of like old times, eh?"

Giving a shrug, Nicole gazed out her window. Ruben took the hint and went back to his binoculars. Seconds stretched into minutes. Finally, she couldn't take it.

"Is this all we're going to do?"

"Excuse me?"

"Just sit here?" she asked.

Ruben cocked his head as if she was speaking a foreign language. "Um… Sitting here, quietly, unmoving is pretty much the definition of a stake-out, Nicki."

Before she changed her mind, she opened her door.

"Where are you going?"

Nicole was not sure, but she had to get out.

Ruben grabbed her arm. "Nicki, what are you doing?"

"I'm going to get some fresh coffee."

Nicole was already down the street as Torres said, "Starbucks is the other way."

She shrugged. "There's one this way too."

The detective quickened her pace so that his next words were just a murmuring in the wind.

CHAPTER 56

Perched in a tree across from Rebecca's bedroom window, Kent watched her disrobe. You know for a "B" cup, the meter maid's bosom was not half bad. Not as good as Nicole's of course, but whose was?

Shaking off the thought, Kent scanned the rest of the neighborhood. The street had settled into the quiet lull of suburbia. The stillness was punctuated by an occasional bark of a dog, or meow of a cat.

Every once in a while the loud sound of wheels screeching would echo off the pavement. Some stupid teenager thinking it proved his manhood because he could step on a gas pedal hard enough to lay rubber.

Kent sighed. Why didn't serial killers target teens? Especially overly macho, testosterone-poisoned ones? If that were the case, he could easily retire. Oh, who was he kidding? Then he'd just be staking out the very teens that annoyed him.

Kent scrutinized the surrounding yards. If his instincts were correct, the killer would be lurking as well.

Watching. Waiting. Just like the profiler.

But the two men had very different agendas. If Plain Jane kept to his pattern, the psycho would be wearing a texturized vinyl overcoat. Something that on first glance would look like a normal coat, but on closer inspection it was made of a slick, low transfer, water repellant material. Just what the killer ordered.

Torres had tracked down manufacturers for months for such an outer garment, but had come up empty. The internet had spawned too much untraceable commerce to be able to follow a lead like that anymore.

In one of the pockets, the killer would have a large scalpel blade. Stainless steel. No rust. Most likely even sterilized. This psycho didn't take any chances.

There had been a great deal of speculation about the type of handle that could hold such a large blade, and the M.E. determined it was not a standard surgical handle. One of the junior beat cops had worked on a ranch and suggested the killer might be using an equine handle. Those were strong and rugged enough to cut through horsehide.

The entire squad had spent a month tracking down veterinarians, to no avail. This killer was too smart. Too thorough to have left a trail as wide and paved in gold as that.

No, the only way to catch this psycho was to get to his victims first. Then lay in wait.

With such a strongly stylized killer like this, if you knew his end game, you had him by the balls. You had him, because he needed to kill again. And not just anyone.

No, Plain Jane no longer needed food or even oxygen. His sole sustenance was the feel of a uterus in his hands.

And any uteri would not do. This psycho needed a brunette of childbearing age with a history of abortion. These select women were his siren. They sent out a call, to him and him alone, that the killer had to answer.

Kent hated to tell the whacko, but he'd picked up the frequency. He had Plain Jane in his cross hairs.

With all this knowledge, why didn't he feel more confident though? Kent knew, beyond a sliver of a doubt, that Rebecca was the next victim. He also knew that the killer would strike tonight. He knew this more surely than the fact he himself would wake up alive tomorrow.

Kent's trepidation had nothing to do with what he knew, but what he did not know. For all this trying, he had yet to nail the 'why'. He could feel his pulse quicken at Rebecca's picture, but he couldn't verbalize why. And the "why" was the all, because the "why" completely consumed the killer.

The "why" was the only reason his heart still beat. And that "why" Kent did not know.

It left him uneasy. He was missing something. Some motivation important enough that it let Joann get killed last night. Something that endangered Rebecca right this moment.

When he looked up again, the meter maid had already changed into her pajamas. His mental anguish had only gypped him of the money shot.

The brunette left the bedroom and moved towards the living room. He'd need to reposition soon, but not until the lights of the neighborhood extinguished, as even those Jay Leno fans went to bed. Then the night was his. The street, his.

Tonight, this would end. Tonight, Kent would have a 'talk' with Plain Jane and put things right.

CHAPTER 57

Nicole's ankle hurt, yet she walked on. Perhaps if the detective had known the second Starbucks was quite this far away, she might have reconsidered the closer coffee shop.

She had wanted to stretch her legs to get some relief from the awkward truce with Ruben. But now she found herself far outside Nancy's block. Closer really to Rebecca's neighborhood.

The street was dark and more than a little menacing. Most of the businesses were long closed. If she was not armed, Nicole might have even felt a little spooked. The only thing that kept her moving was the bright green and white neon sign at the end of the block. Hot coffee beckoned.

Slightly winded, she entered the aroma-filled restaurant. The place was empty except for a lone employee mopping the floors. Her grandfather would have called this type of guy a beatnik. Nicole would say he was more heroin chic.

How looking like a junky became fashionable, she would never know, but this young man fit the bill. Fine, straggly hair. Thin, almost to the point of gaunt. The forest green and tan uniform did nothing for his sallow complexion. Yet for all those faults, the guy was attractive.

As a matter of fact, the more she looked at him, the more he fit Ruben's profile. Could the killer be someone this innocuous? There were so many Starbucks in town that he could transfer all over the city, and they wouldn't know it.

Nicole chided herself for letting her imagination run away. The walk in the dank night had made her more than a little paranoid.

Clearing her throat, Nicole said, "When you get a chance, I'd like a tall latte." Then thinking about the long, late night she added, "And a double shot of espresso."

The employee turned. "Sorry, we're closed."

Confused, Nicole looked to the door. But he was right. The place closed at midnight. Her memory had failed her. It was the store just a block and a half away from Nancy's house that was twenty-four hour.

Okay, she wasn't going back to Ruben without coffee.

"Look, I know you're closed, but I just walked… Like a hella long way. I'll take anything you've got."

"It's the bottom of the pot."

"Even better."

This got a brief smile from the brooding youth. "It's your intestinal lining."

"I'll take the risk."

Nicole rubbed her hands together, trying to prepare for the long walk back as the employee poured her tall coffee. He was about to throw out the rest of the pot when Nicole spoke up. "Is there enough for a second cup?"

The guy swirled the pot. "If you count the sludge."

"We'll have to make due." Nicole watched the he stirred in the hot milk. How she wished Kent were here. He could tell her everything she needed to know about this guy. Like why did he dress like a slacker when obviously he had some intelligence under that grossly over-produced hair?

"The same then?" he asked.

"Yes." Then Nicole thought better of it. "But no sugar."

"You don't want any sweetener?"

"Nope."

The kid just shrugged again and made the second cup.

Little did he know he had helped her have an epiphany.

CHAPTER 58

In the pitch dark, Kent fiddled with the lock on a neighbor's car. It was getting too cold to stay out in the open, and he always liked Buicks anyway. With a final flick of the wrist, the car unlocked, and he opened the door, thankful it was an older model without an alarm. He was not in the mood to crack open the steering column and disengage one.

Settling in, he didn't even flinch when the passenger's side door opened. Nicole had tried to be stealthy, but he had sensed her watching him break into the car. She handed him a cup of coffee.

While he was not surprised by her presence, the peace offering seemed odd. Nicole had been pretty pissed off the last time he had seen her. Usually it would take her days to come down off an anger buzz that high. Kent looked at the coffee with a certain degree of suspicion.

"Double sugar?" he asked.

"Like I wouldn't remember." She gave him that lop-sided grin that got him each and every time.

"What's your El Cid going to say about this?"

Waiting for her answer, the profiler took a huge gulp of the coffee, then started gagging.

Double sugar?

Shit, there was not a granule of sweetener in this sludge. If this had been Nicole's car, he would have spit it out, staining the rug as a fitting punishment.

"That's for ditching me," she stated in a flat tone, then handed him four packets of sugar.

Tentatively taking the sweetener. "And this?" Checking the edges to make sure they had not somehow been tampered with. "What are these for?" Kent asked.

"For helping me out." Nicole took a long sigh. "I know you didn't want to...at least not at first..."

Kent couldn't help himself. He knew she was struggling to share something, but he was happier when she was pissed at him. "And Ruben said you weren't perceptive."

"Yeah. Tonight I realized that I promised if you helped that you could work the case your way. No interference. No ragging. No second-guessing." She looked up. Her eyes just a little melancholy. "That's what we agreed to."

"I believe it was *absolutely* no interference, ragging or second-guessing."

His words came out harsher than he meant, for Nicole's lips turned downward as she reached for the door. "I just wanted to let you know that I remembered the conditions of your assistance, and I'll be honoring them from here on out."

Kent didn't know what to say.

This was uncharted emotional waters for the both of them, and not a life jacket in sight. Finally, Nicole broke the impasse by pulling his comic book from her jacket and offering it to him. "No more bribery. No more coercion."

He accepted the first edition Archie comic. It was in mint condition. Double mint condition. UV protected mylar bag. Acid-free backing board and not even a crease on the spine. It was a one of a kind. By the time he was finished appreciating its pure beauty, she was halfway out the car.

"Nic."

His former lover turned back. Still sad, but a glint of hope. "Yes?"

"Have we discussed the skewed gender modeling of Veronica and Brutus?"

"No." A look passed across Nicole's face that he hadn't seen in four years. "No, we haven't."

So much had happened between them, some of it painful, yet somehow Nicole's expression had exactly the same amount of embarrassment and excitement as she did the first time he asked if she wanted help. Equally surprising was how good it felt to see that look on her face and have her sit back down next to him.

Letting that warmth reach his voice, Kent said, "Well, you obviously need some tutoring then."

Kent pointed out several subtle social cues on the cover and was rewarded by Nicole leaning her shoulder against his. The gesture didn't wash away years of problems, but the profiler no longer felt cold.

CHAPTER 59

Ruben looked down the empty street, then at his watch, then at his cell-phone, then back down the street. Nicole had been gone over an hour and a half. No one had heard from her.

If this were a few months ago, he would have been worried and called. No, that wasn't true. A few months ago, he wouldn't have needed to call because his partner never would have gotten out of the car.

Each and every time he thought Nicole had finally, finally, finally caught a glimpse of what an asshole Harbinger was, some invisible bell would ring and like Pavlov's dog, she would go running back to him.

What kind of hold did the profiler have over her? How much better in bed *could* Kent be?

Frustrated, Ruben rubbed his eyes. It was getting late, and so far this intensive surveillance had come up with squat. After hours of twisting Glick's arm to throw his support and manpower behind his plan, it looked like they were going to leave empty-handed. Most of the attacks had taken place between eleven p.m. and two a.m. They were an hour outside that window.

The grand sum of their accomplishments this evening was having pulled over a guy in a Malibu and finding out he had an outstanding warrant for unpaid child-support.

So while Ruben had gotten a dead-beat dad off the street, there was no sign of Plain Jane.

"Did you see that guy?" the squad's resident techno-geek, Cody, asked into Ruben's earpiece.

Startled, he sat up straight. He'd nearly forgotten the radio in his ear. "No. Where?"

"Ten o'clock. In a trench coat, if you can believe it."

Ruben scanned the street quickly. Cody was right. A man, trying awfully hard to look casual, despite wearing a floor length trench coat and baseball cap, walked down the street towards Nancy's house.

Using the binoculars, Torres confirmed it was an Oriole's cap. Quickly he looked down at the store video stills. Baltimore it was.

Adrenaline flowed through his veins. This was it. This was him. As he grabbed the radio, his finger shook just the slightest bit. Besides catching a serial killer, for a single night Ruben might actually be able to eclipse Kent.

"Blue and yellow teams be ready to move."

CHAPTER 60

Nicole's body felt nice next to him as Kent carefully used a latex glove to turn the comic's page. It was already absolutely hedonistic to open the Mylar bag in a car without humidity control, but Kent wasn't about to add skin oil residue to the damaging mix.

They had been analyzing Archie and his friends for an hour. Long ago they had watched Rebecca go to bed. He was rapidly running out of ways to keep Nicole close. Plain Jane had never struck so late, let alone inside someone's home. He was more of a snatch-and-grab kind of guy.

Kent made sure to do his ten-point check of the perimeter before pointing to Archie's shoe. "Now tell me that isn't a metaphor for male impotence."

Nicole nudged him in the ribs. Even that contact felt good, then she leaned away from him and looked around the car. "So why are we in the neighbor's car?"

"Look at this angle. You could not buy better positioning." Kent continued, happy to have another topic to keep her near. "The rear entrance to her house has a motion detector flood light. The yard to the right has a Jack Russell that doesn't like men. The yard behind hers has a hot wire up for a Labrador which means the only access left is the frontal portal into the house. Hence the car."

"Did you get permission before you--" Nicole interrupted herself. She must have already known the answer. "Never mind."

They sat in silence. A silence that stretched on. A silence that needed to be filled before it became awkward. He went to speak, but Nicole was already there. "Kent, I think we need to...I want to..."

How Kent wished her could hear all of her needs and wants, but off to the left there had been the slightest movement. "Did you see that?"

Nicole's head spun to look out the window. "What?"

"Don't look over there," he chided. "*Feel* over there. Use your peripheral vision. Bring that subconscious into play."

"Is there movement down that alley?"

"Yes." A knot formed in his stomach.

"Maybe it's just a tarp caught in the wind."

Shaking his head, Kent opened his door. "No. I've checked it out already. That was definitely *someone* moving."

He had to give Nicole credit. She didn't miss a beat. Pulling her gun, she got out as well.

"You take the front," Kent instructed as he made his way to the alley.

CHAPTER 61

Ruben caught up with the blue team, his back-up squad, at the staging area behind Nancy's garage.

Stikle, the squad leader, looked behind Ruben. "Where's Usher?"

"Called away." Ruben tried to be brusque enough to halt any inquiry, but one of the squad, a younger guy, snorted. "Yeah, right."

"Excuse me?" Ruben turned. His ego wasn't in the mood for a ribbing, especially from the Harbinger fan club.

The younger cop shrugged. "Nothing."

Ruben turned back to the Stikle. "Alright. We have to let him break in, but we are not, and I repeat, not going to let him hurt her. Understood?"

"Just give the word."

He took the proffered night vision goggles. The trench coat was approaching from the west, the opposite side of the house from Nancy's bedroom.

From this angle, he looked just like the man in the video footage, or was that wishful thinking on his part?

Glancing back, Ruben wasn't surprised that Nicole was nowhere to be seen. She might have set out to get coffee, but Ruben knew his partner had found something else.

***

Gun drawn, Nicole cautiously made her way to the front door. She lightly tapped on the glass. "Rebecca?"

No answer. She knocked again.

Then peered into the windows. The house was dark.

***

Kent kept low to the ground as he made his way down the alley. It was clear. No sign of a break-in.

Keeping to the shrubs, the profiler made his way to the back door. A loud clunk from inside the house caused Kent to drop to a knee. He waited. Silence.

The profiler studied the lock. It didn't look like anyone had tried to pick it, and he had seen Rebecca double check it before she went to bed.

Still, Kent reached out and tried to the door.

Unlocked.

"Shit."

***

Nicole knocked again. No answer. She knew Rebecca had locked the door, but still she tried it.

Unlocked.

"Shit," she whispered to herself as she whipped out her cell-phone. Nicole hit the number one speed dial. Ruben. Her call went to voice mail. No back-up.

She opened the door and stepped inside. "Rebecca?"

***

Ruben watched as the hooded man jimmied the window. This was too perfect. They had him dead to rights. You would be able to eat off this bust, the arrest was going to be just that clean.

The man pried the window open and slipped in.

"Move!" Ruben announced and his squad fanned out, covering the exits, storming the house.

***

Kent checked a closet. Clear. He continued down the hallway towards the bathroom. Was that a sound?

Was there a struggle? The profiler's pace quickened as the noise got louder. "No!"

***

Nicole heard Kent's cry and the sound of a muted shout. Without looking she dialed the number to the station as she ran forward. She didn't even wait for the person on the line to identify themselves. "Usher at 1503 Windham Road, I need back-up, and I need it *now*!"

***

Glass shattered inside the bathroom, but the door was locked. Kent pounded on the door. "Rebecca!"

Backing up, he kicked the door with full force, splintering it off its hinges. In the dim light, all the profiler could see was a smashed mirror and blood streaking the walls.

"Rebecca!"

Throwing back the shower curtain, he found nothing.

A sound from his left brought him swinging around, aiming at the new threat. But it was only Nicole.

"Damn it."

***

Nicole spotted the blood and pushed past Kent into the master bedroom. They were too late. *Again* too late.

"Rebecca!"

A whimper from the closet caught their attention. Kent and she shared a look. The profiler backed up a step and to the side, aiming at the door.

Lowering her weapon, Nicole jerked the door open, she found the brunette crumpled on the floor.

"Oh, Rebecca," Nicole nearly choked on her tears.

***

Kent couldn't move as he looked over Nicole's shoulder at the downed woman. That was five. Five women he had failed.

How in the name of all that's holy had he failed again?

The meter maid's frame rattled. Had Nicole moved her? Then the brunette began sobbing. If she could cry, she could breathe.

Rebecca was alive.

***

Nicole pulled Rebecca up to check for injury. Except for a slash on the hand and a nasty scrape across the neck, the brunette was unharmed.

All that blood, yet she was still alive.

Bawling, but alive.

Behind her, Kent checked the room for Plain Jane as Nicole rocked Rebecca back and forth.

"It's okay. You're safe."

***

Kent tossed the bed. He pulled the dresser away from the wall. No perp. A breeze moved the curtains away from an open window. He ran over as sirens sounded in the distance. Sticking his head out, Kent scanned the backyard. Nothing. No one. Plain Jane had gotten away, yet again.

"Bastard!" The profiler slammed his fist against the windowsill as he shouted at the empty night.

***

Ruben ran full tilt as a scream echoed from the bedroom. Bursting in, he found it wasn't Nancy's cries of distress, but the perp's.

Glick slammed the suspect against the wall again. "Did you really think we'd leave her here for your sick game?"

Hands quivering, Ruben got out his cuffs. The ruse had worked perfectly. Hours ago they had snuck Nancy out of the house and left Glick here as their inside man. They had him.

They had Plain Jane.

With a snap of his wrist, Ruben cuffed the sicko.

"Good work," Glick commented.

Ruben shook his head. "No, sir. It's your bust."

"We'll split it," the Captain said as he patted him on the shoulder, then looked around. "Where's Usher?"

CHAPTER 62

Nicole rocked the brunette back and forth, murmuring reassuringly, as the sirens got closer and closer.

"It's okay, Rebecca."

Kent had disappeared into the bathroom.

"You're safe; I promise," Nicole continued.

Rebecca finally lifted her chin. Her face streaked with tears. "Nicole?" The brunette swallowed. "What are you...?"

She smoothed back Rebecca's damp hair. "I should have told you. I'm not a writer. I'm a cop." Nicole met her eyes. "Rebecca, I need you to tell me what happened."

"I don't..." she stammered. "What?"

"We think it was Plain Jane who attacked you tonight."

For the first time Rebecca seemed to focus, pulling her nightgown tighter around her shoulders. "He... He grabbed me from behind. Tried to cut my neck." She showed her the large red hand-sized splotches and shallow cut. "But I... I lashed out..." As if she had not noticed the wound before, Rebecca looked down at her cut hand. "I missed him but hit the mirror. Shattered it. There was glass everywhere then..."

Groaning, the woman doubled over, rocking again. "Oh god. Oh god. Oh god…"

Nicole held her tight. "You're safe; I promise." She waited until Rebecca's sobs abated.

"I need to know, though, did you injure him?"

"No. He just ran off."

"Ran off?" Nicole looked up to find Kent standing just behind her. "Did we interrupt him?"

The profiler shook his head. "Nope. He's desperate. He would have tried, just like last night."

"Then why did he leave?"

Kent tossed an item to Nicole. She caught it mid-air, then turned it over. It was pregnancy test.

"It's positive," she realized, catching up.

"I don't understand," the brunette said, half-dazed.

Nicole hugged Rebecca. "You're pregnant."

"I know. I mean. That's what I was doing --"

The brunette melted into tears, clutching to Nicole as if her very life depended on it.

"He couldn't take a womb that was already in use."

Nicole's phone rang, startling her. The caller I.D. showed it was her partner.

Brusquely, she answered, "I need you over here."

She couldn't believe her partner's answer.

CHAPTER 63

By Nicole's tone of voice, it could only be Ruben on the other end of the line. "What? No, but we --"

Harbinger knew it wasn't good news by the blotches appearing on Nicole's cheek. She nodded several times, then obviously interrupted Torres.

"We'll be there as soon as we're --" Nicole listened, teeth clenched, then finally, "Okay, okay. Be there in ten."

"More drama?" Kent asked as E.M.T.s rushed into the room and quickly extracted Rebecca from Nicole.

The detective pulled him aside as the medics tended to Rebecca's wounds. "They caught him."

"Who?"

There was a gulp before she answered, "Plain Jane."

"Where?"

"Over at Nancy's house."

That didn't make any sense. Nicole must not have heard Ruben correctly. "But there is no way the killer could have made the thirty blocks in less than ten minutes."

Any relief from finding Rebecca alive had completely drained from Nicole's face. "He did not. Plain Jane hit Nancy's house, *not* here."

Kent backed away as the E.M.T.s loaded Rebecca onto a gurney. "No way. No how. This was Plain Jane."

"We need to head over to the station --"

"I can smell him, Nicole. Smell him. Just feel this room. He was here. Can't you feel it? Can't you?"

Nicole looked away. "They are taking the suspect in for interrogation. I suggest if you want answers, we should head over there."

He watched Nicole head to the front of the house. Kent looked around the dim bedroom one last time. He would go with her. He would look at this supposed suspect, but his confidence was unshaken.

The killer had been here tonight.

Of that, Kent had no doubt.

CHAPTER 64

Ruben sat across from Plain Jane.

The Plain Jane.

The city's worst serial killer in recorded history.

Sure, he had captured other murderers. Interrogated dozens of them. Extracted confessions from many of them. But he'd never actually been this close to a bona fide serial killer before.

It wasn't quite the heady experience he had expected.

The guy looked like any other suspect. Maybe a little calmer than most, but still his eyes darted towards the door. Perps were always the same. Even though this one had declined counsel and signed his waiver, the creep still expected someone to come through that door and save him.

But the door stayed closed. Ruben let the guy stew for a bit. He let the drab gray cinder-block walls press in. Let the guy study the cracked paint and that long red smear behind Ruben. It looked like clotted blood but was actually an old ketchup stain. They left it there for the effect.

For the same reason, Ruben had turned off the room's heater. The northern storm's cold air was quickly seeping through the walls and single paned windows. The perp's respiratory rate increased the longer Ruben just sat there. Let him get cold. Let his balls retract up into his belly.

They had him dead to rights on the break-in and even attempted murder. The D.A. could take this case to trial right now and have the jury come back with a guilty verdict in two minutes flat.

No, that's not what this interrogation was about. It was about the other seven women. Joann, Claudia, and all the rest. For that they were going to need some solid forensic evidence, but even better, a confession.

Without Nicole here to play the good cop, he'd have to take a stab at it himself. Build rapport with the guy. He had studied enough texts, including Harbinger's, on interviewing serial killers to know the stock barrage of questioning was not only unnecessary, but put them at the disadvantage.

Most serial killers wanted to tell their story, you just had to give them their venue. Make them think you cared enough for them to share.

It galled Ruben. Cut across the grain to soften his tone, but he needed to show as much finesse as Harbinger. Even more.

"Martin. Can I call you Martin?" Ruben began.

The perp shrugged.

"Martin, where'd you get the scalpel?"

"It's mine."

"Obviously. Your prints were all over the handle," Ruben commented. This was one interrogation he was going to relish. Even more so once Harbinger arrived. Let the profiler sit in the galley and watch for once. "Well, Martin, where did you get it?"

"A friend."

"Really? Because according to your neighbors, you don't have a lot of friends."

"That's not true!"

Ruben watched Martin's eyes dart. This interrogation was going like clockwork. Now that he had gotten a rise out of the perp, Ruben needed to cajole him. "So? Prove them wrong. Who's your friend?"

"A buddy. He works on Farmshire Ranch."

Ruben couldn't help but allow a small grin to form. He had been right this whole time. It had been an equine handle all along. Kent was going to eat crow for a month.

CHAPTER 65

Kent held the door open for Nicole, obviously surprising her with his newfound manners. When working a case, his gentlemanly skills usually suffered. Oh, who was he kidding? He never held much stock in chivalry.

Bending her head slightly in appreciation, she passed by into the observation room, which looked like any other precinct's. Really it was just a narrow hall looking over two one-way mirrors.

Glick was the only inhabitant, and he didn't even bother to look over to know who came in. "Good thing one of you stayed at Nancy's."

Nicole looked down, but Kent could give a shit what the Captain thought. The profiler was here to confirm that Ruben hadn't accidentally hit the serial killer jackpot, then head back out. Clear his head. Completely wipe the slate clean of all preconceptions and find a new bead on the killer.

Plain Jane had given over so much of himself in the past few days. So many clues. So many tells. The genesis for his uterus craving. The fact he could not take a ripe womb.

So much, yet Kent still grasped at tendrils of smoke. After he dismissed this suspect, he would go back to the beginning. The profiler would do some very specific research.

Arriving at the one-way mirror, Kent stared at the so-called 'Plain Jane' killer. The guy scratched at his palm, eyes darting back and forth like he was watching a tennis game.

"So this is the mastermind that killed over thirty women?" Kent asked to no one in particular.

"Plain Jane," Glick proudly announced.

Kent chuckled. "Yeah, right."

Nicole fired him a look, but he just chuckled as he turned towards the exit.

"Don't you even want to talk to him?" Nicole asked.

"We caught him dead to rights breaking into Nancy's house," Glick chimed in. "Scalpel in hand."

Kent sneered. "Do you really think that's what a prolific serial killer acts like under interrogation? They're cold as ice or warm as peach on a spring day. They're not nervous or worried or even the slightest bit out of sorts. They're more in control than the interrogator."

She took a step closer. "You say that all the time, but couldn't one be different? Couldn't one act just like Martin to throw us off?"

"How do you think Dahmer convinced the cops to give him back his captive? Do you really think he stood there with shifty eyes and itchy palms? Or Vansalez talked his way out of a speeding ticket with three torsos in the back seat?"

Even though he was answering Nicole, he glared at Glick. This was a waste of time. Kent didn't need to go in there and prove Martin wasn't Plain Jane. The evidence would do it for him while he was out actually catching the killer.

"But how?" she asked. "How can they stay so cool?"

As much as he wanted to get out of there, he couldn't resist it when she looked at him with such respect and wonder. You might as well give him some crack.

"It's called purposeful forgetting." How many times had Kent taught the technique to F.B.I. recruits and Special Forces alike. He taught it to special agents to break serial killers and soldiers to be able to endure torture. "How can the cop sense you've got body parts tucked under the back seat, if you, yourself, have forgotten? If you don't remember you're a serial killer it's a little hard to give yourself away."

Nicole went to ask something, but Glick overrode her. "That doesn't change that fact that we're tossing his place as we speak." The Captain's confidence grew. "They've already found human blood in the sink traps. Just waiting to match it to one of the victims."

"Great," Kent said as he turned toward the exit. "Call me when you do, otherwise I'll be out catching Plain Jane."

Glick blocked his departure. "You're that sure that Martin isn't our guy?"

That sure? Kent asked himself.

Absolutely *certain* it wasn't Martin from the moment he'd laid eyes on the puny man. He pointed towards the perp.

"Look at him. Nervous. Palms sweating." Kent geared up as he pointed towards the man's hand on the table. "Look at his nails for Christ's sake. Way too long to be fishing around in someone's belly."

"That's it? This is where you impress us with your brilliant insight, then walk off, leaving us with the mess?"

"Yeah, pretty much," Kent said as he stepped around the Captain.

"Glad to see history can repeat itself over and over again. With the same outcome *over* and *over* again," Glick said as he moved to block the profiler again. "Or wait. Isn't that the definition of insanity? Repeating the same behavior but expecting different results?"

Nicole stepped between them. "Captain!"

"What? Harbinger doesn't get to act this crazy then expect us not to mention the fact he's a pain in the ass."

"Sir!" Nicole might be freaking out, but Kent felt only amusement. Did Glick really think he could try some pop psychology crap and get Kent to comply?

"If you don't believe that's Plain Jane in there, then prove it, Harbinger."

Kent threw a thumb towards the interrogation room. "I'm sure Desperado in there is well on his way to securing a *confession.*"

"Just don't bitch if another woman dies. I don't want to hear your 'I told you so' routine again."

He was nearly out the door when Nicole grabbed his arm but directed her comments to her Captain. "Can we please keep this conversation to the present problem?"

"What? Harbinger's gotten really good at pointing the finger after the fact." Glick stared the profiler straight in the eye. "But not so good at standing up for what he believes in."

Okay, the Captain had gone too far that time. "*That* is bullshit," Kent snapped. "You can say all you want about my emotional veracity, but I speak my mind."

Glick took a step forward, forcing Nicole out from between them. "Usually as you are running out the door."

"Captain!" Nicole unsuccessfully tried to wedge in.

"If you are going to go contrary to the evidence, Harbinger, then make a stand. Make it here. Make it now."

"Or?" Kent couldn't wait to hear the answer.

"Or? You'll stay fucked up forever, son."

CHAPTER 66

Nicole stood horrified. What had gotten into Glick? And Kent was no better. He looked ready to punch the older man, and she wasn't so sure the Captain didn't deserve, at least just a little bit.

Then Kent smiled. "Luckily, that's how I like it."

With that, Kent was out the door. She too stunned to follow. He had abandoned her, *again*.

They had made such progress tonight. In the car she felt that maybe, just maybe, they could overcome the last two years. But now this. Typical Kent behavior. Why stick it out when he could run?

She should have been livid with Kent, but instead she vented on Glick. "What was that about?"

"He's got to change. It's not enough to just be a profiler, even if he's a fucking-mind-blowing-brilliant one. At some point, he's got to be a..."

"A man?" Nicole asked bitterly.

"I was going to say, 'an adult.' A citizen." Glick's face softened. "A partner." When she did not reciprocate the look, her Captain continued, sounding tired. "Until then, he's just another Rasputin."

While Nicole searched for a retort, Glick turned up the audio feed from the interrogation room.

CHAPTER 67

Ruben changed the subject, keeping the suspect off-kilter. "So, Martin, how did your parents get along?"

"Fine."

"Fine?" Ruben hadn't expected that answer. This guy was trying to jack him around. That just wasn't going to fly. Not tonight. "Really? Because I just got this faxed over."

Pulling out papers from a file, Ruben laid them all out in front of Martin. "Looks like the cops were regular visitors at your childhood home, breaking up your little family spats."

The perp shrugged. "Parents fight. It was no big deal."

Ruben shook his head and pointed to the emergency room photos. Some were pretty ugly. Others downright gruesome.

"Your mother was hospitalized three times for fractures and at least once for a concussion."

The man averted his eyes and angled his body away from the photos. Shoving an especially explicit picture of a split lip, Ruben pressed harder. "So it didn't have any lasting effect seeing your mom punched hard enough by your father that she swallowed three teeth?"

The perp squirmed. "It was a misunderstanding."

"Oh, no. It was no misunderstanding. X-rays confirmed. It was three teeth. That time her lip took twenty-seven stitches to close."

CHAPTER 69

Despite her anger, Nicole couldn't help being drawn to the window. Ruben was doing a pretty good job in there.

Glick dialed down the audio. "The guy's pitch perfect for Ruben's profile."

"But exactly the opposite of Kent's."

The Captain indicated towards the door that led into the interrogation room. "So go in there and prove him wrong."

"Which *him*?"

Glick sighed. "Whichever one needs it."

With a set to her jaw, Nicole inserted the earpiece that Glick offered and entered the interrogation room. If Kent wasn't going to hang around to prove this guy was a copycat, it was up to her.

Torres was in the middle of a question when Nicole walked in. "Maybe Martin would rather talk about how he feels regarding women in authority?"

Ruben went to stand up, but she put a firm hand on his shoulder. "No. Stay put," she said, doing her best dominatrix impersonation. "I'm just here to watch."

Nicole strode to the back of the room and positioned herself in the perp's blind spot. Ruben and she had danced to this tune before. Usually he leaned up against the wall while she played the 'good' cop, trying to help the perp. But not now. Not with a possible serial killer. A killer of women. Tonight she got to put the pressure on.

Over their earpieces, Glick spoke in a somber tone. "Sorry, guys. It's female blood alright, but it doesn't match any of our victims."

Nicole wasn't sure if she felt pleased or upset by the news. It hurt Ruben's case but supported Kent's arrogant assessment.

Glick continued, "We can't count on the evidence to prove he's Plain Jane. We're going to need a confession."

By the look on Ruben's face, Nicole knew they had a hard road ahead of them. Torres was as good as anyone in the room, well as good as anyone except Kent. But getting a serial killer to confess?

Unless you had a backbreaking tonnage of evidence, it was hard. Unless the perp was an attention-seeker, it was nearly impossible. Nicole sighed. It was absolutely impossible if the guy didn't do it in the first place.

Her partner rose to the occasion, though, and made a show of pressing his earpiece tighter against his ear as if listening to a long discord.

Finally Torres lowered his hand, shaking his head. "The case is just stacking up against you. You should have cleaned those drains better, Martin."

The perp seemed genuinely unimpressed. "You don't have anything or a D.A. would be here."

Good one, Nicole thought, but Ruben turned it right back on the guy. "Who do you think just told me that he'd be seeking the death penalty?"

That got the perp's attention. His eyes nervously flickered to the one-way mirror. "Then why aren't they in here talking to me?"

Ruben wagged his finger at Martin. "If they were willing to cut a deal, sure. But how's that going to play in the press? The new D.A. making a deal with a serial killer?" Torres leaned back in his chair. "I wouldn't wait on them."

Perhaps Ruben went too far, because the perp nearly peed his pants. "Maybe... Maybe, you know, I should think about getting a lawyer then?"

Nicole moved in before he actually requested counsel and invalidated his signed waiver. "Need protection? Feeling a little guilty, are we?"

She hovered behind Martin, just out of sight. Yet the man seemed to gain resolve. Her eyes met Ruben's.

They were losing him. Soon some high-profile lawyer would take the guy's case just for the headlines, and not only would they never get a confession, but a conviction was equally unlikely.

Then a familiar, sultry voice came over her earpiece. It certainly wasn't Glick.

"Lean forward," Kent repeated.

Nicole's eyes darted to the mirror. Had she really heard correctly? Had the profiler really come back? By the frown on Ruben's face, he thought so as well.

"Do it," Harbinger encouraged.

With a feeling slightly akin to a beer buzz, Nicole leaned in. Close enough she could smell the perp's cheap cologne but was not quite touching his clammy skin.

"Ask him how that feels," the profiler prompted.

She leaned in so that her lips were nearly brushing his ear lobe. "So do you like your women close?" The perp's respiration rate skyrocketed. He did not answer.

"Closer," the voice in her ear whispered as if it were Kent she snuggled up to.

Complying, Nicole brought her chest level with the perp's cheek. "Or closer, Martin?"

Flustered, the guy tried to keep his eyes facing straight forward. Like a compass to the north, he kept sneaking peeks at her cleavage.

"Let that left breast just lean against him."

Ruben's head turned sharply toward the window.

A movement that was not missed by the perp.

"Tell him you found blood mixed with semen."

Nicole did not hesitate. "No biggie. We found more blood in the shower drain pipes."

"You did not."

She "tsked" before she continued, "I was not done. It was mixed with jizz. I can only assume *your* jizz." Nicole moved from the right side of his face to his left. "Did you go and beat off after you killed her?"

CHAPTER 70

"Get that left breast in play," Kent urged Nicole even though he felt Glick's disapproving presence. The profiler watched through the mirror as she leaned in.

But her voice was sexy even muffled over the audio feed as she whispered to Martin. "Does it excite you? Proximity? Being this close?"

The detective worked her magic, but this guy was scared. Even more scared than horny. They needed the big guns. And they needed them now. "I'm telling you, Nic. Get that left breast front and center."

Kent matched his respiratory rate to the Martin's. As her chest glanced the guy's shoulder, his breaths skyrocketed.

"Yes," the man exhaled more than spoke.

The profiler could sense that Nicole knew she had the upper hand, for her tone was coy. Her words soft. "You just wanted to be close."

The guy nearly shook with excitement. "Yes."

Martin was theirs. He was nothing more than clay to be molded. "Told you. That left one has magical properties, doesn't it, Julio?"

Kent smiled as Ruben glowered. Nicole, however, had overcome her reservations and was in such close contact with the perp that even he felt a twinge of jealousy.

Nicole sounded as if it were pillow talk. "Tell me."

Breaking the mood that Kent and Nicole had so carefully cultivated, Torres cleared his throat loudly.

Martin's eyes darted nervously. "I can't."

"You can," the temptress encouraged.

"I'm not saying another word."

As the perp crossed his arms, it looked like Nicole's breast had lost its magic. However, Kent had more in his arsenal than just her mammary tissue. It would take Nicole trusting him, though. Completely. Unquestioningly.

"If you won't talk to me…"

Nicole dutifully recited Kent's words. "If you won't talk to me…"

"Then show me."

Again the detective parroted the statement. "Then show…" Nicole stumbled, then regained her footing. "Me."

The harsh metallic scraping of his chair announced that Ruben was up on his feet. "That will be enough."

Nicole must have known where Kent was leading and she seemed eager to follow. "Maybe you should leave the two of us alone?"

The tall Hispanic clenched his fist. A gesture Kent was sure was meant for him and not the perp. "Never."

"Then sit down." Nicole's tone was dominating. It brooked no argument. Damn, but she had never been hotter, Kent thought.

The perp must have thought so too as his respiratory rate ticked up and his cheeks flushed red.

Once Ruben was back in his seat, Nicole continued in a cajoling tone, "We've got the evidence. We've got the break-in." She sounded almost sympathetic, plus Kent couldn't help noticing that the left breast was back in play. "You're going to prison for a very long time, Martin."

In a move that even impressed Kent, Nicole stroked the perp's cheek. "When's the next time you'll be this close to a woman again?"

Martin looked to Ruben, who still fumed, then back to Nicole. He seemed uncertain, but at least he was not talking about getting a lawyer.

The perp mumbled something.

"Speak up, Martin. Tell me what you want." Nicole encouraged like an experienced pro that wanted her money.

Martin cleared his throat. "You'll need to un-cuff me."

CHAPTER 71

Nicole looked to the mirror. Toward Kent. What the perp asked was well beyond regulations.

"Is it any wonder people think I'm disturbed?" The profiler asked rhetorically in her ear. "If you want a confession, darlin', you've got to go where the weirdoes lead."

With a harsh glare at Ruben to keep him seated, Nicole pulled out her keys. With a click, the perp was un-cuffed.

"There you are, Martin."

The man rubbed his wrists, then looked to Ruben. She had to give her partner credit; he looked away rather than argue and upset the delicate rapport she had built with the creep. Finally Martin turned toward her, but did not approach.

"You're going to show me?" Nicole asked

He licked his lips and nodded. "Oh, yeah."

The perp did not move. Kent remained silent on the other side of the glass. She was on her own. "Do you like them facing you or away?"

"Facing me."

With hands outstretched, the perp came at her. Obviously intent on groping her.

Nicole squirmed, waiting for Kent, but the profiler continued his silence. Had he abandoned her? Was she really going to let this pervert touch her? Her anxiety increased as the man inched forward, almost as surprised that he was going to reach the promised land as she was.

"Yeah, like he ever gets that action," Kent joked.

Relieved, but slightly pissed the profiler had let it go that far, Nicole knocked Martin's hand away. "I don't think so," she said. "This needs to be *just* like you did it."

The perp looked frustrated, and his jaw worked back and forth. The guy probably grew up with a retainer. Probably had a tooth guard at home by his bed. Nicole felt gratified. That was the type of insight that Kent might have had. Being this close to a psycho, the detective's learning curve was steep. Nicole didn't have to wait for Kent's instructions. She knew what was needed next.

Slowly, ever so slowly, Nicole circled the perp, running a finger along his shoulders, then his back. "This is what you want but never get, isn't it?" She came around to face him, her finger still lightly touching his chest. "So close. But they always say 'no' don't they?"

"Don't forget the power of that left breast," Kent reminded her.

As she passed by Martin again, she made sure her breast made contact with his elbow. When the perp spoke, it was so husky that you could barely make out the words.

"They shouldn't have."

"No," Nicole tried sympathize. "They shouldn't."

Martin's voice firmed. "Turn around."

Nicole hesitated, suddenly not so sure this guy wasn't Plain Jane. A possible murderer un-cuffed and inflamed.

"Do it," Kent's instruction was blunt.

Nicole turned around. "You like them to be surprised?"

CHAPTER 72

Good girl, Kent thought as Nicole completely turned her back on the freak. For a second there, he thought she might balk, but Nicole had done her duty.

He knew how vulnerable the detective felt, yet those feelings just fueled this guy's fantasy. In a few moments, Martin would completely forget he was in a police station, and they would see his true colors.

Martin was pressed up against Nicole's back. His hips thrust slightly forward so his crotch was practically between the detective's butt cheeks. Still Nicole held her ground, finally understanding how you had to deal with these psychos.

"You like to take them from behind?" Nicole asked again. Again, Martin didn't answer. Instead his finger traced the length of her neck.

Nicole's face was angled away from Kent, though he knew she cringed. The detective wasn't the most comfortable with physical intimacy under the best of circumstances. This type of contact had to be excruciating.

"Draw him out."

Nicole's tone was a little flat. "Where's your knife?"

"We'll get to that," Martin said as his hand slipped forward, down her sternum toward her cleavage.

"Show me," Nicole urged. "Show me how you did it."

"Do you *really* want me to?"

Oh yeah, we do, Kent thought, but it was Nicole who voiced the answer. "Yes."

With a violence that startled everyone else, Martin grabbed Nicole by the neck and started choking her, screaming hysterically, "You, bitch! You'll pay, just like she did!"

Very un-Plain Jane-like. If there had been doubt in anybody's mind this was their man, it should have been completely dispelled.

In a single bound, Ruben was over the table, pulling the psycho off Nicole. Glick seemed agitated, but Kent was almost bored. "Told ya so. The ugly, stupid ones are easy to catch."

The Captain rushed in as Ruben struggled with Martin.

"Tell Nicole, next time she should believe me," Kent said to Glick as he strode out.

CHAPTER 73

Nicole sat on the floor, still choking a little, trying to convince her throat it was safe to breathe again while Ruben was busy slamming Martin against the wall. Her partner was cursing vehemently in Spanish. Seldom did Ruben let his Latin roots show quite so colorfully.

"He's not Plain Jane," Nicole croaked out.

With another good shove against the wall, Ruben answered. "Maybe not, but he did *kill* someone."

Glick called two other uniforms in. At this point they were there to protect Martin from Ruben rather than the other way around. Nicole knew she should be angry at Kent or even scared of Martin, but she was elated.

She could still feel the killer's hands around her throat. Still feel the adrenaline surge as he closed off her windpipe. It had been a rush. A rush that wasn't over yet.

Martin was no Plain Jane. His actions under stress had proven that. A serial killer still lurked. A smarter one. A true predator. One that she was now ready to help take down.

"Yeah, but he didn't kill our girls," Nicole stated.

Even with Martin re-cuffed and a uniform on each arm, Torres still shoved the man before releasing him into the other officer's custody. "Still, we caught a murderer tonight."

Nicole knew how badly Torres wanted to be the one to bring down Plain Jane. Sadly it was not to be. That killer was well beyond either of their skills.

"Where's Kent?" Nicole asked as she tried to rise.

Dizzy, she had to plop back down. Glick and Torres rushed to her side. "Pulled his 'who was that masked man' routine," the Captain replied.

Nicole leaned back, exposing her bruised neck.

"That bastard," Ruben growled. Nicole was pretty sure that he was referring to Kent rather than Martin.

Now feeling more silly on the ground than excited, Nicole tried to rise again. Ruben put hands on her shoulders. "The E.M.T.s are on their way."

"I'm good," Nicole said as she purposefully removed her partner's grip. Glick offered a hand also. Nicole declined it as well. She was not a damsel in distress. She was one motivated, ready to track down a serial killer kind of damsel who was not going to let anyone get in her way. "Did he say where he was going?"

Glick shrugged. "Just a 'hi, ho, Silver', and away."

CHAPTER 74

Ruben watched as the woman he loved walked out, again. Could he blame Nicole, though? He had failed, yet again. Failed so very publicly. Failed right in front of her. It had taken Kent, riding in on his white horse, to save the day.

Within a matter of minutes the profiler had completely debunked his theory that Martin was Plain Jane and secured a confession regarding whomever he did kill.

But Kent had degraded Nicole in the process. A process which his partner seemed to not only tolerate, but enjoy as well. Ruben never could have put Nicole in that position. Using her body like that? Forcing her to seduce a killer? Then to put her in such physical danger? How he wished the profiler were here. Ruben would show him what physical danger felt like.

Glick cleared his throat, bringing Torres back to the problems still at hand. "You better check the rest of the names on Harbinger's list."

"We're that sure Martin's not our man?" Ruben asked, knowing full well the answer to that question.

With a frown, Glick answered, "Uni's just found his landlady in the dumpster. He got evicted after losing his job."

"Damn it. Then why was he at Nancy's?"

Glick walked out of the room, indicating that Ruben should follow. In silence, they made their way to the Captain's office. Glick made a point to shut the door before turning back to Ruben. Still, his supervisor didn't answer his question.

"Well?"

"Harbinger was..." The Captain couldn't finish.

"He was right? Again?"

How could this be?

Maybe the damned profiler truly was psychic after all.

"Martin told one of his friends last week that Plain Jane was nothing compared to what he was going to do."

"The ugly and the stupid," Ruben murmured.

"Yeah, something like that..." The Captain paused long enough for Ruben to search his face. What else could there be? "And we have a new problem."

"Kent is running for president?" he asked, somewhat sarcastically, and somewhat hoping he wasn't right.

Glick grunted as he sat down. "No, but almost as bad. The uterus from last night's vic, Joann. It's missing."

Ruben stayed standing. "I thought the coroner confirmed it was intact?" A glimmer of hope arose. Had Kent somehow been wrong about Joann? "Harbinger's whole theory rests on that uterus."

"Don't get too ramped up. The uterus was intact last night. The M.E. removed it, weighed it, biopsied it and put it in a jar marked as evidence."

"And now it has miraculously disappeared?"

Glick rubbed his dark circled eyes. "Yes."

Ruben sat down hard on the chair. "Great. So we think the killer got his trophy after all?"

"Who else would want a cut-up uterus?"

CHAPTER 75

Through the window, Joshua saw the coroner's wagon drive up. Dropping his stack of paperwork on the desk, he rushed out to the delivery bay. A new body. It was sights like this that made him glad he ended up coming into work tonight. Especially after the night he had.

Punching in the code, Josh pulled his lab coat around his neck. The night had gone cold. The sliding doors opened, bringing with them a rush of frigid air. The driver was already out of the vehicle, opening the back doors.

"Seriously, dude. Tell them to stop dying," Josh joked. Another perk of the job was yanking this slacker's chain.

"I don't think she had any choice."

The driver, in an unusual show of personality, opened the zipper and pointed to the badly beaten woman with dark purple bruising around her neck. Obviously strangled. Joshua could tell the cops that without a freaking autopsy.

"Fine, but tell the killers to hide the bodies a little better. We are *way* backed up."

Snapping open the gurney, the driver sounded so very unimpressed by Joshua's dilemma. "Sorry, they need the prelim by nine."

Shocked, Josh asked, "Why?"

"They need to be sure the uterus is still in there."

Okay, that was the stupidest thing Josh had ever heard. It was almost insulting that anyone in their right mind could think Plain Jane would kill like this. What did they think he was? A cretin?

"You are kidding, right?" Josh asked as the driver just shut the wagon's doors. The attendant pointed to the body. "This broad was strangled and beaten." Josh was nearly speechless, he was that upset. "This isn't Plain Jane's M.O."

Sighing as if he was bored with the whole conversation, the driver locked the back of the wagon.

"You can never be too sure."

"What do they think?" Josh was not about to let this travesty go. "The guy forgot to take his Ritalin and just started hammering away?"

"Look, I drive just 'em, and you load them on the slab. What do we care what they think? An autopsy is an autopsy."

Josh sucked in a breath. That was sacrilege. Just straight up sacrilege. It took him a few moments to form the words necessary to counter such blasphemy. "Oh... Oh, you are so wrong. They are like --"

"Okay, if you give me your delicate flower analogy, I'm going to hammer *you*."

As Josh stood there stunned, the driver got back into his wagon and drove off. The man obviously didn't understand that death was as important as life. He went to close the bag back up, but patted the woman's cheek before he zipped it. "No one understands us, do they, love?"

CHAPTER 76

Nicole drove toward the seediest motel on the outskirts of town. The neon 'L' in motel was burnt out so the sign flashed 'Mote', which pretty much summed up the place. She parked in front of the lop-sided sign that announced the office. Now no mystery why Kent had not ever let her pick up him up.

Setting her car alarm, something which she seldom did, Nicole went into the office.

Immediately her nose cringed.

She'd searched sewer tunnels that weren't as ripe. Surprisingly there was actually an awake attendant. It appeared besides offering weekly and monthly rates; the 'mote' also had a lively late night "hourly" business as well. The man's greasy nametag read "Arty, Night Manager."

Even though the cowbells attached to the door had rung quite loudly, Arty didn't look up from his 'Max at Night.'

"I need to know which room Kent Harbinger is staying in." Through force of habit she flashed her badge.

Arty just yawned. "I would have told you without that. I've got no reason to protect that freak." He nodded to the left. "He's in number four."

"Thanks," the detective said as she exited.

"And tell him I'm not giving him any other towels until he returns the last ones!" Arty shouted.

Giving a polite wave, Nicole proceeded to room number four. Or at least she was pretty sure it was number four. The metal number was long gone, leaving an outline of rust and faded paint in the outline of a four.

Due to the late hour, she gave a soft knock, although she doubted any of the other guests would hear or even mind if she started yelling at the top of her lungs. Unit number five had porn blasting so loudly that Nicole did not need any visuals to know it was a three-on-one scene.

It was a little disconcerting to know this is where Kent spent his 'down' time. She knocked again. "Harbinger?" Giving up on formality. "Kent?"

Still no answer. On a whim, she checked the doorknob. Unlocked. What profiler didn't lock their door? Especially in the middle of an intense manhunt for a serial killer?

Uneasy, Nicole drew her weapon and entered. She felt for the light switch and flicked it. Nothing happened. She paused, half in and half out of the doorway.

"Damn it, Kent. Answer if you're in here."

Keeping her eyes forward, Nicole fished around in her coat pocket for her flashlight. Turning it on, she swept the room with its beam, looking for an intruder, or worse, a body.

She found neither, though the walls glistened strangely in the low light. Taking a step inside, the detective quickly learned why. Every square inch of the room was covered in photographs. Photos of all the women he had been following. There was Joann. Claudia before that. Maria was there too. All the women that he had 'stalked' and lost. Picture after picture lined the walls.

"Oh Kent," Nicole whispered to the sad, pathetic room. It had not been the urine smell that had kept the profiler from inviting her over, it had been this bizarre, twisted shrine.

A sound prompted her to swing around.

"Hey, hey. It's me," Arty said, hands up.

Nicole lowered her gun. "What's wrong with the lights?"

Turning on a dime, the manager went from anxious to pissed off. "Tell him no electricity until he returns the lamps!"

"That's illegal." Who did this guy think he was?

Arty stepped into the room and indicated to all the walls. "I haven't turned him into the mental health department, so I figure we're even."

Giving up on him, Nicole quickly checked the rest of the room. A small closet and even smaller bathroom. No Kent. Even these rooms were covered in pictures. She turned around to find Arty right behind her.

"And if this tape damages the walls, he's paying to have them re-painted."

"I'll forward the information...Once I find him."

Arty seemed done with the conversation and headed to the door. "So, you staying or what?"

Nicole re-holstered her weapon. "Yeah, for a while."

"Whatever turns your crank," Arty said as he exited.

She wasn't even sure why she was staying, especially when unit three had live-action sounds that put the porn in room five to shame.

As she studied the room in more detail, she realized that many of the pictures were marked as she had been in the briefing room. Red slashes marred many of the pictures.

"Oh Kent..." she said as she plunked down onto the sagging mattress. Nicole lay back even though she had a lingering concern about what might crawl into her hair. She closed her eyes.

This was all her fault. After his release from the hospital, Kent had been in the psychiatric halfway house for over six months, and the doctors said he was adjusting well. Taking his medications without incident. Beginning to socially interact with the other patients.

A stranger might have taken him for a normal person, but no, Nicole had to go and trash all that progress.

Over the reservations of Ruben, Glick, four doctors, two social workers and an assistant district attorney, she had asked the profiler to return to work. What concern was Kent's tentative mental status with so many women's lives on the line? Brashly, Nicole had thought she knew the profiler better than them all.

Opening her eyes, she found hundreds more pictures taped to the ceiling, and realized just how wrong she had been. Obviously she didn't know Kent at all.

Mainly out of a morbid curiosity, Nicole pointed her flashlight upwards. Which victim had won the coveted spot above his bed? But as she studied the photos, she realized these weren't creepy stalker pictures.

These were photos of *her*.

Sitting upright, she craned her neck for a better look. The ceiling was covered with images of her. And these did not have the impersonal feel of surveillance photos. They were great shots. There she was with her friend, Lisa, at a movie. Both laughing in the picture.

Another of her with Monty, a detective from the two-seven. They ran the reservoir weekly. The layout looked like a huge photo spread for a magazine. There was even one of her sleeping. Taking in the scene as a whole, Nicole made a realization; Kent wasn't coming back tonight.

Standing up on the bed, she reached up and pulled down the center photo, knowing pretty damn for sure where Harbinger was camped out.

CHAPTER 77

Ruben shook his head, then shook his head again. "You can't expect me to make the call," he said to Glick.

The Captain looked around. They were the only two left in the bullpen. After the flurry of activity surrounding Martin's arrest, everyone was either back out on patrol or at home catching a few hours of shuteye before coming back to work. They knew they still had a serial killer on the loose.

"Sorry. It's you."

"You could make the call."

Glick shook his head. "There aren't many perks to this job, but not having to make this call is definitely one of them."

Sighing, Torres nodded. No one in his right mind would want to make this call to Nicole. Yet here he stood, hand on phone. Ruben dialed his partner's cell phone.

It only rang once.

"Kent?"

He was unable to control his temper. "Wow, this must be a real disappointment."

Nicole's tone wasn't nearly as sympathetic as her words. "Ruben, sorry."

Trying to regroup, he took a breath before continuing. He had a job to do. "Look, the press is all over our arrest of the possible Plain Jane. Glick doesn't want any dissenting comments until the autopsy confirms he's not our guy."

"You really called me at this hour to tell me to keep my mouth shut?" She sounded in no better mood than he did.

Well, he'd had enough tonight. "Let me be more blunt. The Captain doesn't want *Harbinger* talking."

"Tell him yourself."

Who did his partner think she was talking to? He knew she was tired, they all were. He knew she was stressed. They all were. Ruben worried that Kent's entitlement attitude had rubbed off on his partner.

"His voice mail is full or I would."

No answer. Ruben could hear the low rumble of the car engine as she drove. The soft sounds of the radio floated into his earpiece so Torres knew he had not lost the connection. Why wasn't she answering?

"Nicki?"

CHAPTER 78

It wasn't her partner's fault. As much as Nicole tried to make it his fault, it was not. Per usual, it was Kent's.

"Yeah, Ruben, sure. I'll tell him."

She closed the phone and mumbled to herself, "Who needs voice mail when you've got me?"

Nicole pulled up to her house to find a light on in the kitchen. At least she had been right about one thing tonight. There was only one person who would break into her house, then fix himself a snack.

Quietly she made her way into the house, then into the kitchen. Sure enough, there was Kent standing over the table. Probably making a sandwich.

"I knew I'd find you here."

The profiler looked over his shoulder, an unreadable look on his face. Then he moved to the side, revealing that he was elbow deep into the abdomen of a pig.

A pig tied down to her kitchen table.

A pig whose belly was splayed full open.

"Bet you weren't expecting this."

"What in the..." Nicole couldn't speak. What could she say? There was a dead, cracked open pig on her kitchen table, for Christ's sake.

Kent obviously didn't have any problem, for he pulled up tissue to show her. "This is the uterus."

He displayed the bloody organ like a cat who had caught a mouse and presented it as a display of affection. She could not respond.

"What? You wouldn't let me practice on humans."

Whatever connection she had felt back in the interrogation room, whatever sense of guilt and responsibility she had felt back at the motel room, Nicole snapped, "That's it." She heard herself say. "That's enough."

Nicole tried to pull him away from the pig, but Kent balked. "What's your problem? I put down plastic."

For the first time, she realized what had changed over the last twenty-four hours. "Damn it. Let me see your eyes."

Kent tried to resist, but Nicole persisted. With his hands still inside the pig, she pulled his head back and pried open his eye lids. "I knew it. You're not taking your meds."

She physically pulled his hands out of the carcass and dragged him over to the sink like a small child who had been caught finger painting on the walls. Trying to regain her composure, Nicole silently washed his hands under the tap.

"Drugged, four women died. Almost a fifth." Kent sounded drained but determined.

"The only reason the doctors let you out was because I promised, I *swore*, you would keep up with your meds."

Finished washing the pig's blood off, she grabbed a towel and dried his hands. Now he sounded angry as well. "You're not my keeper."

Nicole was no longer angry, she was livid.

"But you're mine?"

She pulled out the candid photo of herself.

Kent actually grinned. "That's a good one."

Disgusted by so much this night, Nicole dropped the picture onto the kitchen counter. Surprisingly the profiler tenderly picked it up and dried off the corner.

"Don't you agree?"

"You broke into my house to take it." Did the man have no more civility left in him?

"No, I didn't," Kent retorted.

This was all too much. Ruben had been right. The profiler was out of control. "Kent, don't lie. The picture --"

"Was not taken here." He sounded serious for once.

Confused, Nicole looked at the picture in his hands again. "But I haven't slept anywhere else for…" How long had it been since she shared Ruben's bed? "It's been months."

"Yeah, back when you were still having sex with Gaucho-boy."

No. Kent couldn't mean it. He could not. He would not. "You… You broke into *Ruben's* house?"

The profiler casually nodded, like 'duh'. The concept was inconceivable. Kent had broken into her partner's house, no, broken into his *bedroom* to take pictures of her. It was something an obsessed stalker did. It was something people were arrested for.

She tried to express her horror, "Oh, that… It's just…"

"His security system was a joke."

"It's *perverse*." Nicole backed away from him.

"*You are sick.*"

Instead of being insulted or even mildly upset, Kent's tone was almost teasing. "That's debatable, but tell me that you didn't feel the most alive when you were drawing the killer out of that loser back there in the interrogation room?"

Nicole took another step back, less sure of herself. How could the profiler cloud her mind so easily? "Maybe." How could he know her so well, only to violate her privacy? "I would never conceive of stalking you."

Suddenly serious, Kent's eyes gleamed in the low light. "You would if it helped hone your skills." He took another step forward, forcing Nicole to back away again, only this time she bumped into the sink. She couldn't go any further back as the profiler smiled.

"Face it, Nic. As much as you are repulsed by my eccentricities, you want to grow up to be just like me."

"In your medication-hazed, psychotic dreams."

Kent closed the distance. Nicole had nowhere to turn, so she held her ground, glaring, but the profiler seemed unimpressed. As a matter of fact, he was downright seductive. "You want to be able to walk through the Valley of Death and not be afraid."

Resisting his tone, Nicole held her chin high. "I think I was striding pretty confidently in that interrogation room."

CHAPTER 79

Kent looked into her eyes. The detective was trying oh-so-hard to be brave. That made him want her even more. Only Nicole could balance being aggressively vulnerable.

He brought himself as close to her as she had gotten to Martin. Close enough that her left breast pressed against his chest. Close enough that his lips were nearly kissing her ear.

"Only because you knew I was in the shadows, whispering, keeping you safe."

Nicole slipped from their intimate contact, and indicated to her badly bruised neck.

"I would not exactly call this 'safe'."

Ever so gently, Kent traced the outline of the bruise. He noticed she did not step any further away. "A small price to pay for knowing exactly what a victim feels like."

The sexual tension they had generated during the interrogation was pressing in on them, nearly smothering them. He took a step behind her, his left hand finding her belly. Her muscles tightened, which only served to excite them both.

"You must have wondered what it would have felt like if he had cut into your belly. Tugged at you from the inside while you were still conscious."

Bringing his right hand into play, he let it slowly travel up her side, just barely missing the outer curve of her breast. He could feel her tremble under his touch.

She was his.

"Did you know that the hormones released in the fear response are exactly the same as those released during sex and even more so during an orgasm?"

Kent wondered how long it had been since she had climaxed. From what he had seen, Ruben got an "A" for effort, but a "D" for execution. Not that Nicole was not without her own set of skills.

From his memory, he knew she was pretty damn good at self-service. But both knew there was a world of difference between convincing your body to climax rather than surrendering to another and allowing them to coax you there.

"Well?" Kent asked.

Nicole tried to respond, but what came out was just a guttural response. No words. Just desire given breath.

"Is that why we did so well together?" Kent rubbed his five o'clock shadow against her neck. There were other soft, delicate spots where his stubble was going to come in handy.

"Were you a little afraid of what I might do?" He asked her as his left hand slowly made its way down to her waist-line, exploring just under her belt for a window of entry.

"Did the fear double your hormone release? Sweeten the sex? Heighten the orgasm?"

A moan was all Nicole could muster as he found an opening below her belt within the hollow of her pelvic bone. She sucked in a breath as his finger cautiously made its way along her panty-line.

"Feel the blood pounding," he encouraged.

CHAPTER 80

How could she not feel it? Her pulse was just about the only thing she could hear. It roared so loudly that it almost drowned out Kent's voice. It was not his words that drove her heart rate though. It was his touch.

Despite the deep bruises up and down her neck, his light touch there made her nipples harden. So tightly that it almost hurt. Almost. Then his other hand was halfway down her belly. Just the thought of what he could do once he finished his travels sent a shiver through her body.

His hands slowed. His touch more firm. His murmurings had taken on an edge. Nicole tried to regain some semblance of control and listened more closely.

"The killer must have loved this moment," Kent said, his seductive tone waning. "Right when the victim knew that something terrible had begun."

Nicole's pulse raced, only now it wasn't driving it. Worry was. She tried to break free, but Kent's gripped her.

"The vessel of life would be engorged." He murmured against her skin, "So perfect. So ripe."

The profiler's hand moved back up to her belly. Kneading his fingers as if he could touch her womb. This officially was not fun anymore.

"Kent."

"You're not... Not perfect. The womb had been lucky enough to hold life once, but then it was violated. The life ripped from it."

Nicole squirmed beneath his steely grip. He didn't even acknowledge her anymore. Instead Kent pulled her tight against him. Not in sexual conquest, but in domination. Nicole could feel he wasn't even hard against her. This erection was mental.

It was no longer the profiler talking, but the killer. "It was my right to take it. To reclaim it. These women don't understand the precious gift they were given. That they let be torn asunder."

Nicole struggled against Kent's restraint; however, her movement only fueled his mania. He didn't know what he said anymore. Didn't know how he hurt her.

"It's my job to redeem the vessel." His finger sought purchase as if he could reach the precious trophy. "My responsibility to make it pure."

Nicole ripped away. "Stop. Just stop!"

CHAPTER 81

Kent snapped back like a switch had been flipped. He found Nicole shaking, holding her arms tightly over her belly.

"What?" Truly puzzled by her sudden change of mood, Kent smiled. "My intuition usually turns you on."

He reached a hand out. Nicole recoiled.

Not her usual take-a-step-away-to-see-if-you'll-follow kind of retreat, but a true rejection. "Not this time."

Ever confident when it came to Nicole, Kent lowered his tone. "I'm sure we can recapture the mood."

He tried to brush the hair back from her cheeks, but she actually pushed his hand away. What was up? They had just been on the cusp of making love.

Nicole certainly didn't act like she had felt the same way. "Just go." Her tone flat. Not even angry. Just frustrated past the point of caring.

Which only meant he needed to turn up the burner. Remind her of what they had just shared. "My dear, I was pretty set on *coming*."

"Trust me. There is *no* sex on your horizon." Nicole said it like a stripper who had been given a cheap tip. Said it like she actually meant it.

Kent's mojo was in serious disrepair.

No, his mojo had been working just fine. He'd revved the engine, and she had purred. Something was up with Nicole. "Where is this coming from?"

"Just go," she stated as she headed out the kitchen.

"No," Kent said, blocking her exit. "Not until you explain why you flipped an arousal U-turn."

Nicole's face registered shock, then anger. Big anger. Anger like the profiler had never seen from her. "Because you can't handle the consequences. That's why."

"Just because a guy doesn't want to sleep in the wet spot doesn't mean that --"

Kent stopped mid-sentence as Nicole turned away from him, though not before he saw her eyes tear over. There was no joking his way out of this one.

There was something seriously wrong.

"Hey," Kent said as he gently placed a hand to her shoulder. "What did Torres do to you?"

With the back of her hand, Nicole swiped away the tears. "So typical." Her voice dropped, and her lips turned downward. "Point the finger at anybody but yourself."

Wow. What had gotten into her? He was at a complete and total loss. He had tried seduction. He had tried humor. He had tried blanket compassion. The only thing left was honesty and that had never worked well in the past. But he knew he better try something or lose her.

"I usually pride myself on being able to follow twisted feminine logic, but I have to admit, I'm lost."

Nicole sighed and hung her head.

For the slimmest moment, Kent thought he'd won.

"I know." Then Nicole looked up with a sad stare. "That's why I told you to just *go*."

He hadn't just opened himself up to have her turn him out. "No. I came here to --"

"Not to have any kind of honest relationship." Anger rose again as she pointed at the gutted pig. "You came to fulfill your need to have a uterus of your very own, then you were hoping that if I did not notice how profoundly disturbed that was, you'd get your other needs met. End of story."

Kent stared at the woman that he thought he knew. That he thought knew him. Is that what she deduced from all this? A little wounded by her outburst, the profiler pulled back into comfortable territory.

"If you are going to play the swami role, you've got to get a little more imaginative."

Obviously that was exactly *not* what Nicole wanted to hear, for she lost her temper, lashing out at him. "When you left me jobless and --"

Well, Kent had enough of being her punching bag. "You weren't fired."

"They took my badge and my gun, Kent!"

"You got them back." What in the hell was she going on about? Didn't she know the sacrifices he had made? "You got everything back."

"Not everything." Tears rose again, making her eyes shimmer. "Some things can't be returned."

Unexpected, a feeling welled within Kent. He wanted to go over to her again. Pull her into his arms. Tell her whatever the problem, they could get through it together. But he did not. He could not. He could not even find the words to console her as she continued.

"It was not just being broke and jobless. It was…"

Was what? Kent almost verbalized the question, then wisely bit his tongue.

"I was alone and…"

The profiler waited for the end of the sentence. And waited. His empathy drained with each second.

"I was…"

Another eternal silence.

A silence that so loudly blamed him for his every inadequacy that Kent snapped, "Damn it all. How many times do I have to apologize?"

CHAPTER 82

Nicole stood in complete shock at Kent's audacity. She had been trying, really trying to open up to him. Tell him secrets she swore she would never reveal, and he dares to complain? Dares to say he has paid his pennance? How could he? He didn't even fully know his crime.

She struggled to find words. There were so many of them. So many curses she wanted to hurl.

Finally she chose the one closest to the surface. "*Once,* damn it! *Once* would be a fucking start!"

His retort was instantaneous, "I've apologized plenty."

"In your head? Probably," she spat. It was time Kent had a little taste of reality. The gloves came off. "Role playing with your therapist? Possibly." Nicole shoved the snapshot in his face. "To a photograph? Maybe." She threw the picture onto the floor. "To me? To my face? *Never.*"

Unflinching, Nicole stared into Kent's eyes. Daring him to challenge her. Daring him to try and defend his actions. Daring him to say anything at all. As always, the profiler chose a silent, enigmatic response. It took a few heartbeats to realize that he really wasn't going to answer.

More wounded by his current lack of participation now than his hurtful actions in the past, Nicole pointed to the door.

"Get out."

"Gladly." Kent stomped off, slamming the kitchen door behind him.

With one hand on the sink, Nicole took in each breath consciously, slowing them, guiding them. She stood strong. She wasn't going to let Kent get to her. Break her. Break her again. It was best he left. Best he was out of her life. Then a wave of sorrow come up from her gut. A wave of hurt. A wave of disappointment. A wave of loneliness.

Once again she had gotten her hopes up. Hopes that Kent had finally realized that he needed her as much as she needed him. Hopes that he had missed her as much as she had missed him. Hopes that he would take her in his arms and tell her that he loved her as much as she loved him. That was never to happen though, was it?

A sob arose from her very soul and erupted in her chest. She struggled to contain it. Struggled to hold the tears in, but it was effort in vain. Racked in sobs, Nicole couldn't hold herself up. Even the sink became ineffective support. Nicole slumped to the floor, crying, rocking, hugging herself. There was no one else to do it for her.

CHAPTER 83

Kent leapt down the steps and into Nicole's car within seconds. Firing up the engine, the profiler squealed out.

He pounded his fist against the steering wheel. "Don't take responsibility for my actions?" He hit the unforgiving plastic again. "I was voted best in group therapy for that!"

Oh, there was so much he had wanted to tell Nicole. Actually there was so much he had wanted to shout at her, yet none of it would come. What would it have mattered?

Swerving around a corner, the profiler hit the curb and just kept on driving.

Damn it, why couldn't Nicole let go of the past? Wasn't she always harping about *carpe diem*? She was like a freaking dog with a bone about it. But when push came to shove, she was the one who couldn't let go. The detective had to rehash every detail of the implosion that was their break-up.

Kent couldn't help himself, he shouted to the car as if it were Nicole. "Miss 'I was alone. I was…'" Anger built until it exploded again. "How about taking responsibility for finishing a fucking sentence?"

The profiler took a corner way too fast and nearly skidded out. Nicole really should check her tire pressure a little more often. Which reminded him of another affront.

"Oh, and *broke*? My ass. They didn't even have time to foreclose on the house," he yelled at the dashboard.

A fist pounded the steering wheel again. The woman had some nerve. Damn it, he's the one that had been arrested, having blood drawn every hour on the hour to check for mad cow disease and somehow she was the one that went on and on about how crappy her life had been?

"Lost your job? You were on fucking paid administrative leave!" he shouted out the window.

Mildly aware he really was starting to act like he was off his meds, Kent rolled up the window. He wouldn't give her the satisfaction of seeing him in a lock-up again.

CHAPTER 84

Nicole's body spasmed one last time. She had no more tears. Her breaths came in erratic gasps. Her throat swollen and hoarse. She was truly spent.

All she wanted to do was curl up in bed; however, a splayed pig, courtesy of Kent, of course, stared back at her from the kitchen table. There was no rest for the weary. Or was it the wicked?

Shrugging off philosophy, she rose and picked up an embroidered dishtowel, one her grandmother had stitched for her when she first went away to college.

Then she took a good look at the mess. These stains would not come out. Putting the gift back into the drawer, Nicole grabbed an entire roll of paper towels.

This was a job for Brawny.

At least Kent hadn't been joking about the plastic. He had in fact lined the floor with garbage bags before he hacked open the pig. Still there was the splatter. Nicole knew she should really get the pig off the table, but she just could not face that task yet. It was huge. It covered her entire kitchen table with the expansion leaf in.

Where in the hell had he gotten such a beast? She was about to ask how the profiler had paid for it, given that pork was about two bucks a pound, then realized that was stupid question. Kent didn't pay for anything. Ever.

Financially or emotionally.

The profiler had some contact somewhere that not only got him a carcass in the middle of the night, but probably drove it over here for him. Someone like Dolores or even Nicole a few years ago. If someone as brilliant as Kent wanted a pig in the middle of the night, obviously it had to be important.

Finally done with the peripheral clean up, Nicole could no longer avoid the large porcine that had taken over her kitchen. She rolled up her sleeves. Kent wasn't the neatest surgeon. Well, at least it was good to know he wasn't perfect at everything.

As she struggled to untie the pig's front leg, Nicole found her eyes straying to its exposed abdomen. It was truly a disgusting sight. Guts hanging out. What looked like a bladder flopped over the side of the body wall. How did doctors do it? Stare at gore like this? Worse, medical examiners had to look at the most distorted and grotesque bodies imaginable.

Yet with all this repulsion, Nicole found herself pushing her sleeve further up her arm. She couldn't help but wonder what it felt like. To plunge your hand into a belly like that. To find the uterus and hold it in your hand? She had seen Kent's face. Twice. Wonder and satisfaction had radiated from his normally somber features.

Had the killer practiced like this?

Had he possibly even gotten the idea of taking his very specific trophy from visiting slaughterhouses?

Focusing on the victim always opened up so many new avenues of investigation for the profiler. It was Kent's forte.

Even though he had broken over a dozen laws in 2003 by eating the homeless man's brain, it had been just such a bizarre feat that had led Kent to the killer.

How else besides eating fresh brain would the profiler have thought to look up exotic New Zealand spice importers?

Nicole was about to put her fingers into the belly when she remembered Kent hadn't stopped there. He had gone on to eat the killer's brain as well.

"No," she said to herself as she rolled her sleeve back down. Kent had been right when he said she had started down the slippery slope by blackmailing him. If she stuck her hand in this pig, where would it stop? Obviously the profiler didn't know where, but she did.

"I am not going there," Nicole said as she freed the pig and slid the carcass inside a garbage bag. She didn't need to act like a psycho to catch one.

CHAPTER 85

The killer watched as Nicole struggled to lift the pig by herself. Her man had driven off after the fight, leaving her with the mess. No great surprise. From the cracked open door of the pantry, the killer had seen it all.

From the aborted seduction to the soul-tearing fight to the gut-wrenching departure. Through it all, the killer had eyes only for Nicole. Her former lover, the *supposed* profiler, was nothing. He strutted, and he patted himself on the back, but he wasn't even close.

The profiler hadn't even known the killer was only ten feet away. If this was the best opponent the police could find, the killer was not worried. Not a bit.

The detective walked back in, cheeks tear-streaked and flushed from the exertion of hauling the carcass outside. How perfect she looked. Masculine enough to clean up the mess the profiler had left, feminine enough to sob so hard the killer thought Nicole might hurt herself.

The killer snapped to attention as the detective kneeled down on the floor. What was she doing? Slowly Nicole rose with the photo. Using the back of her hand, the detective wiped away some pig blood from the edge.

Would she keep it, the killer wondered?

Nicole went to throw the picture away, but the trashcan was completely full.

"Crap," she said. "Garbage day."

Setting the photo down on the counter, Nicole tugged the bag out of the can and turned away from the killer. The detective's back was ever so perfect. It sloped gently into a full buttock. And her hair was the perfect length. Just past the shoulder. The otherwise straight locks, curved upward at the very end, making the whole of Nicole's hair bounce and sway.

Just like Mother's. Tugging at the ends of the latex gloves, the killer made sure they were on tight.

The time was almost at hand.

Could there be a more perfect final sacrifice?

CHAPTER 86

Kent drove fifteen miles over the speed limit. He needed to just go. As fast as possible. He had controlled the impulse to spontaneously shout out the window, but still he mumbled to himself. That was the one big drawback to being such a loner. When the only person you can talk to kicks you out, there is no one else to grumble to.

"Never told her I'm sorry? What a crock..."

With a glimmer, the profiler imagined making Nicole a tape. A tape of him saying over and over and over again that he was sorry. He'd put it to that old Thompson Twins song, "Hold me now." Or maybe it was "The Gap?"

Whichever the song, it was the one where the singer laments that he'll say he's sorry even though he doesn't know what he's sorry for. Kent could relate to that guy.

A thousand apologizes weren't good enough for her.

Would having said it tonight, one more time, really have made a difference? Had it ever made a difference all the other times he'd said it?

Kent perked up. That's right. She hadn't accepted his apology before. He could throw that fact back in her face. His mind raced, trying to remember the last time he had said he was sorry. Oh, to be able to go back to her with proof of his rebuked contrition.

As he made another right turn, the profiler tried to picture it in his mind. The last time, or hell, *any time* he had been rebuffed when saying he was sorry. Come on, just once was all he needed.

Kent had said those words to her before. Right?

Out loud, to Nicole, right?

With her in the same room, right?

The car slowed as his foot slipped from the gas pedal. In all this time he'd said he was sorry, right? He must have. Sure, he'd said it in therapy. Sure he'd said it to her picture, then kissed it with tears on his lips. The more his mind sorted through their history, the more and more certain he became that he had in fact never, ever, ever apologized to her.

No wonder she was pissed.

Flipping an illegal u-turn, Kent raced back to Nicole's. It might not make a bit of difference. It might not matter at all. Yet at the very least, after everything he had put her through, he would actually say he was sorry.

With her in the room and everything.

Luckily his haphazard route had not taken him far from her home. A left, then a quick right brought him to her driveway. The profiler hopped out and took the stairs two at a time to her front door.

He had to hurry before he rationalized himself out of it. Like somehow an e-mail apology might suffice. Shoving those thoughts from his mind, he picked the lock and rushed inside.

"Nic," he said as he made his way to the kitchen.

He arrived to find the pig gone, but blood still pooled in the plastic bags. Okay, Nicole was slacking. In the old days this room would have been spick and span by now.

Where had she gotten to? He crossed the room and noticed his favorite picture of Nicole tossed on the floor. It was smeared with blood. Had she desecrated it on purpose? Or was it an accident? And why did the answer to that question matter so much to him?

"Nic?"

Hearing a sound, Kent turned, but not fast enough.

A blow came, throwing him forward. He tried to torque to see his assailant, Plain Jane. He knew it had to be, even though his attacker was shrouded in shadow.

Feeling incredibly stupid, Kent lost consciousness.

CHAPTER 87

Nicole raised a hand. "Did you hear something?"

Ruben looked back to her house. He had heard something, but he wasn't about to admit it. For once he had Nicole alone. Granted it was in the middle of the night, under the guise of official business, in her backyard out by the trashcans, and there was a huge hog carcass sticking up out of the trash. A sight they both chose not to mention.

But they were alone, damn it.

"No," he said, trying to sound definitive.

He tapped her shoulder, pulling her attention back. He had no doubt Kent was back. He was like a fucking boomerang. Ruben knew this was probably going to be his only window of opportunity.

Getting back to the matter, he continued, "I'm here to talk to you about something you aren't going to like."

"Please, Ruben. I can't. Not tonight."

"We have to."

Nicole wiped a stray hair from her face. She looked as beat as she sounded. "I'm sure you think we have to, but I've had a really shitty day."

"Me too," Ruben said before he thought it through. "You know, even before we became…" Given Nicole's distant look, he best not get too specific. "More than friends, on a night like this we could go out for a beer and commiserate."

"Those days…" Nicole could not look him in the eye. "And *nights*. They're over, Ruben. I'm sorry."

There was so much he wanted to say. So much he wanted to tell her. So much he wanted to warn her about Kent. But he had to face it. If she said their relationship was over? It was over. "I guess we got to resolve some things after all?"

"Yeah, I guess we did." Her voice gave no inflection. Nicole looked as if she were sleeping were she stood.

"Look, that's not what I came over for. Glick sent me on official business."

"That could not wait until dawn?"

Ruben shuffled his feet. This was not going to go well. Not well at all. "We have two uteri missing."

For the first time, it seemed Nicole had life breathed into her. "What are you talking about?"

"Both Joann and Martin's landlady… Their wombs were stolen after their autopsy."

Instantly, his partner was back on her game. "That means the killer must have access to the morgue."

"Or…" Ruben hesitated. Almost wishing he was not the one discussing this with her. Let someone else get skewered once in a while. Unfortunately, it was his job. "Or someone 'lifted' them for his own personal amusement."

Strangely, Nicole sounded more quizzical than angry. "And you are trying to blame Kent for this?"

Ruben indicated to the dead pig sticking half out of her garbage can. "It's not much of a stretch, Nicki."

"Okay."

Nicole started toward the house. Ruben followed. "What do you mean, okay?"

She shrugged. "If you think it's Kent, then go get him. Interrogate him. Torture him for all I care."

"But --"

"I'm done with men for the night. With you. With Kent. I'm going inside, by myself, and going to bed."

Ruben watched her walk away. He had never seen her like this. He knew how to fight with her. He knew how to sway her to his side.

But how did you overcome complete and total apathy?

CHAPTER 88

Just before she entered her house, Nicole turned to Ruben. "If you are really feeling motivated, you can put out an A.P.B. on my car. He's got it."

Her partner's face clouded over. Obviously confused by her behavior, he gave a curt nod then left.

Actually, after she said it, Nicole realized she wouldn't be displeased at all if they hauled Kent's ass in for taking her car. The sight would give her a reason to get up in the morning. Perhaps he should be as inconvenienced as she was... constantly.

Of course, she'd be the one to bail him out, but still. Nicole was in the mood for a tiny bit of revenge.

Entering the kitchen, the detective found the floor smeared with blood. Damn it, she knew she had heard a noise. It must have been Kent, because the damn stain was in the shape of a uterus.

"Dear God, why can't you just send flowers like every other guy?"

Grabbing the roll of paper towels again, Nicole started cleaning up the red design. She was halfway done when she heard a creak from upstairs. From her bedroom. Putting down the cleaning supplies, she rose.

It was time to get this over with.

"Yeah, this would be your warped idea of an apology."

With little relish, Nicole climbed the stairs and entered her bedroom. Sure enough, there was a lump under the covers. A lump on the left side. Kent's side. You had to give him credit; he had audacity.

"Honestly, Harbinger, your seduction techniques could use some updating."

Or not. Wasn't this how it used to be? They would fight. Fight so badly that they finally told each other to fuck off. Kent would take the car and disappear for hours. Then when it came time for Nicole to go to bed, there he would be. Naked. Warm. Inviting. He would open the covers, and she would crawl in beside him.

Her skin could still remember his embrace. They would just lay there entangled in each other's limbs. Unspoken, each of them asking for forgiveness and receiving it. Then, well then, Kent would make it up to her. For hours sometimes. In ways that Ruben would never dream of.

That was long ago and an exceptional lay was not going to get the profiler back into her good graces.

"Kent," she said as she walked over to the bed. "Damn it, this isn't going to work." Nicole shook the figure. Something was wrong. It gave no resistance. "What the --"

Pulling back the covers she found the lump was no more than a bunch of pillows. Why would Kent do this? Worse, they were streaked with blood. Had he finally lost it all together? She found the note, writing scrawled all over it. Whatever Kent's issues were, they were his. Still, curiosity got the best of her. She read the message. Then re-read it.

It couldn't be.

'I have him. Come alone.'

"No..." Nicole read it again. How could it be? How could someone have kidnapped the most efficient profiler the F.B.I had ever known? It must be a joke. Kent must have faked it. Was pulling some psychological stunt. Make her think he was in danger, forcing her to realize how much she cared. Even as she fleshed it out, the detective knew it wasn't true. Kent was many things, but an attention seeker? Never.

That only left one possibility. The profiler truly was taken. She read the note again. 'Come alone.' Where? Where was she to come? Nicole spun around. What was that noise?

Instinctively she reached for her gun, but the weapon was downstairs. Along with the sound. No, music. Not just music but "Spin Me Right Round."

The tune for an incoming text message.

Running headlong down the stairs, Nicole snatched up her phone and read the scrolling message.
"Felter and Chayma Way. Convenience store. *Alone*."

The alone was underlined, italicized, and bolded.

Nicole guessed Plain Jane meant it.

CHAPTER 89

Kent blinked his eyes, uncertain where he was or even *when* he was. The last he remembered, he'd been at Nicole's.

Nicole!

Snapping fully awake, Kent searched the surrounding room. Dank. Dark. Moist. Subterranean, more than likely. Rough stone at his back.

The glimmering metal more than likely steel.

No Nicole.

Directly across the room a blank screen stared at him. Kent tried to reach out, only to find his wrists chained to the wall. He tugged, then tugged again, hard. The chains were meant to last.

Craning his neck, Kent felt blood trickle into his eye. Good information. He hadn't been unconscious for longer than an hour, otherwise the laceration would have clotted. That knowledge did not diminish the throbbing. A ten-laager-out-until-four-in-the-morning kind of headache.

Blinking rapidly to get the blood from his vision, Kent reviewed his situation out loud, partially to check to make sure his verbal and auditory functions were still working, and partly just to fill the emptiness.

"Alright. Let's see…" He tugged at the chains. "I'm chained up…" His glance took in the small room again. "In a dingy basement…" Sighing, Kent finished, "By a killer who targets brunette women."

He leaned his throbbing head back. "Nope. Definitely did not see this one coming."

Kent didn't feel terribly bad about not divining his fate. Who would have?

The reasons were incomprehensible. He had been seized by Plain Jane, of that he had no doubt. But why? More importantly, was Nicole safe? Had the killer already dispatched her and only took him to prevent any witnesses? Did Plain Jane have trepidation about killing a man?

So many questions rattled around his mind that they only made his head pound more. A sudden light from across the room brought all of this conjecture to a halt. The illumination came from the computer screen.

Once it bloomed fully, words typed as a mechanized Hal-like voice accompanied them. "How's the head?"

How many times had the profiler wished for just this opportunity? An opportunity to talk to Plain Jane. However, he had visualized it under drastically different circumstances.

It was those circumstances that made garnering valuable insight into Plain Jane even more pressing. So against every grain in his body, Kent kept his tone light, almost casual, but inside he was anything but laid back.

"You know, concussed."

"You'll live."

The profiler within him perked at the choice of the killer's words. His own voice took on a more serious tone.

"Will I?"

"Someone has to survive to make them understand why I had to do this."

Kent did not have to pretend to be relieved. "Absolutely, I am your guy. Give me a pencil and piece of paper, and I'm your scribe."

"Don't play me. I know all the tricks you use to lure people out."

Not only did the killer's confidence not intimidate Kent, it galvanized the profiler to make sure he tricked the bastard. To ensnare Plain Jane in a tangle of psychological techniques. "So, no face-to-face? Man-to-man talk?"

"No. I don't think that will ever happen."

Quickly trying another tack, Kent acted as if he had given up. "Alright then, shoot." He looked up instantly. "Not literally of course."

The computer screen remained blank. The killer had not risen to the bait. Perhaps he needed to try an even more direct approach. "Why kill women, then take their uteri?"

Damn, Plain Jane could type fast. The words came faster than Kent could read them. "Why act crazy when you are more sane than I am?"

Kent snorted lightly. "That's faint praise coming from a man who's chained me in his basement."

"You know what I meant."

Kent decided to use his strongest interrogation method. Arrogant indifference. "My head hurts, and I'm not going to do this tit-for-tat Clarise thing with you." He shifted his weight, getting comfortable for the long haul. "You want your story told, tell it, otherwise log off."

"Trying reverse psychology on me?"

"Nope." Kent didn't even open his eyes. "I've just got a screaming headache, courtesy of you, I might add."

There was a long silence. The profiler worried that he might have lost him. Perhaps acting bored worked well in an interrogation room; however, it might not be the best weapon to use when you were chained up.

"Picture loading."

Kent kept his eyes closed.

"Picture complete."

The profiler fought opening his eyes. Whatever the picture was, it was meant to throw him off balance. Meant to rattle him. Horrify him. Throw him off his game. Kent could not let that happen. His life, and possibly Nicole's life, depended on it.

However, he could not ignore it forever. Taking in measured breaths, the profiler opened his eyes and looked at the screen. At first he did not understand why the killer had bothered to show it to him. It was just the picture he had taken of Nicole sleeping.

Sure, it was blood smeared, but Kent already knew that. It took his eyes a few moments to adjust before he realized that there was a message.

'I have him. Come *alone*.'

The computer chimed again. "Copy of text message sent 4:05: Felter and Chayma way, convenience store, *alone*."

"No!" Kent threw himself against his restraints.

"Oh, my. Do I have your attention now?" Plain Jane laughed. A tinny, hollow, computer generated laugh that echoed off the barren walls.

CHAPTER 90

Nicole pulled up to the curb at the corner of Felter and Chayma Way, to find an all-night convenience store. Bars on the window. Probably a shotgun under the counter. There were a dozen such in the city. Why had the killer picked this one? Was there some personal connection?

Was it near his lair?

Having none of the answers to those questions, the detective put the car in park and took in a few deep breaths. The car still held Kent's aroma. It had only been an hour since he had driven off into the night. He must have come back while she and Ruben argued in the backyard. If only she had cut the discussion short. Could she have stopped the kidnapping?

There was no real point in torturing herself anymore. She needed to get inside the store. Nicole tried to peer inside. Not only were the windows covered in bars, but the inside of the glass was lined with beer sales. Beer advertisements. Beer models endorsing the beer. There was not a clear view inside.

Maybe that's why the killer had picked it? She was going to have to go in half blind.

Nicole picked up the stained picture. It didn't seem such a travesty that Kent had taken the photo anymore. If anything happened to him, at least...

No, the detective refused to go down that road. It was time to be cop instead of a woman.

Rising from her car, Nicole threw glances down the road. No one. The streets were deserted.

Confidently, or at least she hoped she looked confident, she entered the store. A greasy clerk grunted in her general direction, not even looking up from his exercise machine infomercial. Unless her instincts were totally off, he was no threat. Quickly she took the first aisle to her right, then proceeded to the back of the store.

Slowly she walked past each aisle, glancing down it as if she were looking for a hard-to-find item. Each empty except the row that housed car engine oil next to the soap and cold remedies. There, a tired mother tried to figure out which syrup would quiet her pre-pubescent son's cough. He hacked and hacked, following Nicole with his eyes.

Continuing on, she reached the end of the aisles. There was a bathroom, locked. No light spilled under the door. So far, besides the clerk, there was only the mother and child.

No sign of the killer.

On edge, as the anxiety amplified in her veins, Nicole asked the clerk, "Do you have a restroom?"

The man grunted at a gold key attached to a large cardboard cutout of a toilet. Classy. Nicole took it and headed to the back corner of the store. Hidden from plain sight, she pulled her weapon.

Jerking open the door, Nicole quickly surveyed the tiny, cluttered, dirty restroom. No one. Another dead end. Re-holstering her weapon, the detective felt close to tears. She was rapidly running out of options.

CHAPTER 91

Kent struggled against his metal restraints. This could not be happening. He took very little comfort knowing that Nicole was still alive, because he was pretty damn certain her clock was ticking down. Obviously he had interrupted the killer. Plain Jane had no choice but to take him, then use him.

Use him as bait.

"Hey!" Kent yelled again, yet the computer screen only showed a peaceful underwater scene.

Ignoring the pain in his head and neck, Kent craned to look up at his shackle. Shit. It was a shiny new 'O' ring, as thick as his thumb. His chains were older, but still solid.

Jerking on them again, he watched the 'O' ring. It didn't budge. Not a speck of dust indicating that it might be loose in the wall. As a matter of fact, on closer inspection, the damn thing had been cemented into the brick. Short of pulling a power drill out of his ass, Kent doubted there was any way he could break his restraints.

His anger grew. "Answer me, damn it!"

In response, the screen filled with twirling hourglasses and flashed , "Busy at the moment."

Throwing all his weight forward, Kent only succeeded in nearly dislocating his shoulders.

"Don't do it, Nic," he whispered to the dank room. He knew his appeal reached deaf ears. Nicole would be racked with guilt. Racked with 'what ifs'. What if they had not fought? What if she hadn't let him walk out?

Nearly a sob, "Don't go, Nic. Don't go."

CHAPTER 92

At the sound of the door chime, Nicole swung around. Could this new customer be him? Be Plain Jane? The shopper appeared to be a young male. It was hard to tell, as he wore his sweatshirt hood pulled up over his head, tied tightly around his face. Gangsta-style.

While his attire screamed 'street cred', his manner was nervous. His steps came too close together. His shoulders slumped too far forward. His chin dipped to his chest as he made a beeline to the magazine stand. Instead of taking a few seconds to scan the racks, he picked one, apparently at random.

Fairly certain he hadn't seen her, Nicole slowly made her way across the back of the store, keeping the aisle displays between her and the new man. She stopped as she came to the last row. There was a good ten feet between her and the magazine rack. Ten feet where he could spot her. Ten feet and her cover would be blown. The man changed position, ever so subtly, shifting his weight to his right leg. His shoulder turned toward the front of the store. He was staking out the door.

Knowing this was her best chance, Nicole cautiously came up behind him, shoving her gun into his ribs.

"Where is he?"

He tried to turn, but she dug the barrel into his side. "Eyes forward."

"Is that a gun?" the man asked. His voice high-pitched and crackly. Certainly not 'gangsta.'

"Yes, and I *will* use it if you don't tell me where he is."

In a whirl of arms and legs, the man knocked the magazine rack onto her and tried to flee out the back door. Nicole slipped on a slick Playboy magazine and lost a good two steps on him. He was fast, sprinting for the exit like a rabbit. If he got out onto the street, he could easily disappear into the night.

That wasn't about to happen as Ruben burst in along with three cops. They easily subdued the suspect.

"Let me go!" he screamed, almost like a little girl.

These psycho bastards didn't hold up too well under real life circumstances. With a certain amount of satisfaction, Nicole re-holstered her weapon.

"Did you really think I'd come alone?"

She wasn't Kent. Every once in a while she did things by the book. Especially when someone's life was on the line. When Kent's life was on the line.

Nicole walked up to the hooded man. Soon he could not hide in anonymity. Confidently she jerked the material away from his face, then took a step back. She knew him. Knew that face.

It was the morgue attendant.

"Joshua?" she asked.

"Detective Usher, what're you doing here?"

"Me?" the detective asked perplexed. "What are…"

Then it registered. She looked to Ruben, whose mind was obviously processing this new information as quickly as hers. The question was on both their faces. Could the killer have been right under their noses the whole time? Could Josh be Plain Jane?

"The missing uteruses," Ruben commented.

"The knowledge of police procedure."

They both stared at the morgue attendant.

"What?" he asked, as if had not just been apprehended at the rendezvous point picked by the killer.

"Joshua, you'd best come with us."

"Are you arresting me?" the young man squealed. "For looking at soft core? If the bondage stuff bugs you, I'll quit. I promise."

Ruben had obviously heard enough. "You have the right to remain silent. Anything --"

"I don't want to remain silent!" Joshua squealed.

"Anything you say can and will be used against you in a court of --"

Josh hopped up and down. "I don't want to go to a court of law!"

Nicole put hand on his shoulder. "This is serious."

"You've got the wrong guy," he implored.

"Then why were you here tonight?" Nicole asked.

CHAPTER 93

Instead of answering Nicole, the morgue attendant squirmed. Ruben had seen enough. "I'll call in for a search warrant on his apartment and locker at work."

"Whoa, whoa, whoa there!" Joshua shook his head violently. "That's just crazy talk, that's what that is."

Both he and Nicole glared at the morgue attendant. So far all of this had been crazy talk.

"Okay, okay, okay," Josh conceded. "But if he strikes because of this, it's your fault. The blood's on your hands."

Nicole squinted. "What're you talking about?"

The attendant went for his pocket, but Ruben was right there. He cranked the man's arm up and behind his back.

"That's enough."

"Ouch! It's in my pocket. The print-out."

Ruben wasn't about to let the attendant go, so he nodded to Nicole. His partner fished through his right pocket and came out with a condom.

"Jeez! The other pocket," Joshua protested.

Nicole found a piece of paper carefully folded into quarters. She opened it and read it out loud. "I'm tired of all this. I can't stop myself. If you wish to meet the real Plain Jane, come to the convenience store at..." Nicole skimmed a section. "Blah, blah, blah... Come alone or else you --" his partner indicated to the bottom of torn page. "It's cut off here."

"I spilled Jolt on it. He said I wouldn't make it home alive if I didn't do exactly what he said."

Ruben could tell that his partner was vacillating. She was considering believing him. He had to cut that impulse off at the pass. "He could have sent it to himself."

"But I didn't. I swear!"

"If this was real, you should have contacted either Torres or myself," Nicole said.

Damn right, Ruben thought.

"Come on, like you would have taken me seriously." Ruben tightened his grip on the attendant's arm to let him know that excuse was not flying. Joshua hurried on. "I had a buddy of mine at forensics trace the e-mail address, but the trail ended an internet café." The attendant was nearly frantic. "Which didn't have any security surveillance. I checked!"

Bored by the attendant's tirade, Ruben glanced to Nicole, but she seemed to be buying it.

"So I thought I might as well try. I mean the meeting was at a public place. I thought --"

Ruben had had enough and shoved the attendant into one of uniform's custody. "We'll see what the search warrant turns up, than have another chat."

Joshua began to rant again, but Ruben turned to Nicole, but she was no longer beside him.

Instead she was strode out. "Usher," he called after her. She didn't stop so he grabbed her by the arm, forcing her. "We'll find Harbinger, but we've got to stay calm. Rational."

But when Nicole turned to face him, tears welled in her eyes. "It's a little too late for that."

CHAPTER 94

Nicole turned away before Ruben could think of another clichéd, patronizing thing to say to her. She strode out and into the crisp night.

Despondent, Nicole leaned against the wall and slowly slid down until she was sitting on her heels.

Cops flooded in and out the door.

Too little, too late.

Or too many, too soon.

She had blown her one chance, and she knew it. Nicole had thought she was safeguarding Kent's life by playing it by the book. Now she could see psychos did not follow any rules.

Kent would have shown up alone. He would have followed the creep's instructions to the letter. Then in a fit of brilliance, Harbinger would have sprung a trap. Of what type, Nicole had no idea. She wasn't that damn smart.

"You Nicole?" a young voice asked.

The detective wiped the tears away and looked up. It was the boy with the cough. "Yes."

"The cop?"

"Yes. I'm sorry if I scared you in there."

The boy shook his head. "Nah. He warned me that would happen."

"I'm sorry, I don't understand."

The kid acted like she was a little slow in the head. "He said you'd probably bring lots of friends with you."

Sitting straight up, Nicole pushed her hair behind her ears as if that would help her comprehend the boy's cryptic statement. "Who said that?"

"The man that gave me twenty bucks to pretend to have a cough so my mom would bring me down here."

"What else did he pay you for?"

"To tell you to go down that alley, but this time, really come alone."

Was it possible that she was being given a second chance? Was this really a message from Plain Jane? "What did he look like?"

The boy shrugged. "Some bum on the street. A guy gave him twenty to tell me from another guy."

Yep, that sounded like the psycho. Covering his tracks seamlessly. Nicole looked down the alley. It was dark and stretched well beyond her field of vision.

Alone, huh?

Down there?

Nicole looked back into the store. Ruben was busy coordinating the cops. She couldn't read lips, but knew procedure well enough to know he was rolling out a canvas of the neighborhood. Should she involve him?

"*Alone*," the boy emphasized the word. "He said he'd be watching."

The detective licked her lips. She bet the killer would be. Nodding, Nicole pointed inside to Ruben. "See that detective in there?"

"The mad one?"

"Yes, that one." Rapidly, she tried to think like Kent. How could she spin this situation to her advantage? "He'll be coming out to look for me in a little while. I want you to tell him exactly what you told me. Exactly. Okay?"

"Okay," the boy said extending his hand. Nicole went to shake it, but he pulled back. "No, I want twenty bucks."

Nicole gave a grim smile, then pulled out her wallet. She pulled out two bills. "Here's forty. Make sure I'm out of sight before you tell him, right?"

The boy pocketed the money so quickly it was almost a slight-of-hand. "Right."

Without hesitation, Nicole walked away from the boy and into the darkened alley. Once out of sight, she drew her weapon and slowed her pace. This guy had taken Kent, and without much of a struggle.

What chance did she have against him?

As Nicole progressed down the alley, the light waned even further. She looked back over her shoulder. Safety was only forty feet away. Everything in her head told her to turn back. Get a strike team to assault whatever structure there was at the end of the alley, but her gut said to go forward. One step at a time. One foot at a time.

Halfway down the alley, a brick wall came into view. And up above that dead end was a small camera, its red light blinking ominously.

Her gut was right.

With more urgency, Nicole covered the rest of the distance to find a large, rusted metal door slightly ajar. She checked all around it. Nothing. The detective opened it further as the hinges screamed in protest.

She was going to have to squeeze through. Not the best strategic position to be in going into an unknown, hostile environment. But what else could she do?

Figuring it was exactly what Kent would do, Nicole shimmied her way through the door and found that it led into a large, dark warehouse. The rafters were so high that Nicole could not clearly make out the ceiling. A sniper could be up there. A net waiting to sweep down.

Anything.

"This is such a bad idea," she whispered.

Taking her first step across the wide space, something scrambled under foot. Startled, Nicole tried to track the movement with her gun, but it was too erratic. Finally it stopped. Two yellow eyes blazed from under a desk.

A cat. A black cat.

A black cat had just crossed her path. She wasn't normally superstitious, but come on.

"Why couldn't he just have kidnapped me?"

Stilling the shake of her hands, Nicole continued across the cavernous warehouse. "Kent is so much better at this lurking crap than I am."

CHAPTER 95

Kent tugged against his chains. Intellectually he knew there were at least four fulcrum points along his restraints where they were the most likely to break, but his chafed wrists were telling him it just wasn't happening. Plain Jane wasn't a risk taker. He wasn't impulsive. Finally giving up, he slumped back against the damp wall.

"You should've kidnapped her," he said.

The screensaver dissolved as letters typed. "Why?"

"Because, *duh*." Kent rattled his chains. "This is a little uncomfortable."

"So sorry to inconvenience you."

Kent sighed and leaned back. If the psycho was busy talking to him, he couldn't exactly be out killing Nicole. He needed to buy as much time as possible.

"So, why uteri?" Kent asked. Slipping back into his I'm-not-laughing-with-you, I'm-laughing-at-you attitude, "Were you an overdue baby? Not breast fed long enough?"

"You would like it if it were that simple."

"Yeah, I would." That was probably the first truthful statement he had made to the killer. This whole typing, mechanized voice thing was not giving Kent the insight he needed. Tone of voice. Cadence. Eye position. Those were the needle on the compass.

"You're going to have to do better than that before Nicole gets here, or I won't let you watch."

That got Kent's attention. He sat more erect. His back stiff. Unfortunately by doing so, he was giving Plain Jane way more information than he was getting.

"You like watching her?" it asked. "Stalking her?"

Kent's mind reeled. How long had the killer been watching Nicole? And him? Without these answers, it was difficult to know which tack to take. He chose cryptic. "We have a complicated relationship."

"So she wanted you to take those pictures at her boyfriend's house?"

It was bad enough to be criticized by Nicole and other cops, but to have a serial killer call you out on your eccentric behavior? "Hey, at least I manage to keep my psychosis within legal bounds."

"Your habit of 'borrowing' other's items?"

Wow, not only called out but bitch slapped as well. "Okay, but at least I keep them under felony level."

"That's up for debate. For now, I must go meet my future mother…"

There was a pause, and the screen saver tried to come up, but another message flashed. "I should thank you, really. I never would have chosen Nicole if it weren't for you."

The screen blurred again. "No!" Kent yelled, then restrained himself. "Damn it, throw me a bone here."

"Why don't I show you?"

A loud sound came from across the room. The grinding, then catch of a motor. The room shook from the effort of the engine.

Kent plastered himself against the wall. What in the hell was happening? Then he realized that the far wall was not really a wall at all, but a door. A huge metal door which was rumbling open.

He squinted. His eyes were so used to the dark that even the soft light peeking in caused them to hurt.

Finally the door opened completely. He blinked to clear his vision, then blinked again. What stood before him seemed impossible. Impossibly huge. Impossibly...

Well, just impossible.

CHAPTER 96

Ruben nodded as a uniform told him what he already knew. The canvas had turned up squat. Just like they did every time Plain Jane struck. He looked over as the sea of blue parted to allow Glick to enter the convenience store. "Captain."

Glick glanced around the room. "Where's Usher?"

"Cooling off." Ruben indicated to the front door.

"Well, when she hears this, she's going to want to come back in and talk to our little Joshua, here."

They both glared at the morgue attendant.

"What?" the kid asked.

The Captain didn't seem to believe the kid's innocent tone either. "We found two preserved uteri in your apartment."

Joshua squirmed. "Yeah, about those." Clearing his throat, his words came out more panicked. "I can explain!"

Glick looked around. "Usher really should be here."

Ruben pulled Joshua to his feet. "I'm through chasing her. If she wants to be a part of this, then she needs stay put."

"Your call," Glick said, then turned to Joshua. "Now, you were going to explain?"

CHAPTER 97

Nicole reached the far side of the warehouse. Nothing. She'd found only abandoned machinery.

Rusted over, abandoned machinery. This place must have been deserted for decades. Then she noticed a shadow deeper than the rest in the corner. A trap door. By the lack of dust, it had clearly been opened recently. Nicole jerked it open. A long flight of stairs descended into darkness.

"Oh, this just keeps getting better and better."

The detective did a four-point check around the opening. She searched for any hidden trip wires or explosives. It appeared clean. Looking over her shoulder, Nicole could barely make out the door she had come in.

Should she go back? The detective looked at the stairs. Or should she go down? There was no question in her mind what Kent would do.

With a prayer on her lips, she carefully climbed down the steps. Once to the landing of the basement level, she spotted a dim light down the narrow corridor.

Still cautious, Nicole crept toward the illumination, keeping an ear open for back-up.

What was taking Torres so long?

"Damn it, Ruben," she grumbled to herself. "The one time I need you up my ass..."

To her shock, a bizarre mechanical voice answered her. "That's your problem, always relying on men."

Spinning around, Nicole tried to get a bead on the sound's source. "Why don't you come out here and face me like a man?"

"It is very unlikely that'll ever happen."

Nicole resumed her forward movement, but tilted her head, trying to get a bearing on the voice. "You can't look me in the eye, can you?"

"Oh, I've looked you in the eye." The voice was so distorted that Nicole couldn't tell if Plain Jane was happy, upset, or proud of the fact. "That's how I chose you. You will be the one to nurture me."

Nicole couldn't help snorting. "Bad call. If you knew me at all, you'd know I'm not the nurturing type."

The detective spotted a door at the end of the hallway to see there was a door. A door that was bolted apparently locked from the outside.

"Quite the contrary. You practically have Kent suckling at your breast, he's that dependent upon you."

With extreme caution, Nicole inspected the locking mechanism. It just looked like a simple bolt and latch.

"You are desperate to find him, aren't you?"

Yes she was, but Nicole wasn't going to admit that to psycho boy. Ever so carefully she unhooked the bolt and slid it back. No explosion. No flying daggers.

"Go on, go inside. See how low your man has been brought down."

Clenching her jaw, Nicole's mind whirred. Clearly it was a trap. God, how she wished it had been her kidnapped.

Kent would know what to do. But he wasn't here. Or at least on this side of the door. Resolved, she transferred her gun to her left hand and jerked the door open.

But it was empty.

There was a computer screen at one end and a set of chains at the other, but no Kent. No anyone.

"What?" Nicole asked as the mechanical voice echoed the question, sounding equally surprised.

CHAPTER 98

"Watch out!" Kent yelled as he tackled Nicole.

As they tumbled to the ground, the glint of a metal garrote narrowly missed her neck. While Nicole's reaction was to fire into the darkness, Kent scrambled up and ran for the door, but it slammed shut in his face.

They were locked in.

Nicole looked down at handcuffs dangling from his wrist. "How did you get away?"

"Like I haven't collected a pair of keys in my travels?"

Nicole's hand flew to her belt.

"Not yours," he reassured her.

"Then how?"

"Purposeful forgetting."

Once Kent had realized he was handcuffed and he had the key, lifted from the meter maid's house, he put that knowledge in the furthest crevices of his mind. He needed to believe that he had no hope of escape if he wanted Plain Jane to believe it him to be captive.

Nicole seemed shaken, confused. "They why the hell didn't you just get out of here an hour ago."

Like most goal-based serial killers, Plain Jane had realized that victory felt hollow without an audience.

Usually they reached out to the press rather than kidnapping their profiler, but the killer liked defying the odds at each and every turn. Kent had felt confident Plain Jane would take no action against him until Nicole arrived. There had been no real reason to escape until the moment was ripe.

"I knew he was bringing you here. Of course I wasn't counting on getting locked in, but hey, I'm still batting five hundred..." He rushed on, "And by the way, I don't take your stuff. Any of it."

"Right," Nicole said as she checked the locked room, as if he'd missed some obvious 'open' sign.

"What have I ever stolen?"

"My car for example."

"That was borrowing," Kent asserted again.

Nicole cocked an eyebrow.

"What?" he asked. "What of yours have I <u>stolen?</u>"

A strange look passed over Nicole's face. It looked like she was going to say something, then pulled up short. Was she angry? Scared? Kent would never know because her attention became distracted as she coughed.

"What's that smell?"

"That would be formaldehyde," he said pointing to the other side of the room, at the opened metal door.

"What's through there?"

There were no words to describe what lay beyond that door. Even if he somehow found the words, Kent knew they would sound ridiculous. And even if he could somehow make it sound plausible, Nicole would never believe him.

"You've got to see it to believe it."

CHAPTER 99

Ruben watched as Joshua gesticulated wildly with his cuffed hands. He had only halfheartedly listened to the morgue attendant's story. This was one of those wastes of time you just had to endure to make sure you covered all your bases.

"See? See? There's no way I'm the killer!"

Glick didn't seem any more impressed by Joshua's lengthy, convoluted explanation than Ruben.

And the younger man seemed to sense it. "Come on. Why would I keep two wombs at home and leave the rest somewhere else?" Joshua jumped up and down in place. "I'm telling you. I just took those two after the women were in the morgue. I did not *kill* anyone!"

"Where's Harbinger?" Ruben asked, already knowing what the kid was going to say.

"I don't know!" Joshua squealed. "I told you! The only reason I came to the store was because of that e-mail!"

The attendant certainly seemed sincere. Where in the hell was Kent? Ruben wanted the profiler out of the picture, but not like this. Not a fucking martyr to the cause. Not a ghost to constantly haunt Nicole.

Glick looked around again. "Damn it, where's Usher? We need her take."

"Yes! Yes!" Joshua agreed emphatically, nodding his head over and over again. "Get Usher. She'll tell you. I might collect body parts, but I'm not a sicko!"

Ruben was about to disagree with the guy when his cell phone rang. It was dispatch. He listened but couldn't believe the news. Tonight really couldn't get much worse.

He turned to Glick. "Joshua may, somehow, someway, be telling the truth."

"He's got two uteri on his bedroom dresser."

"And I'm taking no consolation in being right." Glick obviously didn't understand, so Ruben continued. "But remember Martin? The guy Kent insisted was absolutely, positively not Plain Jane?"

"Yes."

He indicated to his cell. "He escaped custody."

"When?"

"An hour ago. About the time Kent disappeared."

"Oh no. We've got to get Usher."

Ruben put a hand on his Captain's arm to stop him from going outside to find her. "In her state, she's no good to us. No good to Kent right now."

CHAPTER 100

Nicole stood dumbfounded, speechless. The stench of the formaldehyde closing off her nostrils. Kent had <u>not</u> been kidding. The sight was unbelievable.

Perhaps if she had not seen picture after gruesome picture of the real organ, Nicole might not have known what she was looking at. But after being on this case for seven months? She knew exactly what this enormous monument was modeled after.

Before them stood a huge, no, *gigantic* womb.

The thing towered over them. It must have been at least twelve feet tall. An enormous metal scaffolding supported the structure's weight.

"I don't understand..." were the only words Nicole could find in a moment like this.

Kent, as always, had a different perspective. "Looks like he wanted one of his very own."

On closer inspection Nicole realized that the structure was actually a patchwork of tissue. "Oh my..." She paced. "He stitched together the women's wombs."

"The mother of all uteri." Kent made a dramatic gesture like a carnie. "I give you the über-uterus!"

Nicole didn't bother to chide him. She knew the profiler kept emotions at a distance, using his wit to make himself feel invulnerable. But even he must have noted that it had took a lot more than a few dozen uteri to create this massive womb.

How many women had this psycho killed? And Ruben had sneered when Kent had suggested Plain Jane had taken over thirty women.

Nicole would now have to double that number.

The two silently circled the monstrosity. So many women dead. And for what? To build this sick quasi-womb? This nearly *completed*, sick quasi-womb. At the very top she could see one small area of frayed tissue. The place for one last uterus. One last victim.

"Why would he do this?"

Kent shook his head. "Okay, not even I'm whacked enough to understand."

That wasn't very reassuring, though. If the profiler didn't understand, then how could she hope to? Or was this just one of those aberrations that no one would ever understand? The more she studied this towering labor of psychosis, the more so many questions rose in her mind.

"And why pick only women who had abortions?"

"Talking to the wrong guy here."

Finally irritated by his cavalier attitude, Nicole shot back, "Okay, if not you, then who?"

For once Kent sounded serious. "I've gotten so..." The profiler paused as if he had forgotten how to express true emotions. True feelings. "So close to him. To his mind. But I just can't nail this guy's core pathology."

Despite the looming uterus, Nicole looked to Kent. That was the most honest she had ever heard him, so the detective took a risk and began speculating out loud, opening herself up to his potentially harsh criticism.

"It kind of made sense when we were going under the assumption that he thought that the victims did not deserve to have a womb after an abortion, but now this…"

They both looked upward. Besides the sheer horror of that much loss of life, you had to marvel at the audacity of it. How long had it taken the killer to so meticulously stitch together all this tissue? And to stitch the tissue so tightly that it was water-tight?

The center of the uterus bulged, suggesting it was filled with some type of liquid. Almost as if the monstrous organ was pregnant.

"I mean if a guy wanted his very own womb, wouldn't he pick an undamaged uterus? Maybe even a virgin's?"

Kent seemed to feed on her comments. "Unless he somehow didn't feel worthy of a pure womb. Unless…"

Nicole stood silently, anticipating the profiler's next words with bated breath. This is when he shone, eclipsing the stars themselves. She'd seen that look in his eyes. That catch in his throat. His brain worked overtime.

You could almost hear his mind whirling at faster-than-light speeds toward an obscure conclusion. Like looking through an exotic spice importer's sales records to find a cannibal. Or after taking a look at the type of make-up and how it was applied post-mortem to a corpse, sending the cops out to pick up a Ferris-wheel operator. It was a freakish talent, but a brilliant one.

"Unless…" Instead of finishing the sentence, he kicked at the base of the scaffolding. "Damn it! I can taste his pain. The confusion. The *desire*, but not the *man*."

While she should have been crushed Kent hadn't solved it, Nicole instead brightened. Something the profiler had said.

Not the man.

"What if it isn't a man?" Nicole asked before she thought, going purely on gut instinct.

"What do you mean?"

Nicole didn't really know. She let her intuition guide her. "A boy. A transvestite. A transgender. Wouldn't that contaminate the profile?"

Pacing, Kent pondered out loud. "It could... But then we should pick up intense emasculation. Suppressed rage at his gender..." finally the profiler shook his head.

"There's none." Kent pointed to the huge uterus.

"There's just this."

CHAPTER 101

Kent stared up at the grotesque perversion of motherhood. It was demented. It was sick. It was pathological. But...

But in an extremely perverted way, it was beautiful.

Somehow he had to bridge the psyche of a person who could kill dozens upon dozens of women, then spend hours upon hours stitching together an organ of life.

The two extremes didn't seem like they could co-exist in a single person.

Even before finding this mountain of flesh, Kent had considered the possibility of an extreme schizophrenic, a true split personality, though he had abandoned such thoughts. Maybe he had best reconsider.

This guy refused to be categorized. This psycho seemed conflicted, but the crimes were too consistent. Too thorough. The right hand definitely knew what in the hell the left hand was doing.

He'd also considered and thrown out the theory that Plain Jane was actually a two-man team with one member in the shadows. A true submissive, his personality so folded into the dominant partner's that he was nearly invisible. But not quite. There was always some clue. Some ripple in the water as he glided through the killing. Kent had found none. He had been convinced he was dealing with a single, cohesive personality.

But standing before this terrible, ultimate womb, Kent wasn't so sure any more.

"What if it's not a *man*?" Nicole asked, again.

Earlier Nicole had impressed him. She had shown insight, pushing him further, demanding him to think outside the box. Now? Why was she double-dipping? "Um... Refer back to my previous comments."

But Nicole shook her head. "No. I mean *not* male." Kent's frown seemed to speed her words. "Look at the victims. All feminine. Look at this..."

She pointed to the enormous uterus. "A monument to femininity." Kent's eyebrow shot up as Nicole smiled. "A monument in *her* mind."

She looked at him as if for praise, but Kent was too busy to offer positive reinforcement. It was as if his mind had been given an electro-shock. Everything he thought he had known about the killer. A blur. He could trust none of his previous conclusions.

"Wouldn't this all fit if it's a woman?" Nicole asked.

Kent knew she wanted him to speak. To acknowledge or shoot down her theory, but his brain only had so much R.A.M. and it was devoted to resifting through each and every piece of evidence in light of this new theory.

CHAPTER 102

Nicole shifted nervously as Kent stared straight ahead. She felt awkward continuing without input from the profiler, but she didn't know what else to do. "I know female serial killers only represent twelve percent of --"

"More like seventeen, because they are far more secretive about their actions," Kent announced bluntly.

"And I know stabbing is the least likely M.O. --"

The profiler overrode her. "Actually drowning only accounts for six percent --"

Frustrated, Nicole cut *him* off. "Look, I may not know the stats cold, but think of it. Think --"

"No," Kent stated flatly.

Like a child who had finally figured out two plus two equaled four only to get slapped in the face for suggesting such an answer, Nicole snapped, "Damn it, Kent, you need --"

The profiler put a hand on her arm. His tone was suddenly much warmer. "No, I'm not arguing that we're after a woman, I'm trying to get you to shut up long enough so I can figure out which one did this."

Feeling incredibly foolish, Nicole answered, "Oh..."

Kent was back in action, pacing, chewing his lip, having an entire conversation unto himself.

"Okay, women kill for very different reasons. She's not taking these uteri to punish the women, she's helping them. Taking on their guilt." Speeding up, the profiler was an analytical machine. "She has a job that covers the city, access to public records."

Nicole just watched him, remembering why she'd fallen in love with him in the first place. His face shown with a light not of this world. It was almost as if he was channeling an energy that normal humans couldn't stand to touch without getting burned.

"Given her choice of victims, she must be physically close to their height, weight, and hair color."

The profiler stopped pacing and turned to Nicole.

A slight smile spreading across his face.

"Oh my... We've met her, it's --"

CHAPTER 103

Kent watched in horrible slow motion as a metal garrote slipped over Nicole's neck and jerked her backward. The detective's gun flew from her hand and clattered on the stone floor as she flailed. Finally she calmed as the garrote loosened ever so slightly.

"It's Rebecca," Kent finished.

The brunette meter maid poked her head around Nicole. "Surprised?"

Kent was not. "You've been logging license numbers from around abortion clinics for years. Then you faked your own pregnancy test to throw us off."

Rebecca smiled. "Okay, maybe you're *not* that surprised. But imagine *my* surprise when a cop came over and sat next to me in the food court."

Nicole choked as the brunette tightened the garrote.

"Let her go," Kent demanded.

"Oh, I thought you wanted me to take Nicole as my next hostage?"

It physically hurt Kent's own neck as the detective struggled to breathe. "Only so that I got to be the one to shoot you, bitch."

"Now, now," Rebecca said as she slowly backed Nicole to the staircase that led to the top of the scaffolding.

Kent had to find a way to stop her and stop her fast. She was ready to kill. He had seen it in dozens of suspects. There was no fear. No hesitation.

"It's over," he said, but it didn't even sound true to him.

Step by step Rebecca dragged the detective up the stairs. Up the steps to certain death. Kent bent down and picked up Nicole's fallen gun. There was no way to cap the psycho bitch without endangering Nicole.

Rebecca leaned into the detective's ear, speaking loud enough for Kent to hear. "I thought it was over when you started talking to me about regret after abortion." The meter maid chuckled. "I nearly choked on my rice. Then I realized you did not have a clue who I was." She tightened the garrote. "Then you told me you'd had one too."

Still looking for his shot, Kent responded, "She didn't have an abortion, you idiot."

The brunette acted as if she hadn't even heard him. "It was in that moment that I knew."

Kent aimed and re-aimed, but no shot. "She was just drawing you out."

Rebecca spoke almost lovingly to Nicole, "I knew it was you that I needed for my grand finale. It would be you to help transport me from this world into the next."

Kent sneered. "You've made your first and last mistake, Rebecca. Nicole's never had an abortion."

She tightened the garrote, forcing Nicole to choke and gasp. "Tell him. Tell him the truth, or I swear I'll kill you here and now."

Rebecca loosened her grip, but Nicole didn't answer. She wouldn't even look the profiler in the eye.

"Nicole?" Kent asked. Why wasn't she arguing with the crazed meter maid?

"Tell him what he forced you to do." Rebecca's anger grew. "Tell him!"

Nicole took several gulps before answering. "I found out after you committed yourself to the hospital."

Kent took a step back. It wasn't true. It just wasn't. "She's just saying what you want to hear."

Rebecca pinched off Nicole's windpipe, "Convince him you are telling the truth or die."

He didn't even let Nicole start. "We used protection." His tone became less certain as he looked into her eyes. "There's no way."

Nicole's tone was soft, as if it were only the two of them in the room. "Except for the time on the beach. We didn't have a condom with us, remember?"

"But you said…" Kent's breath was coming too fast. It was too hard to concentrate. Too hard to remember. "You said you were on the pill."

CHAPTER 104

Nicole tried to turn away. She couldn't stand to see Kent's reaction, but Rebecca forced her face forward.

"I forgot…" Her voice gave out.

The meter maid hissed in her ear. "Tell him."

"I forgot to take the pill. Then…forgot to bring the case with me…"

Tears welled. She had been so stupid. So enthralled that she and Kent were actually going away together that all else seemed unimportant.

"We were supposed to come home Saturday night…" Nicole made the mistake of glancing down.

The look of horror on Kent's face was a thousand times worse than when he studied the uterus made up of dead women's internal organs.

She had to look away. "We… We didn't come home until Monday…"

How happy she had been. Kent had actually suggested they stay the entire weekend at the bed and breakfast. Screw his deadline for a journal article in the American Psychiatric Journal, she was more important. *They* were more important.

At the time, Nicole had thought that life couldn't get much better. Then, of course, reality hit. Kent was arrested for theft and then for a real dose of reality, cannibalism. In a whirlwind of events, Nicole lost her man, her job, and her sense of hope. Somehow the profiler had avoided jail time, then voluntarily admitted himself into a psych hospital. That was right about the time the morning sickness hit.

"Well?" Rebecca asked Kent, drawing Nicole's thoughts back the even worse situation they were in now.

Kent looked up but didn't speak. He didn't have to. From his tortured look, he believed her. That much was clear. She had convinced him of the truth.

A truth she had hidden from all. No one knew. Not her co-workers. Not her mother. Most of the time, not even Nicole herself. She had almost successfully erased the abortion from her mind. Her own version of 'purposefully forgetting' that she'd ever lain on that awful table with those awful metal stirrups.

Rebecca seemed gleeful. "See? Women know, they always know."

Kent's eyes brimmed with tears. A sight Nicole never thought she would see. "Why?" It was nearly a whisper. "Why didn't you tell me?"

It was no longer the garrote that closed off Nicole's throat, just her welling emotions. Her own desire to never speak these words.

"You *left* me."

CHAPTER 105

How could things have gotten this fucked up?

Kent hurt as he had never hurt before. To think. A child. A family. How could he have been so close to that ideal and not even known it.

"You *abandoned* her," Rebecca corrected Nicole.

Kent's head snapped up. Nicole and he might have some issues to work out, but this bitch? He was pretty much done with her.

"No, I didn't," he stated flatly.

"Yes, you did. Look at her. Look at her face. Look what hell you put her through," Rebecca demanded, then tightened the garrote. Nicole didn't even struggle this time.

"Tell her how sorry you are."

"No."

The meter maid began truly choking Nicole. "Tell her how you inflicted wounds that will never heal!"

"I can't," Kent said as Rebecca nearly pulled Nicole off her feet. "I can't because I didn't *abandon* her."

"Kent.." Nicole could barely get the words out. "Please, be honest for once."

Unflinching, he looked into his lover's eyes. All else fell away. He had nothing else to offer but the truth. Not his version of the truth or a spin on the truth, but the truth. "I made a deal."

Confused, Rebecca's grip slipped, letting Nicole breathe. "A deal?"

Kent spoke only to Nicole. "With Glick." How long had he wanted to tell her? How long had he wanted to scream it at her? How long had he wanted to tell her of the sacrifice he had made for her?

"I'd willingly commit myself, and they'd…"

The meter maid became agitated at the notion a man might actually rise above his selfish nature. "Liar!"

"If I went into the hospital without protest he would remove all reprimands from your jacket related to your assisting me…"

Tears burned hot in his eyes as he watched Nicole's own tears streak her face. He could see she still couldn't quite believe what she was hearing. "If I went, Glick promised to give you back your badge and your gun."

It had seemed like the right thing to do by Nicole. He'd fucked her career up beyond repair. He'd taken her livelihood away from her. And for hell's sake he'd eaten a serial killer's brain. Institutionalization seemed like a pretty damn good idea at the time, but…

"Had I known," Kent found it hard to speak. "I would have made a different decision."

For the first time ever, he spoke the words he needed to say out loud. "I'm sorry, Nic. I really am."

Did he see forgiveness in Nicole's eyes? He wouldn't know because Rebecca snapped out of her shock and dragged the detective up to the catwalk.

"How very touching. Too bad it doesn't change the outcome. She and I are the same."

Trying to get a clean shot on Rebecca, Kent watched as the meter maid prepared to jump into the uterus with Nicole. He couldn't let that happen. "Let her go!"

Unfortunately Rebecca held all the cards and was well aware of it. "Or?"

Luckily Kent had no problem pulling an ace out of his sleeve. He lowered his weapon, and aimed straight at the body of the uterus. Without hesitation, the profiler shot into it. Liquid squirted out the hole.

"Or I'll do that."

"No!" Rebecca screamed as the precious fluid left the bulging vessel.

"Oh ya. I'll put in enough holes to drain it dry."

The meter maid searched his face. If she had done her research as well as he thought she had, Rebecca would know that he meant it.

She swallowed before speaking. "If I let her go?"

"I'll let you jump in. Alone." Kent nodded to the uterus. "That's what you wanted, right? To go back in?"

The woman seemed lost in her own world. "My mother... She said I never should have come out."

Damn it, did psychos never tire of their own self-flagellation? "Yeah, yeah. Your poor sob story. I heard it already. How your mother wished she had aborted you."

Now it was Rebecca who had tears. He needed to leverage that emotional vulnerability and leverage it now.

"And how she forced you to have one." The profiler indicated towards the enormous, adult-sized uterus. "Isn't it about time we wrapped up this whole psycho quest of yours?"

CHAPTER 106

Nicole held her breath, not because she was being choked, by now Rebecca's grip was almost loose. No, it was because of Kent's bizarre strategy. How could he go from being emotionally stripped to the marrow then suddenly taunt a serial killer?

Being downright mean to her?

But somehow it was working. Rebecca appeared distracted. Worried. Uncertain.

Nicole wondered if she should not throw an elbow and knock the meter maid off balance, but this close to the edge of the platform? With a garrote around her neck? It seemed to Nicole more likely she'd hang herself than reach freedom. Which meant that her life was in Kent's hands.

And Kent's hands were tight around her gun. With great showmanship, the profiler leveled the barrel toward the uterus and cocked his head to the side, daring Rebecca.

"No! Don't!"

Nicole saw it in Kent's eyes. He was going to shoot and keep shooting if the meter maid didn't comply. Then he did the strangest thing, he winked just before he fired.

She knew a signal when she saw one. Her hands flew up to her neck, grabbing hold of the garrote just as Rebecca shoved her at the steps. Nicole hit her head on the railing, but managed to free the wire from around her neck. She tried to right herself, and might have succeeded, but Rebecca leapt from the platform into the gaping uterus.

The loss of Rebecca's weight tilted the catwalk and Nicole lost her footing and tumbled headlong down the stairs.

CHAPTER 107

"Nicole!" Kent shouted as he ran forward.

The woman he loved sprawled at the bottom of the staircase. He skidded to a halt and knelt beside her.

"Talk to me, babe," Kent murmured as he kept one eye on the uterus where Rebecca thrashed. "Talk to me."

He smoothed back the hair around her face and quickly checked her limbs. They seemed intact. Nothing broken. At least not externally.

"Come on, Nic."

Her eyes fluttered and her voice sounded pretty much like she looked. "Next time, it's your turn to be the hostage."

A faint smile flickered across Kent's lips. She was going to be fine. "I need you to stay here, okay?"

Nicole grabbed his hand. "Don't leave me."

"I'm not. I'm not going far at all."

The detective's hand fell to the ground as Kent reached his feet and began firing fiercely into the uterus.

"What are you doing?" Nicole asked. "She's drowning already."

Kent kept up his barrage, taking a step closer to the womb. "No. That's what she wants us to think"

The thrashing stopped as the uterine walls began to undulate. Kent hated it when he was so fucking right.

"She's giving birth…" he explained, then realized that wasn't quite right. "Giving birth to herself." Okay, that sounded even more lame. Kent shrugged as he looked back at Nicole. "Whatever. You get the point."

By now the uterus was having violent contractions. Kent emptied the clip, and knelt down beside Nicole to get another one from her belt.

"I thought she wanted to end her life," the detective said, her voice weaker than before.

Rapidly loading the clip, Kent returned to firing, then answered Nicole. "Female serial killers are neither fame seekers nor suicidal."

"I don't understand." The detective was fading, Kent could hear it, but what could he do?

Rebecca was getting away.

Running forward, the profiler quickly emptied the second clip as the uterus collapsed on itself.

Grabbing the walls of the womb, Kent gained purchase in a bullet hole and ripped the vessel open. He wasn't surprised by what he found.

A drain.

An empty drain.

Large enough for a woman to squeeze through.

"Damn it!"

He looked over his shoulder to tell Nicole to stay put, but her head was bent back at an odd angle.

"Nicole!" No response.

Rushing to her side, his heart stopped as he waited for a breath. "Don't you dare do this to me."

Finally her chest moved up and down. A good deep breath. He checked her pulse. Regular and strong. She was just unconscious.

Sounds from the sub-basement made him look towards the drain. A serial killer was getting away. The love of his life was knocked out, possibly critically injured.

Did he haul Nicole out or go after the nutty?

Ruben would stay. The cop would never leave Nicole. But Kent wasn't Ruben. He wasn't that man.

Quickly removing his coat, he placed it under Nicole's head. Kissing her forehead, "I'm sorry, babe, but I've got to go after her."

He looked down the dark hallway that had brought them here. "Torres can't be far behind."

CHAPTER 107

Ruben was still wrapping things up at the convenience store. It was amazing how many details there were when not only did a profiler get kidnapped, but a city employee was caught with stolen body parts. Ruben wanted to be out in the field. Out of this damn store, but Glick had put him in charge. He couldn't leave until everything was in order.

Yet another uniformed officer came up. "Have you got the western perimeter set?" Ruben asked.

"Sorry, no"

Ruben groaned. Did he have to do everything?

"This kid stopped me before I could get it done. Says he has information."

This was all he needed. Even the ten year olds were weighing in. Ruben walked over to the child and tried to be polite. It was not the kid's fault it was nearly four thirty in the morning. "Yes?"

"Look, for all this effort, I'm going to need another twenty bucks."

The boy had guts, though Ruben wasn't in the mood. "Sorry, we don't pay for information."

The kid cocked his head to the side. "Really? Even about the lady cop?"

Damn. Still, Torres wasn't going to give in that easily. "I'm going to need a little more information than that before I part with a Jackson."

"He told me to tell her to go alone."

Shit. Plain Jane. Ruben's wallet was out in a flash. He handed the boy a crisp twenty.

"She went down the alley."

"When?" Torres asked.

"A while ago."

A while ago? "Why didn't you tell me this earlier?"

"She told me to wait outside. That you would come looking for her."

Fuck.

"Glick!"

CHAPTER 109

Kent crept down the dark, dirt tunnel. He could hear muffled scrapes up ahead. Rebecca hadn't gotten far. He must have winged her while she was 'giving birth.'

Unfortunately the sub-basement was made up a patchwork of natural catacombs. Noises traveled through a tangled maze down here. Rebecca could be twenty yards away or right beside him.

"Was it worth it?" No verbal response, but the steps quickened. "All those lives for that loser experience?" He cocked an ear. Had she stopped? "You're so not going to be able to sell tickets to that ride."

"You would be surprised."

Before Kent could turn towards the sound, Rebecca lashed out with her scalpel blade, slashing the profiler's gun hand. The thin slice hurt like a bitch as he spun away; however, he held onto the weapon.

"That's cheating."

Rebecca was now the one to taunt him. "That's why I have the upper hand. I know no rules."

Kent stopped as he came to a juncture of tunnels. Which way? He needed to keep her talking. "Darlin' you've got a lot to learn about me."

The glint of the blade caught Kent's attention. He pivoted out of the way as Rebecca lashed out again.

Continuing the arc, he fired three shots in quick succession. A muffled scream was his reward. With any luck, a body shot. Fuck hitting a leg to slow them down. A bullet in the kidney was much more effective.

The meter maid didn't sound quite so cocky any more. Blood loss and pain tended to do that. "You need me alive."

The tables had turned. Kent could feel it. It was she who was unsteady now. Unnerved.

He planned to keep it that way.

"Don't you know what I was hospitalized for?"

No answer. Kent spotted a thin blood splatter on the floor. "I was on the trail of another serial killer. A Lecter wannabe or House of the Dead groupie, anyway, he was killing people and eating their brains."

"So you decided to see how it felt?"

Spinning around, the profiler realigned his shot. The voice had come from behind him. There must be smaller access tunnels. He'd have to be more careful.

"Yeppers. I went into the morgue, found some homeless guy's body."

Kent stopped and listened. Rebecca was having to support herself along the wall now. Her pace had slowed. "I mean his brain was just sitting there on the scale. I figured who's gonna miss a few ounces?"

"But they did," Rebecca said, but he had a hard time deciding which direction her voice came from. Sound traveled strangely in these convoluted tunnels.

"That time? No, but once I got it home and ate it, I had a revelation."

He adjusted to the left as Rebecca spoke, "The power of consuming another's center of reason?"

He had the bead on her. "No... It tasted bad. I mean really bad." She had stopped again, so he paused his feet as well. "I figured nobody is going to eat three pounds of this crap, at least not like that."

"So you went back for more?"

Kent was pretty damn sure she was up ahead about ten feet, down to the right. "Oh yeah. I figured the M.E. was done with it. We might as well progress behavioral science."

He waited. No footsteps. No hands sliding down the wall. Her shallow breaths echoed off in the tight space. "Anyway, I tried everything. Sautéed, basted, even deep-fried the stuff. No better."

Movement. She was trying to backtrack again. Kent adjusted his course. "Then it came to me. The killer was following ancient traditions. So he was probably following an ancient recipe. So to make an extremely long story a little shorter, I tracked down an importer of exotic ingredients and 'boom' I've got my man."

"Captured alive?"

Rebecca couldn't have been further off. Kent snorted, "No, I shot him *twice*."

"Oh, I'm so scared."

"Once in each eye," Kent clarified. "Just as he had done to his victims. You can imagine how hard that was to sell as self-defense."

"That's when they figured out your brain cravings?"

"No."

Oh, she was so very close. He could feel it. Another step forward, turn to the right. Striking out, Kent grabbed Rebecca from behind, putting his gun to her temple.

He pulled Plain Jane close to him and whispered in her ear, "It's when I stole a chunk of the perp's brain...and was cooking it up at home when they found me."

Kent tightened his grip on her neck. "So don't think for a second I won't shoot *you.*"

Rebecca lashed out with her knife, flailing, trying to hit anything she could. "And don't think I won't kill *you.*"

Keeping himself behind her and out of reach of the sharp blade, Kent couldn't help himself. "But you promised you wouldn't."

"That's before I got to know you."

She struggled fiercely, forcing him to lower his gun. But that was exactly what she was angling for. With an expert lunge, Rebecca knocked the gun from his hand. It skittered away into the darkness. His hand slipped from her neck. The only one armed, it was Rebecca who now had the advantage.

"Guess you got a little rusty," the meter maid commented as she lashed out again, forcing Kent back.

"Padded walls do tend to make you a little soft."

Kent blocked her attacks over and over. She was a maniac with the blade. And well practiced. He couldn't find an in, but he was not about to admit that to her. "Fighting off the nurses at meds time? Now *that* was combat training."

And there it was. His window. Kent realized whenever Rebecca was recovering from a back-handed downward slope, her follow through was exaggerated. He just had to wait for it to come back around.

Kent hyper-focused not on the meter maid's knife, rather on her shoulder. She slashed down, than rapidly reversed direction and came back up. There was that hitch. That momentary shift of weight as she tried to bring the blade back around to bear.

Kent sent an elbow into her side, throwing her off-balance and with her shoulder already back, it opened up her abdomen. He jabbed at the blood stain. Rebecca cried out. Each time she tried to slash, he blocked early, causing her to abort her swing, the knife now neutralized.

And he would have snatched the damn weapon, if he hadn't slipped in a pool of blood. His left foot went out from under him at the same moment he had brought his right fist back to prepare for a punch. The combined momentum threw him backward, hard into the wall.

Rebecca didn't miss her golden opportunity and leapt. Knife against his throat before he could recover.

"I'll tell Nicole your last thoughts weren't of her."

The blade dug in. Kent's skin screamed as the edge cut the most sensitive outer layer. In a moment he would be bleeding. A few more moments he'd be dead.

Then Rebecca's blade hand flew outward, away from him, her arms flailing like a wheelhouse. It was then that he saw the strange ligature around the meter maid's neck. The 'rope' was made of tissue.

Uterine tissue if he was not mistaken.

CHAPTER 110

Nicole tightened the tissue around Rebecca's neck. Let her know what it felt like to be strangled. "You know, at one point I actually felt sorry for you, bitch."

The meter maid didn't retort. She couldn't. She was too busy choking, clawing at the ligature. The detective tightened it even more. Not to kill. Oh, Nicole would have loved to kill the psycho, but the cop in her was aiming to knock her unconscious. But the tissue began to fray. Nicole put her full weight into it.

Which meant she wasn't prepared to defend herself when Rebecca raised her knife to the ceiling, then plunged it deep into Nicole's leg. Before she could override her reflexes, Nicole dropped the bloody noose and grabbed hold of her injured thigh. Rebecca tried to bolt, but Kent was there, grabbing the meter maid by the hair. "Where ya going?"

Nicole began to slump. Her leg couldn't support her weight. With his free hand, the profiler grabbed her elbow, propping her up.

The meter maid's smile became savage. "What are you going to do, Kent? Let me go or prove to Nicole, once again, that's she's less important than your work?"

"Neither," Kent said. A pretty damn confident grin on his face as well. "I'm getting myself a weapon."

Nicole was surprised when Kent chose to release Rebecca and stay with her, but she should have known it wasn't for long as Kent used his free hand to grab the handle of the scalpel, then jerk the blade from her leg.

Screaming from astonishment, Nicole fell to the floor.

Kent looked over his shoulder. "I'd put some pressure on that." And then he was off chasing Rebecca.

Gone into the darkness again.

CHAPTER 111

With a single sweeping backhanded stroke, Kent sliced Rebecca's throat. Deep but not too deep. The woman stumbled backward, hands clutching her now crimson, pulsating neck.

"How's it feel?" Kent asked as he circled his prey. It was one thing to threaten him, but to hurt Nicole? This bitch was going down.

"How does it feel to be losing your life's blood between your fingers?"

In the distance a voice echoed, "Nicole!" From the frantic tone, it could only be Ruben.

"Help!" Rebecca cried out coarsely, not seeming to care who it was. Anyone but Kent.

"Keep trying. Maybe he'll hear you? Rescue you?"

Kent closed in on the meter maid. Rebecca staggered back. One hand still at her throat, the other trying to push the profiler away. Her strength seeping out along with her blood.

"Feeling light-headed?" Kent asked, already knowing the answer. "Room spinning?"

"Don't," Rebecca begged hoarsely. "Please, don't."

"Is that what they begged?" Kent asked, already knowing the answer.

How many times had this bitch heard that plea? Had it ever stopped her? Had she ever shown a sliver of mercy to any of her victims? Kent knew he could take her alive. He could subdue her right now. But what would that accomplish? She'd be deemed insane. And the mentally ill could not be executed.

Which made absolutely no sense whatsoever. It was the crazies that were the most fucking dangerous. Whack jobs couldn't be reasoned with. They had spent most of their adult lives stalking people they picked out using their distorted mirror of the world, then torturing and ultimately killing them. No serial killer was sane. And no one was more dangerous than a successful serial killer. Yet they were never executed.

Go figure.

At least not by court order.

Rebecca lurched, nearly falling.

"That would be anoxia. You don't have enough blood to carry oxygen to your brain."

Kent closed in, his voice barely above a whisper. "Don't worry. I'll get to the coup de grace before you lose consciousness."

A look of horror crossed Rebecca's face. For the first time she realized Kent really and truly was her equal. Letting go of her neck wound, she launched at him.

Kent was quicker. The knife sunk deep into Rebecca's belly. Blood poured around his hand, yet he didn't pull the blade out. The meter maid's eyes jerked open. Her visage twisted in horror.

"There we go," Kent whispered. "That was the look I was waiting for."

Behind them a faint voice, "Nicole!"

He'd have to hurry before Ruben spoiled his plan.

"Feel that?" Kent asked as he tugged the knife upward, mimicking the wound she had inflicted on dozens upon dozens of innocent women.

He tugged again as Rebecca gasped in agony.

"That's karma, babe."

As if dropping a sack of potatoes, Kent let the woman fall from his grip. She slumped to the floor, motionless. He stared, watching, waiting for a breath. None came. Rebecca would not be gutting anyone else. Would not be stealing anyone else's uterus.

He was victorious.

Then the rush was over, and his muscles betrayed him. Kent staggered back until he hit the wall. It was the only thing holding him up.

"Damn, but killing takes it out of ya."

CHAPTER 112

Nicole tried really hard not to panic. Kent had been gone way longer than he should have, and, perhaps more topically, she could not get her leg to stop bleeding.

"Usher!" That baritone had to be Glick.

She shouted, "Here!" as loud as she could.

But it was Kent that rushed into the room. His hands were covered in blood, and his shirt streaked with it. Was it his or Rebecca's?

As if reading her mind, he shrugged off his blood-soaked shirt. "Profiler, one. Psycho Bitch, zero."

Relieved, Nicole hauled off and slugged him. "That stunt of yours fucking *hurt*!"

"Tell me about it," Kent said as he shook out his wrist. "I think I gave myself carpal tunnel."

Despite the continued oozing from her wound, Nicole still tried to push him away. For some reason, she didn't want to seem helpless. She didn't want him to see her weak.

Kent persisted. "Let me."

He was actually gentle as he tended to her wound. Concern framed his features. Was this really Kent? Quickly he rigged a makeshift bandage, and the blood flow stopped.

Then he looked up, and their eyes met. So many life-changing moments had come to pass this night, and very few of them had to do with bringing a serial killer to justice. There was so much to say, yet she couldn't get her lips to work. Not when Kent was looking at her like that. Like he used to. Like he did that weekend they went away together to the beach. Like he did when she thought they might actually make their relationship work.

"Nicki!" That was Ruben.

"Here," Nicole yelled back but not quite so enthusiastically as before. Could Kent and she not just have a little time alone? Time to sort through the mess of their relationship before Internal Affairs got involved?

Kent patted her good leg. "I'm telling you, he's no Magellan. I better go get them before *they* end up needing to be rescued."

Nicole couldn't let him go. Not yet. Not until at least one thing was cleared up.

"Wait," she said as she took his hand in hers. "Before…" how could the feeling she had be so strong inwardly, yet so difficult to say outwardly? "Before when you said you'd never stolen anything of mine…"

Kent's eyes searched hers, his expression unreadable as usual. It was up to her. If they were going to break this deadlock, it would be up to her to do it. Kent was absolute crap at expressing himself.

Not that she was all that much better.

"Nic, you need an ambulance."

She ignored his words. "You did steal this…" Nicole brought Kent's hand up to her chest and laid it gently there against her breastbone. "You stole this."

Kent got defensive. "Your bra? No way... Okay, maybe one pair of underwear, but that was for --"

Nicole shook her head, quieting the nearly panicked profiler. She moved his hand over her heartbeat then looked up. She didn't have the words. Would he understand?

CHAPTER 113

Kent could feel Nicole's heart beating beneath his touch. So fast. So strong. Given the complete look of anguished sincerity on her face, he was a little ashamed about the underwear admission.

"Oh, that…"

More than embarrassment, he was tongue-tied. How many ways had he practiced telling her how he felt? His therapist had insisted that women needed to hear about a man's feelings, not just be helped to have a lot of orgasms. Which to the profiler did not seem fair. Wasn't that kind of attention proof enough? Obviously Nicole needed something more. Something he had never given another woman.

Kent squeezed her hand. "Then you're quite the thief yourself."

He leaned over as his lover tilted her head, parting her lips, ready to receive his kiss. His hand cupped her cheek and he held her eyes until the very last second when their lips met, then he could not help but close his eyes.

Everything he loved about her was summed up in that moment. Her soft lips, without a hint of shyness. The horrors of the day melted away, leaving only their kiss.

"Nicole!" Ruben shouted, sounding further away than he did the last time. Leave it to the idiot to not only be lost, but ruin the moment as well. Yet Kent knew from the warmth of that kiss that they'd have plenty of time to work things out.

He pulled back and met Nicole's smile. "I'll go fetch him before we have to bring out the search dogs."

She nodded bravely, but frowned. He knew that look. The look of well-deserved mistrust.

"I'll be back."

"Promise?" she asked.

"Promise."

CHAPTER 114

It took Kent five minutes and seven switchbacks to find the wandering cops. Not only were they lost, they were a very mobile bunch of lost cops.

Ruben didn't even bother to apologize or ask what had happened. "Where's Nikki?"

"Where the hell have you been? We left you a blood trail as wide as the Mississippi."

"Where's Detective Usher?" Ruben growled.

"She's been choked and stabbed, but, you know, other than that, stable."

Ruben pushed past, but Kent was not quite sure where the guy was going. Wasn't the point of this whole exercise that Ruben was directionally challenged? Kent turned to Glick and gave a friendly nod as if they had just met on the street.

"Why don't we catch up with Ruben and collect Usher?" the Captain suggested, but Kent shook his head.

"Sorry, if the detective wants to the girl, he's gotta learn to ask for directions."

Glick glowered, "Harbinger."

Given what they were going to find deeper in the tunnels, Kent realized maybe he shouldn't piss off the Captain right now. Kent would prefer to stay out of the psychiatric ward for a while.

"Okay, okay," Kent said as he easily found Ruben. Once again off course. "She's *this* way."

Kent took a little too much pleasure in the look of embarrassment and frustration on the tall detective's face.

Quickly Kent navigated the labyrinth-like tunnels. Which wasn't too hard if you just knew what arterial blood looked like. Within a few minutes they were back to where he had left Nicole.

"Ta dah!" Kent announced with a flourish. "This is how you rescue a fair maiden."

Great barb, only there wasn't any maiden there.

"Damn it, Kent, this isn't funny."

He knelt over, searching the floors for clues to where she might be. "She was here."

Kent knew he wasn't lost. There was the torn uterine ligature. Nicole's gun. A large blood pool and the remains of a tattered sleeve they had used as a bandage for her leg. Everything was here. Everything but Nicole...and Rebecca's knife. Kent was certain he had dropped it near the detective. Kent had also been pretty damn sure Rebecca was dead.

"Nic!" he yelled as he rushed deeper into the tunnels.

Her response was pained, but close by. "In here."

Ruben burst past Kent, reaching Nicole sitting next to Rebecca's body. Ruben skid to a halt when he took in the scene. Scalpel in hand, the detective looked like hell. Shit, they both looked like hell, but Nicole was alive, and her bandage looked like it had stopped the tide of bleeding.

"I told you to stay put," Kent reminded her as he strode past the stunned Ruben.

"I just..." Nicole looked over at the body. "I had to make sure she was dead."

As did the Captain. He knelt down and felt Rebecca's neck. Glick nodded. "She's gone."

Kent went to help Nicole up, but Ruben elbowed him a good one. He stumbled as Ruben offered his partner a hand.

A hand which Nicole declined.

"It's okay," she said as she reached out to the profiler. "Kent's got me."

In perhaps the single most satisfying moment of his life, Kent helped Nicole up, then supported her as they walked past the ruddy-faced Ruben.

"So if you don't mind, I'll get her to the hospital."

Elbow that, ya prick.

CHAPTER 115

It was what Kent didn't say that stung Ruben. The profiler didn't have to give his feelings voice. His expression was crystal clear.

Fuck you. *I* won.

And the profiler was right. Ruben had lost. In so many ways that he couldn't even keep track of them anymore. Kent had been right about Plain Jane. He had been right about Nicole's feelings.

Still, his pride would not let Harbinger off the hook. Ruben stepped in front of the couple. "We'll need statements."

"The whacko's dead, and we're alive," Kent said as Nicole moaned, a hand on her bandage. "In pain, but alive."

Glick stepped in before it could get nasty. "It's all right. We'll get their statements at the hospital."

Angry at his Captain, but also a little relieved that his superior had stopped him from embarrassing himself further, Ruben stepped aside and let Kent and Nicole by.

He stared at their backs, Nicole leaning heavily into the profiler's chest, until they disappeared around the corner.

"Don't go face down yet, Torres. We've still got another killer to catch."

Crap. In the flurry of activity, Ruben had forgotten to relay the news. "No. I got a call. Martin went back to his place. Uni's picked him up a few minutes ago."

Glick shook his head and patted Ruben on the back.

"The ugly and the stupid."

Yep.

Not surprisingly, Kent was right, yet again.

CHAPTER 116

The sun crested the horizon as Kent drove Nicole home from the hospital. She was leaned back in the seat. Her cheek resting against the headrest.

Half-asleep, half awake.

It took some effort for him to keep his eyes on the road when she had her bedroom eyes like that. Bedroom and morphine-for-the-pain eyes, Kent reminded himself. There would not be any make-up sex this morning.

"I just want acknowledgement that I was right," Nicole said out of the blue. Was it the drugs talking?

"Right about what?"

Nicole smiled a broad, lazy, sedated smile. "You stole my car... Again."

Kent kissed her hand. "It's not stealing if it's *ours*."

Her lips spread into a full smile as the car stopped. "We're home."

Normally not the gentleman, Kent thought stabbing victims might demand slightly more attention, so he hopped out of the car and ran to the other side, opening the door for

Nicole. He then helped her up the steps, through the door, and onto an oversized chair.

"My, my" she said as he lifted her leg and set it upon the ottoman, then gave her a selection of some of his very finest comics to read.

"Now don't expect this kind of service forever."

"Why not?" Nicole asked. "You owe me."

That he did, Kent thought as he leaned over and kissed those lips one more time. Could life get better?

"I'll go fix us some breakfast."

"The meat is from the store, right?"

Kent didn't let his expression change.

"Funny. Now read up."

CHAPTER 117

Ruben squinted. Where was that light coming from? He glanced over. Shit, it was the sun rising. He'd been up for nearly twenty fours hours, with no end in sight, as Glick approached. Ruben got up out of his seat and stretched.

"Turns out you were right, Captain."

"How so?"

He pointed to the towering stacks of paperwork on his desk. That's what happened when your profiler gutted your suspect. "Harbinger ended up needing me for something."

Instead of giving a grin, Glick shuffled his feet. "Yeah... Well... Speaking of Kent..."

No. He couldn't deal with anything else from that man. But his Captain didn't look like he was going away soon.

"What now?" Ruben asked.

"Rebecca's uterus..."

"Showed signs of an abortion, right?"

"Well, we don't know," Glick said.

What was the Captain getting at? And what did it have to do with Kent. "So the report isn't back yet?"

"No, it's back. It's Rebecca..." Ruben's look prompted Glick to finish his sentence. "She didn't have one."

Okay, that didn't sound right. Rebecca's abortion was the lynch pin of Kent's theory. It was the thread that sewed the entire case together.

"She'd had a hysterectomy, then?"

"Um, yeah. On the day she died." Glick strongly emphasized the next part. "*After* she died."

"Oh my..." The implications ricocheted. Kent's last case. His self-admitted cannibalism. "He took it?"

Glick shrugged and toyed with a paperclip on Ruben's desk. "There were a lot of people who had access to the body before the coroner got to it."

Ruben just gave his Captain a 'you've got to be kidding' look. "So are we going to go over there and bust him?" When Glick didn't answer, Ruben emphasized, "*Again?*"

But all the Captain did was shrug.

CHAPTER 118

Kent nudged the meat with his spatula as it sizzled and crackled. Nicole wasn't going to be too thrilled by his selection, but hey, he had to use what was on hand.

"Do you want O.J.?" Kent called over his shoulder.

He waited for her response, but it didn't come.

"Hey, Nic," Kent said as he slid the meat onto a paper towel lined plate. He didn't need her whining about the fat content as well.

"Hon?"

Figuring she must have fallen asleep, the profiler buttered the toast and set it out on the table. The scrambled eggs and fruit were already in their serving dishes. It was a table even Martha Stewart would have approved of...well, except for the meat. Hopefully with all that food, Nicole would not notice that portion of the breakfast.

"Darlin' the doctor told you to eat with that medication," Kent said as he entered the living room.

Not only was Nicole not asleep, she was up, digging through her purse. He rushed over. Kent knew she wasn't used to his new and improved knight in shining armor gig, though surely she must have known he would've gotten her purse for her.

"Babe, I've got it."

Just as he came up next to her, he noticed she was cramming something back *into* the purse. His profiler senses began to tingle.

"Whatcha got there?"

Biting her lip, Nicole lifted the sealed baggie from her purse. The contents were pink, bloody.

It was a uterus.

To be more exact, it must have been Rebecca's uterus.

Kent stood shocked. Pinned in place. His lips wouldn't move. Nicole hadn't gone back to check Rebecca's pulse, she went back to take her womb.

Quickly shock transformed to pride. That was doctorial level stalking in action.

He kissed her forehead. "Coffee, hon?"

Nicole's worried look transformed into a grin. "Maybe some milk?"

"Whatever the lady wants," Kent said as he walked back to the kitchen. Out of the corner of his eye, the profiler watched Nicole stroke the tissue through the plastic, then toss it into the crackling fireplace.

That was his girl, all right.

28089079R00177

Made in the USA
Lexington, KY
05 December 2013